Fo

This is the third in a series of 1920s murder mystery adventures featuring assistant private investigator Marjorie Swallow. I hope you enjoy it.

A word about spelling: I'm a British author and the series is set in 1920s London, so I use British spelling and grammar. Marjorie's employer Mrs Jameson is American but she's lived in Europe for many years and doesn't object to Marjorie writing up her adventures in British English.

You can find out more about the books, get free short stories and a prequel novella when you sign up to my Readers Club newsletter on my website: https://annasayburnlane.com/.

ANNA SAYBURN LANE

Death At Chelsea

A 1920s murder mystery

STARLING
STREET BOOKS

First edition

This book was professionally typeset on Reedsy.
Find out more at reedsy.com

Chapter 1

The scent was sweet and slightly cloying, like lily of the valley that had started to decay in its vase. I moved closer, fascinated by the sapphire trumpets with their speckled throats. The petals were the deep blue that you sometimes see high in the sky on a perfect July afternoon. I reached out a hand, half-expecting to feel summer warmth emanating from the flower.

'Don't touch it, Marjorie,' called Mrs Jameson. I drew back. Little escaped my employer's sharp eyes.

'I'm so sorry,' I said, turning to our hostess, the renowned gardener Constance Hall. 'I didn't think.' To my relief, I saw she was smiling.

'It is rather poisonous, I'm afraid,' she said, her gruff voice holding a hint of amusement. 'Every part – the leaves, the flowers, the bulbs. It has to be, to withstand the yaks and the mountain goats where it comes from. We will need to warn people to keep their pet cats and dogs away from it.'

We strolled through the Victorian glasshouse, with its precious ranks of Himalayan Sapphire Lilies, *Lilium bucklerianum*, standing straight as soldiers. The glasshouse was twenty feet long, and there must have been forty or fifty plants growing in tall pots. The perfume was rather overwhelming. The high windows in the roof had been opened for ventilation, although

1

the doors at either end were closed and locked.

It was May, but unseasonably chilly. I was glad of my wool jacket and skirt. Constance Hall, tall and lean, strode ahead of us in a rather peculiar outfit, which Mrs Jameson had told me was her habitual attire. She wore knee-high riding boots, men's tweed knickerbockers, a thick Argyle sweater and a jaunty fedora hat over her greying auburn curls. A sturdy drill apron was tied around her waist, its pockets bristling with gardening tools. Every so often she stopped by a plant, inspected it closely and removed a discoloured leaf or plucked away a fading flower. I noticed she was wearing thick leather gardening gloves.

'And how long have you suspected sabotage, Constance?' asked Mrs Jameson.

We had been summoned to Hawkshill Manor in the depths of the Kent countryside to investigate why several of Mrs Hall's prized Himalayan lilies had died. It certainly made a change from investigating murder, and I was rather glad at the prospect of a less perilous quest. However, Mrs Jameson had warned, Mrs Hall might be as concerned about the death of her plants as she would be at the death of her nearest and dearest. Especially as they were expected to be the stars of the Chelsea Flower Show, where she would be unveiling them in a display garden in just a couple of weeks' time.

She paused and brandished her secateurs. 'It began in early January,' she said. 'I knew it couldn't be too cold – the lilies grow up in the mountains, for goodness sake. But they don't like the wet.

'The first three lilies that died had damp compost – almost waterlogged. Harry swore he'd told all the gardeners not to water them over the winter. So, he started checking last thing at night. They were all dry. But some mornings, he would come in early and find a group of them had been watered. Those were the ones that sickened. Some he could save, others just went yellow and rotted away.'

'It couldn't have been a leak? A window left open during the night, rain getting in?' Mrs Jameson looked pointedly at the ventilation windows.

'No, it bally well couldn't. Come,' said Mrs Hall, her handsome face creased with annoyance. We followed meekly. It was a new experience for me to see Mrs Jameson being ordered around. I was more used to seeing her commanding others, usually me.

Mrs Hall unlocked the doors and led us to the next glasshouse, where pots of rhododendron, from small bushes with pure white flowers to monsters blooming with vivid pink globes, packed the floor space. At the far end, an old man in an apron straightened, rubbing his back. Sundays, it seemed, were not a day of rest at Hawkshill Manor.

'Morning, Mrs Hall.' He touched his cap.

'Now, Harry. Tell my guests what you discovered back in January. This is Mrs Iris Jameson, the private detective, and her assistant Miss Swallow. They will help us get to the bottom of this dastardly business.'

I took out my notebook, which Harry eyed with suspicion.

'I already told Mrs Hall,' he said.

I tried a winning smile. 'It would be so helpful if you could tell us again,' I said. 'Mr…?'

'Smith, Miss. Harry Smith.'

I wrote it down. 'Thank you. I'm Marjorie. What did you find out back in January, when the lilies started to die?'

He rubbed his eyes, which had enormous bags underneath.

He looked very tired. I suspected Mrs Hall was a demanding employer.

'I set up outside the glasshouse one night, with a flask of tea and a packet of sandwiches,' he said, pointing. 'Over there, between the potting shed and the yew hedge. Didn't see nothing for the first two nights, and the lilies were right as rain in the morning. All I had to show was lost sleep.' He seemed to be warming to his audience.

'Then the third night, round about three in the morning, I seen him. He crept up, unlocked the greenhouse and hefted in a big watering can. I followed him, caught the blighter red-handed. He struggled and got away, but I knew who it was, all right.'

We waited. 'Who was it?' asked Mrs Jameson, impatient. I hid a smile. She usually told me to wait for an interviewee to speak, rather than filling the silence. You got a more truthful answer that way.

'Blooming Dick Cooper,' he said, shaking his head sorrow-fully. We waited for more information. Harry Smith, however, had finished his tale. He bent his back to a rhododendron bush, pushing his thumb into the compost with an experienced air.

'Cooper was one of the gardeners,' explained Mrs Hall. 'We had a team of three – we need more, of course, but you know what it's been like getting staff since the War. Harry is our head gardener, then there's Bert, his son, and Dick Cooper was the second under-gardener. We had to sack him, of course. So now we're down to just Harry and Bert. And me.'

She led the way out into what should have been warm spring sunshine, but was chilly drizzle. Mrs Jameson shivered. Her jacquard-print silk coat and turban, although immaculately tailored, were insufficiently warm. Like me, she was an urban creature. Unlike me, she had been born and grown up in America, then spent much of her adult life in Italy where, I was given to understand, rain and cold were not expected during May.

'Perhaps we could hear the rest of the story inside?' she suggested. Mrs Hall looked surprised.

'Yes, if you prefer. It's about time for coffee, anyway. I usually bring a flask so I can stay out until luncheon, but let's go in. You remember the way, Iris?'

Mrs Jameson hurried towards the side entrance to Hawkshill Manor, a big brick-built pile dating from Tudor times, with twisty chimney-stacks, low gables and leaded glass in the small windows. I saw Frankie, our chauffeur, hurriedly flick away her Woodbine and whip out a cloth to polish the windscreen of the Lagonda. A young man was lounging against the wall next to her, a cigarette cupped in his hand and his cap pulled down over his thick dark hair.

'Bert!' called Mrs Hall, sharply. 'What are you doing? I don't pay you to stand around chatting, you know.'

He straightened up and touched his hand to his cap, his eyes bold.

'I'm just on my way, Mrs Hall,' he said. 'It's Sunday, remember? I've been to church.'

'That's your other gardener?' asked Mrs Jameson, as we continued to the house.

'Yes, far from ideal, I'm afraid. But what can you do? He learned at his father's knee. He knows his plants. But he hasn't been the same since he came back from France. His attitude really verges on insolence.'

Bert strolled across the yard, whistling. It was a catchy tune which nagged at my memory. I'd heard it before somewhere.

Chapter 2

The morning room was grand but shabby, in the style of old English families who would rather sit on an uncomfortable upright wooden chair from the time of Charles I than do anything so vulgar as buy new furniture. There were great bunches of lilies – not poisonous Sapphire Lilies, I was glad to see – on the stone mantelpiece, and a small fire had recently been lit in the grate.

Linenfold oak panelled the walls, one of which was hung with a huge tapestry. It was so dark and dusty that it was hard to make out which mythological scene it depicted.

'Diana and Actaeon,' said Constance Hall, seeing me frowning at it. 'Just before his hounds tear him to shreds.' I recoiled.

A middle-aged man entered the room, his bald head shining, and his face wreathed in smiles.

'Welcome, Iris. Goodness me, how many years have passed since you were last at Hawkshill? And who is this young lady?'

Mrs Jameson accepted his kiss on her cheek. 'Walter, it's splendid to be here again. This is my personal secretary, Miss Marjorie Swallow. Marjorie, Mr Walter Hall, lord of the manor and proprietor of Hall's Horticultural Supplies. We danced together at the hunt ball, back in the dark ages of the last century before either of us married.'

He rubbed his hands together. 'We certainly did. Connie, have you rung for coffee? Or should we have something stronger? It's almost twelve. Everyone will be down for luncheon before long.'

'Coffee, first,' said Mrs Hall firmly. 'We still have business to discuss.'

I cupped my hands around the delicate china, warming myself and breathing in the rich aroma. We'd never had coffee at home when I was growing up, but I had rather got the taste for it since working for Mrs Jameson.

'Now,' said my employer, 'tell me more about this Dick Cooper fellow. Why was he sabotaging your lilies?'

'Do you remember an awful pill called Norman Alperton?' asked Mrs Hall, eyes fierce. 'Lives over at Kingsmead Place, towards Faversham. Fancies himself a gardener.'

Mr Hall's mouth twitched with amusement. 'Sir Norman is a garden designer,' he said. 'Much in demand, especially in the last few years. A bit of a rival to Connie's crown.'

Mrs Hall drew herself up, her nostrils flaring in her long face. 'I expect he'd like to hear you say so, Walter. He has all sorts of notions about Arts and Crafts, using only dreary English cottage plants and leaving a load of old stones lying around. Broken Greek columns and so on. Despite this, the Royal Horticultural Society saw fit to award him a Gold at Chelsea last year. I cannot imagine what they were thinking.'

I glanced at the row of awards on the mantelpiece. There were three Chelsea Flower Show gold medals from before the War, and one from 1920. Nothing from 1921 or 1922, I noticed. No wonder Mrs Hall had been cross.

The Chelsea Flower Show, the great event of the London spring calendar, marked the start of the social season at the end of May. It was held in the grounds of the Royal Hospital, the home of the red-coated Chelsea Pensioners, former soldiers who had retired to live in the hospital. I'd never been, but I'd seen photographs of the show in the illustrated papers and was very keen to attend. I hoped this investigation would give me that chance. My mother would be beside herself with envy.

'And the sabotage?' asked Mrs Jameson, trying to steer the conversation back to the point.

'Well, it was Alperton, of course. Dick Cooper wouldn't have the wit to do it on his own. Someone must have put him up to it. And Cooper worked at Kingsmead Place before he came to Hawkshill. His father was head gardener there until he retired. The family still lives in the village, I believe.'

Mrs Jameson finished the last of her coffee and crunched a ginger snap biscuit. 'So, you think that Norman Alperton paid Dick Cooper to over-water your lilies, Constance? What for?'

'Well, it's obvious. To prevent me from winning Gold this year, of course. Which I will do, when I show the Himalayan Valley Garden. There will be no more nonsense about using only English plants once people see what you can do with a bit of ambition.'

She crossed to a bureau and pulled out a large sheet of graph paper. 'This is my plan.' She gestured to sweeping lines on the paper, broken up with blocks of colour. 'Rocks built up either side of the garden at the back to represent the mountains, inter-planted with white rhododendrons. A mountain stream running through the centre, with rare primulas, Himalayan poppies and other alpine species on the banks. And here, either side of the stream where the gravel will be raised in terraces, the Sapphire Lilies.'

Her cheeks were aflame, her eyes bright. She looked

handsome and rather splendid. I saw that her husband was watching her with admiration.

'It looks marvellous,' said Mrs Jameson. 'And the lilies are spectacular. "Solomon in all his glory was not arrayed as one of these." But are you sure that Sir Norman was really behind the sabotage? Perhaps this Dick Cooper simply made a mistake.'

'In the middle of the night?' scoffed Mrs Hall. 'I don't think so. Anyway, he was a good plantsman. He knew bally well what would happen if he over-watered those lilies.'

'The thing is,' said Walter Hall, his mild voice breaking in as his wife took breath, 'it's rather important for the firm that the lilies are a success. Hall's Horticultural sank thousands of pounds into sponsoring the expedition to find them. And it's been three years since they arrived. We've spent all that time cultivating them, in the hope they will sell like billy-oh. So, if the launch goes badly – or if word gets around that the plants are too delicate for the British weather – we could lose a fortune.'

Mrs Jameson's eyes snapped to his worried face. 'And can you afford to lose it, Walter?'

He looked away and put down his coffee cup. 'I would prefer not to find out,' he said.

'Well,' said Mrs Jameson, her voice gentler than usual. 'We shall endeavour to ensure you don't need to. Now, what happened after Dick Cooper was given his marching orders? Did the sabotage stop?'

Constance Hall stood up and kicked the fire iron, moodily. 'It did. Until a week ago, when Harry found another three lilies half-drowned first thing in the morning. There's been another one since.

'I've asked Harry and Bert to keep a watch, but Bert has

outright refused. He says he'll only do it if we set up a shift system, give him the day off after working nights, and pay time and a half for unsociable hours. Which obviously is out of the question; I need them working full time on the garden during the day until after Chelsea. Harry understands that, but unfortunately, he fell asleep on Tuesday night and the saboteur managed to get past him.'

My sympathies for Bert were growing. No wonder Harry had looked so very tired. The lilies might not toil, but the gardeners certainly did.

'Marjorie could help watch tonight,' said Mrs Jameson. I sighed inwardly. Maybe I should ask Bert's advice about labour relations with my employer. 'And did you say you have other guests staying? We could set up a rota system. What do you think?'

'Excellent idea,' said Mrs Hall. 'Here they come now.'

Chapter 3

Two men walked through the door. Ernest Buckler, the cele-brated plant-hunter who had discovered the Sapphire Lilies, was wiry and thin-faced with a drooping sandy-coloured moustache and straight fair hair that was thinning on top. His skin was pale and there were deep shadows under his blue eyes. I'd seen photographs of him in the newspapers, above articles reporting on his intrepid travels in China and India, and the exotic plants he had brought back.

His companion had a round boyish face and curly chestnut hair that he had tried to plaster down with water. He looked much younger and more cheerful.

Walter Hall greeted them. 'Tommy, Ernest, come and meet our friend Iris Jameson. Mrs Jameson and her assistant Miss Swallow have a plan to help us get to the bottom of this business with the lilies.'

'Oh, good show,' said the younger man. 'Glad to hear it. Poor Constance has been beside herself.' He shook our hands. 'I'm Eversholt, Tommy Eversholt. I was Ernest's partner on the expedition to Tibet when we found the lilies. I've been trying to persuade Walter here to let me have another bash at it. There's so much more to find there.'

Mr Hall smiled. 'One step at a time, Tommy. Let's see what

happens after Chelsea.'

Ernest Buckler nodded curtly at us. 'How d'you do.' He reached for a glass of the whisky that the butler was handing around and knocked it back, wiping his moustache with the back of his hand.

'Where have the girls got to, eh?' asked Tommy, looking around as if there might be women hiding under the side tables or behind the day bed. 'Gossiping about their husbands, I suppose. Or showing off their new hats.'

Two women walked through the door arm-in-arm. One, exquisitely pretty with a pink and white complexion and big blue eyes, looked young enough to fit Tommy's description of a girl. She did indeed have a very stylish hat perched on her blonde curls: a pink silk number about the size of a saucer that matched her charming organdie frock. She must be frozen, I thought, and noticed she made straight for the fire. To my surprise, she took Ernest's arm and smiled shyly at us.

'Mrs Buckler,' said Mr Hall, introducing us. 'Lavinia, dear, this is Mrs Iris Jameson and Miss Marjorie Swallow.'

'Hello.' Her soft voice was barely audible.

'Tommy, you do talk utter rot,' said the second woman. 'As if I've ever taken the slightest interest in hats.' She held out a black cigarette for Mr Eversholt to light.

She was striking rather than pretty, with a sun-tanned face and dark, arched eyebrows that gave her an expression of ironic amusement. Her straight dark hair was bobbed short like mine and she wore a simple velvet cloche in bottle green, along with a belted cardigan and jersey skirt.

'I'm Diana Eversholt,' she said, holding the cigarette at arm's length and wafting the smoke away from us. 'Tommy's wife. Formerly Mrs Ernest Buckler, as I expect someone will soon tell you, if they haven't already.'

I was startled. Not many people admitted to being divorced with such insouciance, and even fewer socialised with their former husband and his new wife. Mrs Eversholt noticed my surprise.

'Don't worry, we're terribly modern and civilised about it,' she said. 'Lavinia's much better suited to Ernest than I was, and I keep Tommy on the straight and narrow.'

Mr Eversholt laughed and rubbed his hands together. 'Diana likes to shock people,' he said. 'But she's right; we're all good friends now.'

Watching Lavinia's strained laugh and Ernest's thin-lipped smile, I wondered how true that really was.

Seeing the design on the graph paper, Diana Eversholt moved to the table and was soon in conversation with Constance Hall about the progress of the lilies and her plans for building the garden at the Chelsea show. Mrs Jameson joined them, while Walter Hall made small talk with the Bucklers.

I was left with Tommy Eversholt. 'Diana came with us to Tibet,' he said, watching his wife fondly. 'That's how we got to know each other. She's a bit of a free spirit. Works as a journalist, writing up stuff for the newspapers. She'll get a good commission to write about Chelsea.'

'Goodness.' I looked at her with new respect. 'That must have been very exciting. Did you have to climb up into the mountains? Was it very cold?'

'Colder than you can possibly imagine, even in this old ruin with this blasted weather. Diana got sick, so she had to stay behind in Lhasa. The capital city, if you can call it that. Ernest and I climbed up the pass from the Salween valley on to the plain. It was grim. Weeks of riding or walking with no shelter anywhere, just exposed screes and snowfields, narrow paths and granite boulders. And then this amazing monastery perched high up above the valley.'

'A monastery? Are they Catholics?' I asked.

He laughed. 'Wrong religion. Buddhist monks. Very hardy fellows: go around dressed in ochre-coloured robes with their heads shaved, carrying begging bowls for alms and food. That's all they possess – their robe and their bowl. Admire them tremendously.'

Living halfway up a mountain with only a robe and a bowl to my name wasn't my idea of fun, but I could see it was a romantic prospect for an explorer.

'And you found the lilies there?'

He seemed to have lapsed into a kind of reverie. I had to repeat the question before he answered.

'Oh, yes. The lilies.' He smiled, but there was something a little off about his expression. His lip twisted as if at a painful memory. 'Completely extraordinary. We'd been hunting around without much luck. Seemed impossible, that anything should grow on those scree slopes. But there they were, on the sheltered side of the valley. A field of blue like you've never seen. Thought I must be hallucinating.'

He paused and his glance flickered from me to Ernest Buckler, then to his wife. She caught his eye and smiled, a firm smile as if to remind him of some agreement. He turned back to me, his face bright again.

'But, of course, they're growing in Constance's glasshouses, so they must be real. Have you seen them, Miss Swallow?'

I was trying to find the words to express how lovely I thought the lilies, but I didn't get the chance to say more. A very young man slouched through the door, his expression dark, his demeanour moody.

Chapter 4

Walter Hall crossed the room and straightened the young man's tie. His long face and pale auburn hair proclaimed his close relationship to Constance Hall.

'Finally,' said Mr Hall. 'Iris, Miss Swallow, this is our son Peregrine. Perry, we're about to go through for lunch. Where have you been?'

'In the gardens,' said the boy. 'I see Mater has Bert and Harry hard at it.'

'Two weeks to go,' said Mrs Hall, looking up. 'Some of us have no time to waste. Come, let's eat.'

The dining room at Hawkshill Manor was as gloomy as the rest of the house. Dark crimson walls were hung with paintings of slaughtered stags and game birds, their glassy eyes shining out from the frames in a disconcerting manner. Above the mullioned windows were mounted five stag heads with enormous pointed antlers. I supposed it was too much to hope for chicken or fish for luncheon. The butler and footmen served from platters of dark pink roast venison, with glossy thick gravy. But the roast potatoes were excellent and even the meat was quite delicious, if I avoided meeting the reproachful gaze of the stag on the wall facing me.

Walter Hall and Ernest Buckler sat at opposite ends of the

polished oak table. I was pleased to be next to friendly Mr Hall, with Mr Eversholt to my right. I was something of a spectator to the conversation between the two men about unexplored parts of Tibet that Mr Eversholt wished to visit next, although they were kind enough to include me when they remembered. Meanwhile, I saw Mrs Jameson manage to draw out the taciturn Mr Buckler at the far end of the table with questions about his travels.

Young Peregrine Hall almost ignored Diana Eversholt on his right, so enraptured was he with Lavinia Buckler's angelic profile. He seemed quite tongue-tied, and Mrs Buckler herself was so timid that they appeared destined to complete the meal in silence. Eventually, Mrs Eversholt began talking across Peregrine, drawing Lavinia out with funny stories about interminable dinners at the Royal Geographical Society, where Mr Buckler was apparently a valued member. The two young people joined in, and the ice was broken.

After the venison was cleared away, Mrs Hall's voice carried down the table. 'Mrs Jameson has made a most sensible suggestion to help us protect the Sapphire Lilies from further damage,' she called. 'I hope I can count on everyone to play their part tonight.'

We paused in our conversation. Mrs Jameson cleared her throat.

'I should like to propose a watch system,' she said. 'The gardeners are working all the hours of daylight to prepare for Chelsea. Therefore, those of you who are less occupied – especially the gentlemen and the younger members of the party – should take turns to sit up with the lilies in the glasshouse overnight.'

'Excellent idea,' said Tommy Eversholt at once. 'Sign me up.'

'Suits me,' said his wife. She grinned. 'I like a bit of cloak and dagger. It'll add colour to my article. Round-the-clock protection for the precious Sapphire Lilies. House guests rally round to defeat unknown saboteur. Really, I should be paid double for this.'

Ernest Buckler shrugged. 'All the same to me.'

Walter Hall was looking unhappy. 'I have a shareholder meeting in the morning. I really need to be fresh for it, my dear.' He appealed to his wife. 'I'm sorry – it does sound like a good idea. Any other time I'd have been keen to do my bit.'

'Well, there's no need for you to be involved, Walter.' Mrs Jameson turned to address the rest of us around the table. 'If everyone does two hours each, we will only need six of you to cover the hours from eight in the evening until eight in the morning,' she said. It did not escape my notice that she had not counted herself in the watch party. Mrs Jameson liked her sleep.

Constance Hall was counting on her fingers. 'I'll take the first shift after dinner until ten o'clock. Then I can check with Harry that everything is in order before he goes home. Marjorie, you or Diana can come after me.'

'I'll do the later shift,' said Mrs Eversholt, somewhat to my relief. 'I never go to sleep before the early hours, anyway.'

'Nor does Perry,' said Walter Hall, who was scribbling times and names on a scrap of paper. 'You can put all your practice at late nights to good use, my boy. Marjorie does ten until midnight, Diana does midnight till two, and you do two till four. Think you can manage that?'

Peregrine nodded. 'Might as well,' he said.

'I'm not awfully good in the dark,' began Lavinia, turning her headlamp eyes on Mr Hall. 'I'd be worried about coming up from the cottage on my own.'

'No need for you to lose your beauty sleep, my dear. Ernest and Tommy, you can manage the rest of the night, can't you?'

'I'll take the next shift,' said Mr Buckler. 'Tommy can get a decent night, then rise early and do six until eight.'

Mr Eversholt looked surprised. 'If you like. I'm happy to do the earlier shift though, old man.'

'That's settled, then,' said Ernest Buckler. 'I'll do four until six. Now, Mrs Jameson, perhaps you can tell us who you think we might catch creeping into the glasshouse overnight?'

She pushed back her chair as the plates were cleared away. 'Too early to say, Mr Buckler. But I would be most interested to hear what you all think about it.'

'Alperton,' said Mrs Hall at once. 'Kingsmead Place is only seven miles from here. Either he comes himself or he sends over one of his staff.'

Peregrine Hall rolled his eyes. 'You're obsessed with Norman Alperton. Ten to one it's Bert. He's right here on site, and you should hear the way he talks sometimes. I can't say I'd blame him, given the way you work the staff.'

'Don't be ridiculous, Perry.' Mr Hall looked quite angry. 'Bert Smith has been with us since childhood. I know he's become a bit of a firebrand, but he wouldn't do anything to upset his father. And don't you think Harry would have spotted it, if Bert had been damaging the plants?'

Diana Eversholt leaned across the table. 'Who is Bert? This sounds very exciting.'

'The under-gardener,' said Mrs Hall. 'But I agree with Walter. Why would the boy do such a thing? I mean, we've looked after him. We even paid for his time in the convalescent home, when he came back from France.'

'And now you're working him half to death,' said Peregrine, pushing his floppy hair out of his eyes. 'You know his lungs won't stand much. I don't blame him for joining the Party. I've been talking to some fellows at Oxford about it. Might even join the communists myself.' He leaned back with an air of insouciance, which I suspected was intended to impress Lavinia Buckler.

The tune that Bert had been whistling in the stable yard floated back into my mind... that was it. *The Red Flag*, the anthem of the British Communist Party. Goodness. Was Bert really a communist? And was Peregrine serious about joining?

Mr Hall rolled his eyes, but his wife rose to the bait. 'You bally well will not, Peregrine. After what those beastly Bolsheviks did in Russia? What do you want – to see the King and Queen murdered, and Princess Mary and the princes alongside them?'

'I'm sure Peregrine doesn't want any such thing,' said Mr Eversholt, heartily. 'Do you, old chap? Personally, I'm rather excited about the prospect of meeting the Royal family at the show. Aren't you, Lavinia?'

She smiled prettily. 'Oh, yes. Do you think we will really have the chance to talk to them?' she asked.

Mrs Hall was mollified. 'I certainly hope so. King George was most gracious when I won Gold in 1920. He very much admired my alpines in the rock garden. He said he was going to introduce a rockery at Buckingham Palace.' She turned her gaze sternly on her son. 'So, I don't want to hear any more nonsense about Bolshevism, Perry.'

Mrs Jameson had been watching the back-and-forth narrowly, her grey eyes darting around the table to capture every nuance and reaction.

'What are your thoughts, Mr Buckler?' she asked. 'Who do you suspect of sabotaging your precious discovery?'

He started and colour mounted in his sallow cheeks. 'I really haven't the slightest idea,' he said. He gazed over our heads at the paintings of wildlife carnage, as if trying not to look at anyone in particular. 'It comes down to jealousy, I suppose,' he added. 'Unfortunately, that happens when you're successful in your field. Jealousy, and spite.'

The table lapsed into a rather uncomfortable silence. Lavinia's smooth face creased with distress, and she looked down at her clasped hands. Diana Eversholt reached for a cigarette. As she lit it, I saw her hands were trembling slightly. What on earth could scare an intrepid reporter who had travelled across the Himalayan mountains?

'Well,' said Walter Hall, after a moment. 'I'm sure Iris will get to the bottom of it. Here's to the success of the scheme, and to success at Chelsea.' He raised his glass and we all toasted. But Ernest Buckler's words had left a chill that lingered for the rest of the meal.

Chapter 5

The party dispersed after luncheon. The rain had stopped, so Diana Eversholt asked her husband to walk over to the village with her to post a letter. Walter Hall retired to his office with Ernest Buckler to discuss plans for the marketing and supply of the Sapphire Lilies after their debut at Chelsea. Constance Hall returned to her glasshouses. In the drawing room, Peregrine was teaching Lavinia a new variation of rummy. Watching their heads together over the card table, hearing their young voices and laughter, I couldn't help feeling they were a better suited pair than Lavinia and her gloomy husband.

Mrs Jameson wanted to visit the gardener's cottage. While she was upstairs looking out a warmer jacket, I nipped down to the kitchen. There I found Frankie, boots up on the fender, polishing off the last of a bowl of steamed sponge pudding.

'Very decent grub here, I must say.' She grinned and passed her bowl to an awe-struck scullery maid. 'Thanks, sweetheart.' The girl blushed and scuttled away.

'Stop teasing the staff,' I said, sitting next to her and trying to get closer to the fire. The kitchen was considerably warmer than the sitting room upstairs.

Frankie laughed. 'They like it. I'm giving them something to talk about for weeks to come. They don't get much entertainment, down here in the sticks.'

Frankie O'Grady was an East Ender and something of an eccentric. She'd trained as a motor mechanic during the War, chopped off her hair to a boyish crop before it became fashionable, and she dressed in men's overalls and work wear. She was also a lethal practitioner of the martial art of jiu-jitsu. Mrs Jameson had taken her on as a chauffeur who was also handy as a bodyguard when occasion arose. Frankie had got me out of a tight spot more than once in the past year. She looked extremely dashing in her chauffeur's uniform and peaked cap, currently hanging on the back of her chair.

'I wanted to ask you about Bert,' I said. 'The under-gardener. You were chatting to him when we came in from the gardens.'

'Seems like a sound bloke,' said Frankie.

'Apparently he's a communist.'

She shrugged. 'Lots of people are. It's not against the law.'

'No, but sabotage is. Aren't the communists rather keen on wrecking machinery and so on?' There had been an article in one of the periodicals that Mrs Jameson subscribed to, describing a campaign of industrial sabotage in America, aimed at getting the factory owners to recognise the trades unions.

She laughed. 'Watering a few plants is hardly in that league, Marge. Anyway, what's in it for him? He told me he wants to go to Chelsea. He won't get there if they don't have any lilies to take.'

'Hmm.' I stared into the fire. The Chelsea Flower Show was primarily a social event attended by all those who were in high society, including the King and Queen. 'Why, though? I wouldn't have thought mixing with the toffs was his sort of thing.'

Frankie shrugged again. 'He's a gardener. Why wouldn't he want to see the biggest flower show in the world?'

'I suppose so.' I checked the clock. 'I'd better go. Mrs Jameson wants to talk to Bert and his dad after their lunch.'

The Smith family occupied the gardener's cottage on the far side of the stables. I was glad I'd accepted the housekeeper's offered loan of rubber boots. The horse dung, puddles and mud as we crossed the stable yard would have ruined my shoes. Fortunately, I'd also procured a pair for Mrs Jameson.

We waded through the muck to the cottage with its low roof, tiles furred with moss. We were halfway down the path when the green-painted door flew open and Harry strode out, his weathered face red and his expression furious.

'I'll not have it, lad,' he shouted through the open door. 'And you can forget about coming to Chelsea, and all.'

'Mr Smith…' called Mrs Jameson. But he did not stop, stamping his way past us without a second look.

A grey-haired woman with an apron tied around her ample waist appeared in the doorway. 'Harry!' she called, looking distressed. He ignored her, too.

Mrs Jameson led the way to the cottage door. 'Mrs Smith? I'm Mrs Jameson, and Mrs Hall has asked me to investigate the problems she's been having with the lilies. I wanted to speak to your husband, but I can see he is very busy. Is your son at home?'

She glanced back into the house, tucking stray strands of hair behind her ears. 'I'm sorry, madam. You've just missed him. He's gone out.'

That seemed unlikely, given that Harry had clearly been shouting at Bert.

'Perhaps we could come in and wait,' said Mrs Jameson,

smiling pleasantly. 'I don't suppose he's gone far.'

'Well, I think he went to see a friend,' said Mrs Smith. She seemed very uneasy. 'I don't know what time he'll be back, you see. Being a Sunday, and everything.'

We all heard quite clearly the sound of a door slamming at the back of the cottage. Mrs Smith looked down, her face red.

'Never mind,' said Mrs Jameson, kindly. 'Some other time. I don't suppose I could trouble you for a glass of water? My throat is rather dry.'

Minutes later we were sitting by the kitchen fire in our stockinged feet, boots outside, while Mrs Smith made a pot of tea.

'I'm sorry about Harry,' she said. 'He's been that busy, what with this Chelsea business. He gets worked up. It isn't good for him, with his heart. And Bert – well, you know what young men are. They don't always see eye to eye. It upsets Harry when they argue.'

'Perfectly natural,' agreed Mrs Jameson, sipping the tea. It was far stronger than she liked, and I saw her shudder slightly as she swallowed the brick-red tannic brew. 'It can't be easy, having both of them living at home now that your son is grown.'

'It isn't,' said Mrs Smith with emphasis. 'Especially since the army. He was quite happy at home before that, working with his dad. But he's got all these notions now. Harry doesn't like it.'

'Notions about politics?' Mrs Jameson asked.

Mrs Smith looked wary. 'I don't understand all that talk,' she said. 'I just know it makes them both disagreeable. I can't be doing with arguments over dinner.'

I saw a photograph on the otherwise-bare mantelpiece. 'May

I?' I rose and picked it up. It was Bert, looking as if he was barely out of short trousers, well-brushed and polished in a khaki uniform. He wore a big grin, as if he couldn't wait to get out to France. My parents had a similar one on their mantelpiece. But my brother James had not come home.

'He looks very smart,' I said. 'Mrs Hall said he needed time in a convalescent home afterwards. Is he quite recovered now?'

Mrs Smith took the photograph from me and stroked the frame. 'I don't think any of them are, do you?' she asked. 'He got caught in a gas attack, poor boy. His lungs are bad. And so are his dreams.'

I nodded in sympathy. 'I'm sorry. And you're right. None of them came back quite the same as they went away.' My thoughts went to my friend Freddie, who still suffered from neurasthenia attacks on bad days.

She patted my hand. 'We do the best we can for them, don't we, duckie? Now, I mustn't keep you. You'll find Harry up at the glasshouses, Mrs Jameson, if you want to talk to him there.'

Chapter 6

Harry Smith had calmed down by the time we found him. He apologised for not stopping to speak to us at the cottage.

'I've been at it since daybreak,' he said, rubbing his arm. He winced, as if it pained him. 'And there's still so much to do. I was up half the night with this watch system that Mrs Hall wants. I'm not as young as I was.'

Mrs Jameson nodded in sympathy. 'I do understand. And I hope I'm the bearer of good news. You won't need to watch tonight, Harry. We will all take turns to sit in the glasshouse with the lilies, from eight o'clock. So, you should get a good night's sleep for once.'

To my surprise, he didn't seem that pleased. 'Well, if that's all right with Mrs Hall. But folks have to be careful with them lilies. I don't want anyone leaving the doors open and letting the foxes get in or messing around with the ventilation system. I've got it just how it should be.'

I tried to reassure him. 'Mrs Hall will take the first shift. And we will all be really careful, I promise. We're going to lock the door each time we come in and go out. And we won't touch the windows.'

He still seemed dubious. 'I'm sure you'll do your best, Miss.'

'Well, that's all arranged,' said Mrs Jameson. 'Now, why

don't you tell me why you were so cross with your son earlier? Do you think Bert has something to do with this sabotage business?'

He straightened up and looked at her steadily. His face flushed red again and his mouth twisted in an obstinate line.

'No, I do not,' he said. 'And I'm sure I hope never to hear anyone say such a thing again.' He clamped his mouth shut and turned his back, then made his way along the rows of lilies, checking them over one by one.

Mrs Jameson watched him for a moment, nodding thoughtfully to herself. We slipped quietly out of the glasshouse. A watery sun had broken through the clouds.

'Let's walk in the gardens,' she said. 'I want to think.'

We passed through a gate and into a long garden hedged with yew, the dark leaves neatly trimmed. By contrast, the flower bed was a jewelled tapestry of every colour imaginable, arranged with an artist's eye. I recognised tulips and irises, but there were many other plants I didn't know. I bent to look at one particularly fine specimen, an iris so darkly purple that its frilled petals were almost black.

Although I'd never lived anywhere with a garden before, I did appreciate flowers and often bought a posy from the flower sellers at Piccadilly Circus to keep by my bed. Freddie and I had been in the habit of strolling through Regent's Park, watching the daffodils coming through the lawns and the first rose buds appear. But I'd never seen anything as beautiful as this before.

'It's so lovely,' I exclaimed. 'I can see why Mrs Hall gets excited about gardening.'

Mrs Jameson looked up from the pattern she had been tracing in the gravel path with her walking cane.

'Hmm? Oh, yes. Very pretty, aren't they? Now, Marjorie, why do you suppose Harry doesn't want his son at the Chelsea Flower Show?'

I considered. 'Do you think he is the saboteur? He'd certainly have the best opportunity.'

'It's possible. But if Harry thought that, he'd be sending his son away from here, not worrying about him visiting London.'

'I asked Frankie about Bert,' I said. 'They were talking earlier, in the stable yard. She says she wouldn't be surprised if he was a communist, but he told her he really wants to go to Chelsea. And that he won't get to go if the lilies are damaged.'

Mrs Jameson nodded thoughtfully. 'Well, perhaps Frankie can find out more. Now, let's think about tonight. There are three possibilities for the saboteur.' She counted on her fingers. 'An outsider, as Constance suspects. In which case they will not expect to find a watch, so we may catch them creeping up to the glasshouse. I shall ask Frankie to keep a look-out from her room in the stable block. But once they see someone sitting in the glasshouse, they will probably leave without attempting entry.

'Bert, or another of the staff. Bert knows about the watch, or will do soon enough from his mother or father. And the kitchen is to provide coffee and sandwiches tonight, so the indoor staff will all know. Any insider on the staff would be unlikely to try anything this evening.'

She raised a third finger. 'And, of course, it may be a member of the family or the house party, who all know about the watch. But if the saboteur is one of the watchers, they might just be tempted to try something. It would be foolish, of course, and point the finger of suspicion straight at them. But fanatics are not always careful. If the lilies are harmed tonight, we will

29

know where to begin our search.'

It made sense. 'But why would any of the house party harm the lilies?' I asked. 'Mr Hall says his business could lose a fortune if they are not a success. Mr Buckler and Mr Eversholt travelled all that way to discover them, and they want funding for more expeditions. Everyone should want the garden to be a triumph.' Mrs Hall's suggestion of an outside rival, or Bert's obscure political sympathies, seemed more likely to me.

Mrs Jameson resumed her walk. We crossed through the yew hedge and into a small apple orchard festooned with pink and white blossom. It smelled heavenly. The path through it led down to the lake and a picturesque white clapboard cottage. I supposed that was where the Bucklers were staying.

'I wonder whether Mr Buckler knows more than he has told us,' said Mrs Jameson. 'He spoke as if he did. Jealousy, he said, and spite. Both of which are powerful motives for wreaking destruction on someone else's dream.'

I thought at once of young Peregrine Hall, arguing with his parents about politics and gazing with adoration at Ernest Buckler's pretty young wife. The way he and Lavinia had laughed over the card game together. Was he jealous of Mr Buckler, and if so, would destroying the lilies be his way of attacking him?

'You suspect Peregrine?' I asked.

Mrs Jameson laughed. 'We have been here only a few hours,' she said. 'At this point in the investigation, I suspect everyone.'

Chapter 7

Up in the chilly bedroom that had been allocated to me – a small box of a room with a connecting door to Mrs Jameson's larger suite – I pulled on woollen stockings and a flannel petticoat, before dressing in my warmest knitted jersey, tweed skirt and jacket. The rain was coming down harder, pattering against the windows. I pulled my felt cloche hat over my ears and tucked a woollen scarf under my collar. Since cutting my hair in January, I'd noticed how much colder the wind felt on the nape of my neck.

Dinner had been lively, in the way of a party that is set on a new adventure. Everyone seemed excited about the night to come. Those who were not going to watch pretended to be relieved, but I think Mr Hall in particular was slightly disappointed not to be able to take part in the fun.

Mrs Hall had departed at eight o'clock sharp to tour the glasshouse with Harry Smith and ensure all was in order for the night ahead. The cook had prepared six packages of sandwiches in waxed paper and six vacuum flasks of hot coffee, which one of the footmen had delivered to the glasshouse with as much ceremony as if he was serving at a formal dinner. After discussion, it had been agreed that the watchers would keep an oil lamp burning overnight, and a whistle in their pockets.

'We only want to protect the plants,' said Mr Hall. 'I don't want anybody putting themselves in danger. Stay inside the glasshouse, with the door locked. If you see anything suspicious, blow the whistle. One of the grooms will come out to see if anyone is lurking around. No heroics, please.'

Mrs Jameson and I had briefed Frankie, whose window in the stable block looked out over the yard where the glasshouses were set. I felt reassured to know that any blast of my whistle would bring her running.

I picked up an umbrella from the porch and scurried across the yard in my rubber boots, head down against the rain. A comforting glow came from the glasshouse. Mrs Hall let me in and locked the door behind us.

'Good show, Miss Swallow. All's well. Do you want a quick tour with me to check?'

We walked the length of the glasshouse, oil lamp swinging in her hand.

'Harry and I had a look around before he retired for the night,' she said. 'I haven't seen or heard anything suspicious since.' She showed me the table with the sandwiches and coffee. 'And you have your whistle with you? Excellent.' She smiled. 'You know, all this reminds me of when I first met Iris, just after I was married. She visited with her aunt for the old Queen's diamond jubilee. There was a most unfortunate incident involving a missing silver chalice, and she sorted it out so neatly.'

I smiled proudly. I'd heard the story on the drive down. 'Mrs Jameson doesn't miss a thing,' I said. 'And she's an excellent judge of character.'

The smile left Mrs Hall's face. 'Yes, well. That's a hard-earned trait.' She hesitated, obviously wondering whether to be indiscreet. I kept quiet, hoping the cosiness of the dark and the oil lamp would encourage her. 'Unfortunately, not one Iris had acquired before she married Julian Jameson,' she said, rewarding my patience.

'You knew him?' I asked. Mrs Jameson never spoke of her late husband.

She shook her head in distaste, her lips compressed. 'I met him once or twice. He was quite a well-known artist in his day. Notorious, even. But there's no stopping Iris when she is set on a plan.'

She stopped, perhaps realising how inappropriate it was to discuss her friend's past with her employee.

'Anyway, that was a very long time ago,' she said, briskly. 'Do you have everything you need? Remember to blow the whistle if you see or hear anything.'

She departed, leaving me with the hissing lantern, the pattering rain on the glass, and new information. Mrs Jameson, married to a famous but disreputable artist! This was news indeed. I didn't recognise the name of Julian Jameson, but I felt sure that my friend Hugh Williams, a painter who taught at the Slade School of Art, would. I would have to ask him when we got back to London.

I poured myself some coffee, more to keep warm than because I was thirsty. Then I paced up and down for a while. My feet felt like lumps of ice in my Wellington boots. I wished I'd put a pair of woollen socks over my stockings.

The night seemed unnaturally quiet. I strained my ears, but could hear nothing from the house. There was an occasional whinny from the stable block. No shouts from the street, no clatter of carts or rattle of trams, no motor cars tooting their horns, no footsteps, voices or music from neighbouring houses. It was almost never silent at home in London, I realised. There was always someone or something making a racket.

I gazed at the lilies, my only companions for the next two hours. There was something unearthly about their upright perfection, especially in the dark when their vivid colour was dimmed. The sweet perfume seemed to hide within it a trace of rottenness, as if the flowers grew out of spoiled flesh. My mother wouldn't have lilies in the house. They're only fit for a graveyard, she said. Flowers for the dead, not the living.

An unearthly shriek ripped through the night. I gasped, raised the lantern and ran to the end of the glasshouse. It seemed to have come from the stable yard. My sweaty fingers scrambled in my pocket for the whistle, heart hammering in my throat. What on earth could make such a beastly sound? It sounded like someone was being murdered.

The noise came again. Something was moving. Something – two things – circling. I held my breath as they separated and turned towards the lantern, the light catching on their eyes.

I breathed and set the lantern down. A pair of fox cubs, scrapping over something they'd found in the yard. They yowled again, a horrible sound that could almost be human, then whisked away, their white-tipped brushes disappearing into the night.

My heart thudded back to its normal pace. How did anyone sleep in the countryside, when the silence could be shattered by such a noise? Give me the hubbub of London any day or night.

I walked back to the table and took one of the packets of sandwiches from the pile. It hadn't been that long since dinner, but the shock had made me peckish. The sandwiches were rather decent: tangy cheddar cheese with onion chutney and lettuce fresh from the kitchen garden. I shook the crumbs from my coat, checked the time on the carriage clock Mrs Hall had placed on the table. A quarter past eleven – three quarters of an hour still to go. Time seemed to be passing jolly slowly.

Something roused me. I jerked my head up with a shock, realising with shame that I had almost fallen asleep. I was cold and my legs felt stiff as I rose to my feet. What had I heard?

I listened, straining my ears, then gasped as something swooped overhead above the glass roof, white and silent. Then I heard the noise which had woken me from my doze. A mournful hooting, an owl out on the hunt. I followed it with my eyes as it drifted towards the woods. I'd never seen an owl before. It disappeared and I was turning back to the table to see what time it was now, when another movement caught at the corner of my eye.

Something pale glimmered, then disappeared by the dark hedge that housed the gate to the flower garden. I stared. What had it been? Another owl, perhaps? But it was not high enough to be an owl. A goose, maybe, or a sheep? I wasn't sure whether livestock roamed freely around the countryside. Although I had only seen it for a second, it left the impression that it had been upright, like a person dressed in white. A ghost, if I believed in such things. Which I didn't, I told myself firmly.

I felt in my pocket for the whistle and raised it to my lips.

Then I stopped. I was being ridiculous. I'd frightened myself half to death over a pair of foxes and an owl. I'd almost fallen asleep, and I was still drowsy. It would be too shaming to raise the alarm over a goose. I looked hard into the darkness. The cobblestones of the yard gleamed black and wet, although the rain had stopped. Perhaps I'd imagined it.

A moment later, a figure crossed the stable yard with a jaunty stride. I ran to the door and unlocked it. Diana Eversholt raised her hand, a grin on her face.

'I say, this is a lark! How did you get on? Any suspicious saboteurs lurking around? Let's have a coffee together before you go, if you're not too tired. It isn't quite midnight yet.'

Chapter 8

I was relieved to have company. Diana Eversholt would not have panicked over the local wildlife, I told myself as we poured coffee from our flasks.

'This makes me think of camping up in the mountains,' she said. 'An oil lamp in the dark, and the stars shining overhead. It's stopped raining, thank goodness. You can see the Plough and the Pole Star.'

I smiled. 'You'll have to show me. I'm afraid I don't know what they look like. You can't usually see any stars in London, what with the fog and the glow of the street lamps.'

'True.' She stretched out her legs, clad in thick woollen stockings and sturdy lace-up boots. 'I don't suppose I should smoke, in case I'm accused of trying to choke the precious lilies to death. So, what's been happening? Any excitement?'

'You didn't pass anyone on your way from the house?' I asked, tentatively. I was still wondering about the pale thing I'd thought I'd seen.

'Not a dicky bird. Why, have you seen someone?'

'I don't think so. Probably an animal of some sort.' I explained my scare over the foxes, and the owl that swooped overhead, trying to make it a humorous story and play down how frightened I'd been.

'God, those foxes,' she laughed, 'they do sound awful. Almost human, don't you think?' She sipped her coffee. 'I remember the first time we camped out in the Himalayas, and I heard the yaks grunting around the fire. They sound just like old men, grumbling away to themselves over a glass of port. Then every now and then, one of them would give this enormous bellow and you'd jump out of your skin.'

She grinned. 'And then there was the day we saw a snow leopard pounce on a baby goat. The poor kid bleated like billy-oh, but the leopard was rather beautiful.'

I felt even sillier for my fright about fox cubs. 'I think you're awfully brave, going to all those strange places,' I said. 'I haven't been further than Margate. Not even across the English Channel.'

'Really?' She looked at me in surprise. 'But then you get involved in all those gruesome murder cases that Constance was telling me about. That's what I call brave – facing up to murderers and whatnot.'

I shrugged modestly, secretly rather pleased. 'I'm getting used to it. Guarding a few lilies is tame by comparison with some of our investigations.'

'I'll wager.'

She sat in silence for a moment, scuffing the gravel up with her boot. She frowned down into her coffee, as if she was trying to read a message in the steam.

'Marjorie, what would you do, if you thought someone might have committed a murder and got away with it?' she asked. Her tone was light, but I didn't think she was asking out of idle curiosity.

'Well,' I said, cautiously, 'I suppose I'd try to find out more. And if there was any evidence, I'd tell the police.' I thought of the first investigation I'd undertaken with Mrs Jameson, one result of which had been a man's conviction for the previously undiscovered murder of his first wife. My only regret was that his second wife, the woman's sister, wasn't tried alongside him.

'But how do you find out?' she asked. 'What if the only evidence is something somebody saw?' I noticed the hand holding her cup was trembling. Her face was carefully blank, but a muscle twitched at the corner of her mouth. Something had frightened the redoubtable Diana Eversholt.

'Well, you need to think about motive,' I said, reciting Mrs Jameson's principles of murder investigation. 'And opportunity, and then about their character. Did they have a reason for wanting someone dead, did they have the chance to do it, and are they the sort of person who might? And, of course, you need to think about the person who saw something. Are they a reliable witness?'

She nodded. 'I see. And if the answer to all those questions is yes...'

'Then,' I said, 'you should be very careful who you tell. But it might be a good idea to talk to the police.'

She shivered. 'But the person who saw something… they would be in danger. Would they not?'

I set down my empty cup and screwed the lid back on the flask. 'Mrs Eversholt, is there someone in particular you are worried about? Because the answer is yes. The witness would be in grave danger, if they knew that someone had committed an undiscovered murder, until the suspect is safely in police custody.' I thought of the killers we had encountered. 'When they have killed once, it becomes much easier to do it again.'

She rose. 'Call me Diana, won't you?' She turned away,

gazed down the rows of lilies, standing like sentinels. 'I am
worried... yes, a little. Don't mistake me – not for myself. I'll
be all right. I always am.' She flashed me a grin and I could see
her intrepid nature reassert itself.

'Can you at least tell me whom you suspect? Is it someone
here?'

Diana laughed, a rather cynical chuckle. 'You've just said I
should be very careful whom I tell. And I don't want to put you
in any danger. No, it's just a theory. Go back to bed, Marjorie.
I've kept you up long enough. I will think it over.'

Back in my little room, I found my desire for sleep had left
me completely. I saw a line of light under the connecting door
to Mrs Jameson's room and tapped lightly.

'Come,' she called. I turned the handle and put my head
around the door warily. I was never sure of my reception if
Mrs Jameson had been sleeping. But I saw she was still up,
wrapped in a warm cashmere dressing gown and sitting at a
desk, browsing through a large gardening book that Mrs Hall
had loaned her from the library.

She beckoned me in. 'Anything to report?'

I sat in the upright chair she indicated and explained about
my curious conversation with Diana.

'And I think it would take a lot to scare Mrs Eversholt,' I said.
'She talked about camping up in the mountains and hearing
yaks bellowing.' I wasn't entirely sure what a yak was, but I
could well believe they would be alarming. 'Not to mention
seeing leopards eating goats.'

Mrs Jameson tapped her chin with her index finger. 'How
very interesting. She's right, of course. People are far more
dangerous than leopards. She didn't tell you when this
suspected murder happened?'

I shook my head. 'She put it in theoretical terms. But when I asked if she was worried about someone, she said she was. Although not for herself. And she wouldn't tell me whom she suspected.'

Mrs Jameson walked to her window. There was nothing to be seen in the darkness outside, except for a waning moon.

'I wonder whom she is worried for, then. Who has seen something they shouldn't have that might endanger them? And what bearing does it have on the sabotage?'

She turned to me, her large grey eyes shining. 'Well done, Marjorie. You've made this rather dull investigation a whole lot more interesting. Now, you get some sleep. We may have a busy day tomorrow.'

Chapter 9

Fortunately, I had brought an alarm clock. After lying awake
thinking until gone one o'clock in the morning, I'd fallen into
a deep sleep and was momentarily disorientated when the bell
clanged next to my ear at half past seven.

Downstairs, Mr Hall was already tucking into scrambled
eggs and bacon, the newspaper propped up in front of him.

'Good morning, Miss Swallow. Do help yourself from the
sideboard. How did your watch go last night?' he asked.

'Uneventful, thank you.' I loaded my plate with bacon, egg
and fried bread. It smelled heavenly. 'Except for scaring myself
silly when a pair of foxes started yelping in the stable yard.'

He laughed. 'Yes, they do make a racket. I thought I heard
them last night. Cubbing season in August will see them off.'

I felt rather sorry for the fox cubs, but thought it best to
keep my sympathies to myself, knowing that country people
had different attitudes to city folk when it came to animals. I
tucked into the bacon, which was crisp and extremely tasty.

'Constance will be with us shortly,' he continued. 'She went
to see Harry before he starts work. Tommy will have finished
his watch by now, I suppose. Iris went for a walk, but she said
she'll be back for breakfast. I haven't seen the other watchers,
but I suppose we'd have heard by now if anyone had caught

a saboteur lurking in the grounds.' The lines around his eyes deepened with a mischievous smile. Although I knew how important the lilies were to him commercially, I suspected he found the whole cloak-and-dagger business of trying to catch someone over-watering the plants rather funny.

Mrs Hall, Mrs Jameson and Tommy Eversholt all arrived together.

'What ho! Splendid breakfast,' said Mr Eversholt, heaping his plate high. 'Gives one an appetite, all this skulduggery.' He sat opposite me and began to demolish his pile of food.

'Well, the lilies are all fine,' said Mrs Hall. 'Harry arrived at eight and we checked the plants. No sign of Bert, although they're supposed to start at the same time.' She took her seat and reached for toast from the silver rack. 'So, we managed to protect them, Iris, but we're no closer to finding out who did it.'

'Not completely true,' said Mrs Jameson, spooning scrambled egg onto buttered toast. 'We didn't see anyone crossing to the glasshouses from the main house, except for the watchers. My chauffeur kept a look-out on the back of the gardener's cottage and says nobody left it before Harry this morning. That tells us that, if it was an insider, nobody attempted sabotage last night.'

Mr Hall stood. 'Well, they all knew about the watch,' he observed, rolling up his newspaper. 'Please excuse me. I need to run up to London this morning. Shareholder meeting. They will be most anxious to hear about our progress.' He strode out of the room.

Mrs Jameson finished a mouthful. 'Neither did we see any traces of anyone attempting to come in from outside. If they had come close, the watchers would have seen or heard them,' she added.

I suddenly remembered the white shape I'd seen. But I wasn't even sure if that had been a person. I would tell Mrs Jameson later. I'd quite forgotten about it in the intrigue of Diana's conversation.

'Which proves nothing,' said Ernest Buckler, entering the room. 'Except that the blighters didn't get close enough for us to see them. We should have kept the lights out.' He sat and stared at his partner. 'You've got quite an appetite this morning, Tommy,' he said.

Mr Eversholt grinned and wiped his mouth. 'Certainly have. I'm starving after all that watching.' He looked over at me. 'I apologise for this revolting display of greed, Miss Swallow. Ernest knows what I'm like. We were at school together, you know, although he was a prefect when I was still in short trousers. I've always liked my food, what?'

Mr Buckler grunted and cracked open a boiled egg. 'You'll get fat. You don't want to be carrying too much weight in the field.'

I had noticed yesterday that Lavinia Buckler barely ate a thing at mealtimes. Perhaps Ernest Buckler didn't approve of his wives carrying too much weight, either.

On cue, Diana strolled into the room. She wore a neat navy-blue cardigan belted over a simple white blouse and pleated navy skirt, like a particularly chic schoolgirl. She regarded her current and former husband for a moment with a quizzical expression, and then helped herself to bacon.

'So, we all survived the night,' she said, lightly. 'And so did the flowers, I take it. What's the next step, Mrs Jameson?'

'I think I will drive over to Kingsmead Place,' she said. 'See if Sir Norman Alperton is at home. Marjorie, you will accompany me. If, as Constance suspects, the sabotage is being organised from Kingsmead, we had better inspect the lay of the land.'

Mrs Hall beamed. 'Finally. I told you to start with him,' she said. 'I told that blasted policeman from the village, too, when Harry apprehended Dick Cooper red-handed. But he said it wasn't a police matter. He wouldn't even arrest Cooper, never mind Alperton. He had the cheek to tell me that watering plants was a domestic affair for the landowner, and not for the constabulary. Those are valuable plants, I told him. Would he have said it was my responsibility if it was actual sapphires that had been destroyed?'

I hid a smile, imagining the likely response of Mrs Jameson's favourite policeman, Inspector Peter Chadwick of Scotland Yard, if he'd been summoned to investigate the over-enthusiastic irrigation of a greenhouse.

Mrs Jameson checked her wristwatch. 'It's gone nine o'clock now. Marjorie, tell Frankie to have the car ready for half-past nine.'

I rose, pushing my plate away. 'Of course, Mrs Jameson.' I'd have a quiet chat with Frankie first and see if she'd seen any white-clad figures drifting about before midnight.

The breakfast room door slammed open, bouncing off the sideboard with a clatter. We all looked up in surprise. Standing in the doorway, cap clutched in his hands, was Bert Smith. His eyes were wide with distress, and he was badly out of breath.

'Come quickly,' he said, as soon as he could get the words out. 'Please. It's my dad. He's collapsed.'

Chapter 10

Bert and I raced down to the glasshouse with Ernest Buckler, Tommy Eversholt, and Diana at our heels. The door stood open. Harry Smith was sprawled face down on the stone flags.

I dropped to my knees and turned him over. 'Can you hear me, Mr Smith?' His skin was pale and clammy, his eyes staring glassily up at me, their pupils wide. His lips were tinged with blue. I put my fingers to his neck, felt for a pulse. I couldn't find one. Oh, no.

I laid him flat and leaned over, placing my cheek close to his open mouth. No air stirred. Bert hovered next to me, desperation in his face.

'I'm awfully sorry.' I looked beyond him to the other three. 'Has anyone called for a doctor?'

'I'll run back and ask Mrs Hall,' said Diana. 'But... is it too late?'

I looked down at the man's lifeless gaze, his grey cheeks. I remembered what Harry's wife had said the day before about his heart and thought of the way Harry had gripped his left arm as if it hurt him.

'Did he have heart problems?' I asked Bert.

He sank to his knees beside me and took his father's limp hand.

'Yes,' he said, his voice gruff. 'The doctor said he should take it easy. But how's he supposed to do that?'

My throat constricted. Poor Bert, and poor Mrs Smith. I thought of her now, tidying away the breakfast things, getting on with the laundry, with no idea of the calamity about to break up her life.

'It's my fault.' Bert's voice was fierce. 'I should have told him to rest and come myself. But I wanted my porridge and said that she couldn't expect us to work on empty stomachs. And Dad was worried about being late, so he came running over to be here at eight for the handover. Mrs Hall's orders.'

He looked up and his face hardened. 'She blooming well killed him. Worked him to death. It isn't right. And I don't care who hears me say so.'

'Come along, old chap,' said Tommy Eversholt, uneasily. 'Could have happened any time, eh? It's rotten for you. Shall we go back to the house, get you a cup of tea? It's been a shock.' He reached out a hand to pull Bert to his feet.

'No.' The man turned his face away. 'I'm staying with him till the doctor gets here.'

I looked around at the crunch of gravel on the path outside. Mrs Jameson and Mrs Hall stood in the doorway, shock on their faces.

'Oh, my godfathers,' said Mrs Hall. 'When did this happen, Bert?' She hurried over and crouched beside us.

He looked away, his mouth sulky. 'Found him like this when I arrived. Couldn't wake him.'

'Run and telephone for a doctor, Tommy. You know where it is – in Walter's office,' said Mrs Hall. I saw her glance quickly around the glasshouse. Even faced with this disaster, she thought for the welfare of the flowers. 'Shut the door behind you, please.'

'Of course,' said Tommy.

'I'll come with you,' said Diana, briskly. 'We need to start packing. I had a message from my editor before breakfast. He wants me in Scotland tomorrow, so we'll have to head back to London.'

'No,' said Mr Buckler, suddenly. We turned to look at him. He was staring down at poor Harry, his face almost as pale as the corpse.

'What do you mean?' asked Diana.

He looked angry. 'Surely your packing can wait? A man's just died, for goodness sake. Why is everything about you and your career?'

Mrs Jameson's voice rang sharply through the glasshouse. 'Mr Eversholt, please go at once and telephone for a doctor and the local police.'

'The police?' Mrs Hall protested. 'Surely not, Iris.'

Mrs Jameson ignored her. 'Please go right away. Tell them a man has been found dead, suddenly and unexpectedly. We shall need them here.'

He nodded and disappeared, Diana at his side.

'Iris, what on earth are you doing? The poor man probably had a heart attack,' said Mrs Hall. 'Whatever do you want the police for?'

'They can arrest you, for a start.' Bert got to his feet. His breath was coming fast and shallow and I could hear it wheezing through his airways. 'Working a man to death.' Sweat had broken on his brow, although the day was far from warm.

'Now, listen to me, Bert,' began Mrs Hall, her colour mounting.

'You listen,' he said. 'About time you did, I reckon.' He paused and I saw he was struggling to speak. Bad lungs, his mother had said, from a mustard gas attack. Bad lungs, bad heart. The Smith men didn't seem to have much luck with their organs. 'My dad worked… You ought to…' He wheezed to a halt and his face went pale.

I grabbed a folding chair from beside the table where we watchers had sat the previous night. Sandwich wrappers were strewn across its surface and a cup of coffee had been knocked over, the liquid spreading a dark stain across the gravel.

'Sit down, Bert. Don't try to speak,' I said. His eyes were wide with fear. 'Slow breaths, counting to five.' I crouched before him, trying to remember the nursing I'd done in the VAD service during the War.

'What's wrong with the man?' asked Ernest, his voice irritable.

'Gas damaged his lungs,' said Mrs Hall, more kindly. 'Bert, do as Miss Swallow says. I am very sorry about your father. I will make sure you and your mother are all right, I promise.'

Bert slowly regained control of his breathing and his colour began to come back. I let out my own breath in a rush. As Oscar Wilde would say, to lose one gardener in a morning might be regarded as misfortune, to lose both looks like carelessness. I felt rather shocked at my inappropriate thought, and hoped I wasn't getting cynical.

'Someone should tell my mum,' Bert said between breaths. 'It's not right that she doesn't know.'

'Do you want me to go with you?' I asked. Poor Mrs Smith. This was going to be a horrible shock for her.

'I'm staying here with him,' he repeated. 'But someone should tell her.'

49

'I'll go,' said Mrs Hall, brusquely. 'It's my responsibility.' She turned on her heel and marched out of the glasshouse.

'Well,' Ernest Buckler looked around, 'not much I can do here, I suppose. Maybe I should find my wife. She gets very upset about such things.' He stalked out, leaving Mrs Jameson and me with Bert and his father's body.

My employer and I exchanged glances. I knew what that meant. Although Harry's death seemed to have been natural, Mrs Jameson had taught me to take nothing for granted, especially when an investigation was underway. We would need to establish a timeline of events. She passed me my handbag, which I'd left in the breakfast room, and I extracted my pencil and notebook.

'Can you remember what time it was when you came down to the glasshouse, Bert?' asked Mrs Jameson. 'And do you know when your father left the cottage this morning?'

He hunched over in his chair and clasped his hands between his knees.

'We both woke late. Dad usually sets his alarm for seven, but he must have forgotten. He's been dead on his feet these last weeks.' He realised what he'd said and shuddered. 'Anyhow, the first thing I heard this morning was Dad yelling that it was ten to eight and we were going to be late. I stuck the pillow over my head. Then he came in and pulled off the blankets.'

He sighed and sat up, running his hands through his hair.

'I told him to leave me be, didn't I? I said I'd get up when I was ready and have my porridge, and he should do the same. We had a bit of a row, then he went off. I took my time over breakfast, I admit. I suppose I was making a point. Had a second cup of tea with Mum. Then I walked over here at about five to nine.'

He sighed heavily and looked down at the older man. 'Soon as I got to the door, I saw him lying there. I tried to wake him, then I ran up to the house.' He turned his gaze to me. 'You know the rest.'

'Marjorie? What was the situation when you arrived?' asked Mrs Jameson.

Briefly, I recapped. 'His colour, and the clamminess of his skin, suggested a problem with circulation,' I said. 'And the way he was lying with his arm across his chest, as if he was in pain. That's typical of a heart attack.'

'He had one last year,' Bert interjected. 'Doctor said he shouldn't get over-excited or work too hard.' He hunched over again and spoke to the gravel path. 'I shouldn't have argued with him, should I? But he's so blooming... I can't stand it. "Yes, Mrs Hall, no, Mrs Hall, whatever you say, Mrs Hall." I just wished he'd show some backbone for a change.' Bert lapsed into silence.

Mrs Jameson was prowling around the glasshouse. She stopped by the table.

'How many flasks were there, Marjorie? And how many packets of sandwiches?'

'One for each of us. Mrs Hall's flask was empty when I arrived, and I drank mine during my watch, and ate my sandwiches. So, there were four unopened flasks and four packets of sandwiches when Diana Eversholt arrived.'

I made a note in my book. Mrs Jameson liked to have a thorough record of a possible crime scene. She counted through the empty wrappers.

'All accounted for. There are four empty flasks on the floor there,' she pointed with her cane, 'and two on the table.' She counted the mugs. 'Six cups, including that one that's been

51

knocked over. I don't suppose that was there when you left, Marjorie?'

I shook my head. 'But there were still three more people to come after Diana. Peregrine Hall, Ernest Buckler and Tommy Eversholt.'

Mrs Jameson nodded thoughtfully. 'And Tommy handed over to Harry when he arrived from the cottage at eight. Constance arrived around eight o'clock too, and I met them shortly afterwards in the garden. I estimate it was around quarter past eight when the three of us came in for breakfast, don't you think?'

I nodded. 'I came down at about ten past eight, and Mr Hall said he needed to leave by half past at the latest.' I scribbled the timings in my notebook. 'We can ask Mr Eversholt if he spilled the coffee. And see if Mrs Hall noticed it when she checked the plants with Harry.'

Bert looked up. 'What are you talking about? Why do you care about who spilled the blooming coffee?' he asked.

I hesitated. Mrs Jameson took a chair and sat next to him.

'We need to know for sure how your father died,' she said, her voice gentle.

He frowned. 'What do you mean?'

'It may have been a heart attack,' she said. 'But when someone dies during the course of an investigation, I've learned to take nothing for granted.'

Chapter 11

'That's daft,' said Bert. 'He's been working too hard. If you want to blame anyone, blame Mrs Hall. Or me, for winding him up this morning. He didn't drink coffee, anyhow. Nasty stuff, he called it.'

Footsteps sounded outside. Constance Hall, holding Mrs Smith by the arm. Bert rose to his feet. Mrs Smith's face was composed, her gait steady.

'Mum,' called Bert, his voice breaking.

She held out her hands. Her son took them and led her towards her husband's body.

She sighed, a long sigh, bent and caressed his cheek. 'Harry, my love.' She straightened. 'It would be thirty-four years, this summer, since we were married.' She looked at her son. 'We had to wait ten years, till you came along. And barely a cross word between us.'

She turned to Mrs Hall with dignity. 'Thank you, madam. Please ask if some of the stable boys will help Bertram to take him to the cottage. I'll go to the church this morning and speak to the vicar. There's a spot in the churchyard, by the far field. We've talked about it before. We used to sit there together, when we were young.'

'I'm afraid that may need to wait for a while,' said Mrs

Jameson, her voice kind but firm. 'The doctor is on his way from the village, and so, I hope, are the police.'

Mrs Smith turned, her expression puzzled. 'The police? Whatever for? No, that's not needed. Leave him to us.'

'That's what I told her,' said Bert, taking his mother's arm.

Mrs Jameson looked unusually uncomfortable. 'I understand, but there are processes for sudden deaths, Mrs Smith. I'm sorry, really I am. But you can't just take him away.'

Mrs Smith regarded her for a moment with disdain, then turned to Mrs Hall. 'I should like to make arrangements for my husband to be properly buried, like the respectable man he was.'

'And I'm sure he will be, very soon,' said Mrs Hall. She turned to Mrs Jameson. 'Are you sure all this is needed, Iris? It will cause so much upset. Not to mention gossip, which we could really do without.'

I knew how stubborn Mrs Jameson could be, but feared she had met her match in Mrs Hall and Mrs Smith. However, as was often the case, I'd underestimated her.

'We must await the arrival of the doctor and the police,' she said. 'Think how strange they will find it if they arrive to discover that potential evidence has been removed. If you wish to keep gossip and upset to a minimum, Constance, I suggest you enable the authorities to do their jobs quickly and efficiently. Isn't that how England works?'

The words 'authorities' and 'England' seemed to work a kind of magic on Mrs Smith. 'I don't mind waiting for Doctor Barnes,' she conceded. 'And he can tell the constable about poor Harry's heart.'

'Well then, that's settled,' said Mrs Hall, with relief.

Bert shook his head. 'It's not right. You don't have to agree to anything you don't want to, Mum. We should get him home, like you said. I'll go and find some of the lads to help. It's not right, leaving him lying out here where anyone going past could see.'

I'd been thinking much the same. 'Perhaps I could fetch a blanket from the house,' I suggested.

Mrs Smith glanced at me with approval. 'Please get one from the cottage, Miss. There's a crocheted blanket folded over his armchair.' She turned to her son. 'No more arguments, Bertram. Let the authorities do their work.'

I sprinted across the yard past the rows of glasshouses, heedless of mud and puddles. The door to the cottage stood open. The stone floor was swept clean, the grate emptied of ash and the breakfast things had been cleared away from the round table under the window. Before the fireplace stood two green armchairs, both of which had been neatly patched over the arms and on the seats, where Mrs Jameson and I had sat the day before. A multi-coloured blanket was folded over the back of the chair closest to the fire.

I picked it up, imagined Mrs Smith settling it over her husband's knees when he came in cold and wet after a long day's work. I thought of her patiently wielding her crochet hook, using up scraps of wool left over from other projects to make a cheerful patchwork of colours. My eyes blurred with tears, and I had to swallow down the constriction in my throat. It seemed so unfair. Why should Harry have to work until he dropped? Old age pensions had been introduced for men before the war, but you had to be seventy to qualify. I wondered how old Mr Smith had been.

As I turned to go, a book on the mantelpiece caught my eye. It hadn't been there before. Someone had placed it neatly next to Bert's army photograph. I hoped Mrs Smith had a photograph of her husband somewhere.

Curious, I picked up the book. It was a drab cardboard-covered thing, barely more than a pamphlet. Plain text in red letters on the front read: *Manifesto of the Communist Party*, by Frederick Engels and Karl Marx. Price: One penny.

I'd heard about it, of course, but never seen an actual copy before. My parents were fervently anti-communist. Feeling rather daring, I opened it.

'A spectre is haunting Europe – the spectre of Communism,' I read, with a shiver. I scanned down the page. *'The history of all hitherto existing societies is the history of class struggles.'* Was that what Bert believed – that we were all fighting against each other, worker against employer?

I turned the page, and a scrap of paper fell out. Quickly, I stooped and picked it up. After a very brief struggle with my conscience, I read it.

'The Royal visit will be on the morning of Tuesday May 22,' read the copperplate handwriting. 'You know what to do.'

'I say, what are you doing here?'

I jumped guiltily and replaced the book on the mantelpiece, closed my fist around the paper, and turned to see who had caught me.

Chapter 12

Peregrine Hall lounged in the open doorway, eyeing me with curiosity.

'I came to collect a blanket for Mrs Smith,' I said. He frowned with confusion. Clearly, he hadn't heard the news.

'What were you doing with that book, then?'

'Mr Smith has died,' I said, hoping the news would distract him. 'Poor Bert found him in the glasshouse when he arrived for work.'

'Oh, Lord. What a rotten business,' said Peregrine. 'I saw the doctor's car. Wondered who'd been taken ill.' He eyed the book again, but let the matter drop. 'Are you going there now?'

He fell into step beside me. Had he seen me take the scrap of paper? I transferred it to my skirt pocket under cover of the blanket. With luck, Bert would not notice it had gone.

As we rounded the corner, a policeman wobbled across the yard on his bicycle.

'Hullo! What's old Perkins doing?' My companion stopped in his tracks. 'I say. This hasn't got anything to do with the sabotage business, has it? They couldn't sabotage the plants, so they sabotaged the gardener instead?'

I looked at him in surprise. Even Mrs Jameson hadn't suggested such a thing.

'I don't know,' I said. 'Excuse me. I should take this blanket to Mrs Smith.'

Inside the glasshouse, the doctor confirmed death, and Harry Smith's history of heart trouble.

'I've been warning him about it for months,' he told PC Perkins, the policeman, who seemed to have little idea why he had been summoned. 'Poor chap had been working too hard. He had an attack last year. All too common for a man in his sixties, unfortunately. I'm sorry it's come to this, Mrs Smith. I'll write the death certificate this afternoon.'

'One moment,' said Mrs Jameson. 'Could I have a word with Dr Barnes and Constable Perkins outside?'

They both looked to Mrs Hall, who nodded, her face troubled. The four of them retreated to the path. I helped Mrs Smith, who had been clutching the blanket to her chest, spread it over her husband's body.

'What's this all about?' she asked me, after she'd gently smoothed Harry's hair and adjusted the blanket over his face. 'I'm not daft, you know. Why has your American lady called for the police?'

I glanced outside. Mrs Jameson and the two men seemed to be having an argument. I had little doubt about who would emerge victorious.

'She's had a lot of experience with investigating deaths,' I said, carefully. 'She wants to be sure everything is as it seems.'

Mrs Smith fixed me with her sharp blue eyes. 'She suspects that someone caused my Harry's death?'

I shook my head. 'Not exactly. She wants to be sure there are no grounds for suspicion. The thing is, she was here to investigate whether someone had been deliberately damaging the lilies. And then Harry died right after the first night of watching in the glasshouse.'

Bert looked up from the chair he'd sunk into. 'So what?' he asked. 'Why would someone do away with my dad?'

Peregrine had been wandering around the glasshouse. He returned, a gleam in his eye.

'All part of the sabotage, don't you think? I mean, this will put Mater's plans for the garden back, won't it?'

I winced at his insensitivity. Bert got to his feet, knocking the chair over.

'Now, love…' began Mrs Smith, warning in her voice.

'Don't talk soft,' said Bert, his voice low. 'You might think you sound very clever at *university*,' – his tone as he pronounced the word was beyond scornful – 'but you don't know what you're talking about here.'

Peregrine flushed. 'I know you and Harry weren't getting on, anyway. I know you'd been having rows about going to Chelsea. Maybe the police should investigate your motivation for murder.'

Bert grabbed Peregrine by the collar and pulled back a fist. His mother and I scrambled to our feet.

'Stop it, Bert,' called Mrs Smith.

'Oi! What's happening here?' PC Perkins crossed the glasshouse in a flash, his speed belying his rather advanced years. 'Bertram Smith, you stop that nonsense. You should be ashamed, with your poor father lying there not yet cold.'

Bert dropped his fist and released his hold on Peregrine. He clamped his jaw shut and turned away. Peregrine, looking aggrieved, rubbed his neck.

'Nothing I can't manage, Constable Perkins. Just a little altercation.' He took care to get well out of Bert's reach, all the same.

'He's very sorry. It's the shock,' said Mrs Smith, grabbing her son by the arm. 'Now, you go and find some of the stable boys to help us carry your father home. Do you hear me?'

PC Perkins coughed apologetically. 'I'm afraid not, Mrs Smith. And I'm afraid I must ask you all to leave here, except for Dr Barnes. There are things we need to do. I shall have to call for help from the police station at Faversham.'

Mrs Hall looked mutinous. 'We shall need access to the glasshouse today, Constable. It's two weeks before the opening day of the flower show. The lilies need tending to.'

Constable Perkins swallowed hard. 'I will try to make sure it is free for you by the end of today, Mrs Hall. And Mr Smith's body will be available for burial as soon as possible, but I need to request a post-mortem examination.'

'What? No, you blooming well don't,' shouted Bert, pulling away from his mother. 'I won't have it. No-one's cutting up my dad.'

'I'm afraid it is a necessary precaution...' began Dr Barnes.

'Precaution?' Bert was running short of breath again. 'He's dead, isn't he? No point in taking precautions now, is there? You couldn't keep him alive, so you're not blooming well having him dead.'

Mrs Smith stepped forward. 'Bertram, I've known Dr Barnes since before you were born. He brought you safe into the world, young man, when I couldn't manage it without help. If Dr Barnes and Constable Perkins say that's what's needed, then that's what's going to happen.'

The dignity in her bearing was in no way undermined by the tear that was now making its way down her cheek. 'Dr Barnes, I trust you to make sure my Harry's looked after properly. I'm going home now, and Bertram will come with me.'

She bent to smooth the blanket again, and then walked slowly out of the door, her son following sullenly at her heels.

'Come on, Constance,' said Mrs Jameson. 'We should leave these gentlemen to make their arrangements.'

Mrs Hall, Peregrine, Mrs Jameson and I turned for the door. In the doorway, Mrs Jameson paused and spoke to Constable Perkins.

'Be sure to retain the sandwich wrappers and flasks, Constable. They should be tested. Please don't hesitate to ask me if I can be of any more assistance.'

Chapter 13

Back at the house, Mrs Hall ordered coffee and we sat in the morning room, absorbing the tragic turn of events.

'I should tell Walter,' said Mrs Hall. 'And he should tell the shareholders. They won't be pleased. Goodness knows how we're going to get the garden ready in time now. I'll have to get the stable lads to help, but they don't have the first idea about gardening. I suppose I'll need to put Bert in charge of the plants and direct the building work myself.'

Mrs Jameson sipped her coffee. 'I'd let the boy calm down a bit before speaking to him,' she advised. 'He has just lost his father. And he was very agitated.'

'I'll say,' complained Peregrine. 'The man's out of control. You should be warning him he risks being sacked for insolence, not putting him in charge.'

Mrs Hall gave her son a long, cool look. 'And you should be apologising for whatever you said that upset him so much. I don't know what goes on in that noddle of yours, Perry. But I'll need you mucking in, too. So, you can bally well bury the hatchet with Bert Smith.'

It was perhaps an unfortunate choice of words. I mused over Bert's behaviour. Peregrine had been insensitive, but was he right? Bert had been particularly against Mrs Jameson calling in the police, and the idea of a post-mortem. And his anger had ignited quickly into violence when Peregrine suggested that Bert might be involved in his father's death. I thought of the communist pamphlet I had found at the gardener's cottage, and the note about the Royal visit to the Chelsea Flower Show. I'd not had a chance to tell Mrs Jameson about that, yet.

Harry had told Bert that he could forget about going to Chelsea, when we interrupted their row at the cottage the previous day. And, of course, Bert had found his father's body. One of Mrs Jameson's precepts was that most murders are family affairs, and that you should always be suspicious of the person who discovers the corpse. Had Peregrine, in his clumsy way, hit on the truth, or something close to it? I wondered if you could kill a person with heart trouble by giving them a fright or hitting them in the chest. Had Bert somehow caused his father's death, so he could carry out whatever he had planned at Chelsea?

Lavinia joined us, her beautiful eyes wide. They were the exact colour of the pattern on her blue-and-white sprigged day dress, I noticed: a blue almost as intense as that of the lily flowers.

'Ernest says something has happened to one of the gardeners,' she said. 'How horrible. Is it all over with now?'

She took her coffee and opened the pack of cards she'd been playing with last night, setting them out for Patience. Peregrine looked up, then moved to the card table and watched as she shuffled the deck and started to deal.

'Oh! It's never going to come out,' she exclaimed after a few minutes of playing. 'Shall we have another game of rummy? I think I was getting better at it, don't you?'

Ernest Buckler entered the room quietly and stood by the

door, watching his wife laughing with Peregrine Hall. His eyes were cold. He picked up a newspaper and took it to the window seat without a word.

Minutes later, Diana and Tommy came down to the morning room. Diana had changed into a travelling suit that I instantly coveted – plum-coloured tweed with matching velvet trim, a toque hat and smart crocodile-skin button boots. She held a waxed mackintosh over her arm.

'We must be off,' she said. 'So sorry to leave you suddenly, Constance. You know what it's like. When the big boss calls, you jump.'

'I didn't hear a telephone ring this morning,' said Mrs Jameson. 'When did your call come through?'

Diana's smile flickered slightly. 'I expect you were out in the gardens,' she said. 'My editor likes to 'phone early, to make sure I'm not slacking. He wants me up in the Highlands of Scotland, for the opening of a new golf course. Apparently, the Prince of Wales is backing it. If we motor back to London now, I can get tickets for the night train and be there first thing tomorrow morning.'

'That's a pity. I shall miss you,' said Lavinia, looking up from her card game. She seemed quite sincere; her mouth quivered a little.

'Don't worry, dear heart. We shall see you again at Chelsea,' said Diana. 'Won't we, Tommy?'

He beamed around the room. 'Oh, rather. Wouldn't miss it for anything,' he said. 'First unveiling of the lily and all that, eh?'

Ernest Buckler threw down his newspaper. 'Golf,' he said scathingly to his ex-wife. 'Really?'

She returned his gaze coolly. 'Really. You should learn,

Ernest. It's tremendously useful for making social connexions. A most convenient sport for a journalist.'

Mrs Jameson gestured to me to open my notebook. 'I'm sure it is, Mrs Eversholt. Now, could you please give me your address in Scotland? I'm sure the police will require it, and I'm happy to pass it on.'

Diana looked stumped for a moment, then took the pencil from me. 'Of course. I'll write it down for you.' She scribbled in my notebook. 'Don't go showing everyone, please. You have no idea how many enemies you can pick up, in my profession.'

She laughed, but the look she gave me was serious, and she pressed my hand as she returned the book and pencil.

'Good luck with your investigations, Marjorie. Do let me know what you discover. I shall take a great interest in your career. Who knows, I might even write an article about you one day.'

I smiled, knowing full well how much that would annoy Mrs Jameson. As my employer liked to make clear, she considered herself the brains of our operation.

'Thank you. Safe travels,' I told Diana. I looked down at the book, half-expecting to see some kind of message, but it simply gave the address of a hotel in Inveraray.

Mrs Jameson's second precept: be suspicious of anybody who disappears as soon as a murder is announced. Their departure was precipitate, and I hadn't heard a telephone call come in before they arrived for breakfast, but why on earth would Diana or Tommy Eversholt want to murder Mrs Hall's gardener?

As they departed, I remembered our conversation of the night before. Did Diana think that someone had just got away with murder a second time? In which case, was her departure down to guilt – or fear?

Chapter 14

With all the disruption caused by Harry Smith's death, we didn't get to Kingsmead Place that day. Mrs Jameson had a long interview with Constable Perkins' superior, a sergeant who came over from Faversham. Luckily, he was young and ambitious, and seemed keen to leave no stone unturned in his investigation.

A police ambulance took Mr Smith's body away during the afternoon, after a visitation including the sergeant, a police surgeon and a constable with a camera who took careful photographs of the scene from every angle. This last was described to me by Frankie, whose room above the stables had a perfect view of the glasshouse.

'If only I'd been looking this morning, after Mrs Hall and Mr Eversholt left Harry on his own,' she said, handing me a short length of metal encased in white ceramic. 'Hold that, will you?' For want of anything else to do, she had the bonnet folded up on the Lagonda and was fine-tuning the engine. I twiddled the thing in my fingers, wondering how on earth she knew which bits did what.

'You didn't see Bert arrive?' I asked.

She shook her head. 'I was having breakfast in the kitchen. Did you have the bacon?' She took the length of metal back and started to attack it with a wire brush, dislodging oil and muck.

'Delicious. What are you doing?'

'Cleaning the spark plugs. Do you want a go?'

I looked at my clean fingernails. 'Maybe another time. Frankie, you didn't see anything last night, did you? I thought I saw something white, dodging around the corner of the hedge towards the flower garden.'

She looked up. 'What time?'

I tried to remember. 'Before Diana came over. Maybe a quarter to midnight?'

Frankie considered. 'I saw an owl. Scared the blooming daylights out of me. Never seen one before.'

I smiled. 'Same here. This was about the same time as the owl, but down in the yard. I only got a glimpse, out of the corner of my eye. I don't know if it was a person, or maybe an animal.'

Frankie fixed the spark plug back in place and took out another. 'I don't remember anything. It's weird, though, isn't it, all those animals wandering around? And it's so quiet – until something gives an almighty screech. I couldn't have slept if I'd tried.'

Mrs Jameson arranged another night's watching in the glasshouses, with Mr Hall taking the place of Tommy Eversholt and Lavinia standing in for Diana. Mindful of Lavinia's nerves, I took the midnight shift and tried to get a bit of sleep after dinner. When I arrived at ten minutes to midnight, Lavinia was pacing the glasshouse in borrowed rubber boots and an enormous cream-coloured raincoat, which wrapped almost double around her slim figure.

'Oh, I'm so glad you're here,' she said. 'I hate being on my own in the dark.' I saw she'd left her flask and sandwiches untouched. 'Perry walked me over. He's going to come and see me back to the cottage. It's so kind of him.'

That was one word for it, I thought. 'I'm sure there's nothing to be scared of,' I said. 'Although I must admit all the noise from foxes and so on is rather alarming. I grew up in London, in a flat above my parents' shop. I'm not used to the countryside.'

She really did seem frightened, however. 'I wish Diana and Tommy had stayed,' she continued. 'Diana's so wonderful, isn't she? I don't think anything scares her.'

Except, I thought, something had. 'She's very brave,' I agreed. 'It's nice that the two of you get on so well. It could have been awkward.'

She gave me a quick smile. 'She and Ernest were already divorced before I met him. She was engaged to Tommy. So, there was nothing for anyone to be jealous about, or anything silly like that.'

'How did you meet Ernest?' I couldn't imagine their social circles coinciding. Mrs Jameson had told me that Lavinia was from a very wealthy manufacturing family from Birmingham, and her father had settled an enormous inheritance on her when she married.

She smiled a little wistfully and gestured at the rows of lilies. 'I suppose you could say these lilies brought us together,' she said. 'Mamma and I were staying in London for the season. She thought I should attend some improving lectures, as well as going to receptions and dances. So, we went to a lecture on the flora of the Himalayas, at the Royal Geographical Society in Kensington. Mamma is rather keen on flowers.

'Of course, Ernest was the lecturer. Afterwards, Mamma went to talk to him. And a day later, he called and asked us

69

to go to tea.' She shrugged. 'That was it, really. I thought he was very clever and brave, and my parents admired his achievements.'

Her description of their first meeting wasn't exactly swooning with romance. It sounded as if Lavinia's mother had been more taken with Ernest than her daughter. I wouldn't marry someone because my parents admired them, and they seemed clever. And surely Lavinia, with both beauty and fortune, would not have been short of suitors.

'And will you accompany Mr Buckler on his next plant-hunting expedition?' I asked. 'It must be very exciting.'

She shuddered. 'Goodness, no.' Then she pulled herself together. 'I mean, I'd only be in the way. I'd be better off making sure everything is nice at home for when Ernest comes back. He's likely to be away for a year or more, next time, he says.'

She seemed rather relieved at the prospect. Poor Lavinia: a hasty marriage to an unsuitable, unsmiling older man with whom she had nothing in common. And the best she could hope for now was that he would go away for years at a time and leave her alone in London.

'Here he is now,' exclaimed Lavinia, jumping to her feet. 'The dear.'

But it wasn't Ernest Buckler hurrying across the yard, bearing a huge umbrella like a sword he was carrying into battle, but Peregrine Hall.

I watched them retreat towards the path to the apple orchard, huddled together under the umbrella. Lavinia's big cream coat shone in the moonlight. I frowned. Had it been her I'd seen going into the garden the night before? But why would she have been out after dark when it frightened her so?

I settled down to another two hours' watching. Peregrine would be back at two o'clock, he promised. I resolved to be ready to go as soon as he returned. The last thing I wanted was to give him time to quiz me about my presence at the Smiths' cottage that morning. Although now I came to think of it, he hadn't explained why he was there, either.

Chapter 15

I picked up my flask of coffee and poured myself a cup. On Mrs Jameson's suggestion, we were each to take the coffee directly from the kitchen and bring a flask over to the glasshouse ourselves.

'Nothing against your hospitality, or your guests,' she had told Mrs Hall, who was looking more and more as if she regretted asking us to get involved. 'But I do think a few precautions would be wise, in the circumstances.'

My watch, thankfully, was uneventful. Peregrine arrived to relieve me at two o'clock, but didn't seem in the mood for chat. I then managed to get a few hours' sleep before breakfast. When I came down, the rainclouds had finally parted.

By half past nine, we were motoring along the Kentish lanes. The hedgerows were laden with creamy swathes of hawthorn blossom, the sky a deep blue and the sun sparkled off every raindrop, as if the trees were hung with diamonds. The Lagonda purred happily after Frankie's attentions. Orchards full of apple-blossom danced in the sun, lambs gambolled in fields full of daisies, and I began to see the point of the English countryside in springtime.

'Smell that air,' shouted Mrs Jameson over the roar of the engine. 'Glorious!' I sniffed. It smelled green and damp, with an undertow of manure.

'Look at that.' She pointed over the fields to an elegant stone mansion, set in wide lawns with a lake shining before it. Woodland clumped around the lawns, separating the grounds from the fields. We turned a corner and the house disappeared.

'Very nice,' I said politely.

'Otterling. It's mine,' said Mrs Jameson.

I looked at her in shock. She'd never mentioned owning an estate in England before.

'I often stayed at Otterling with my uncle and aunt,' she said. 'That's when I got to know Walter, and later Constance. Of course, I visited less frequently once I was married. I spent a few weeks there when my aunt was dying. And then my uncle made me his heir, because they had no children.'

She gazed back over her shoulder. 'I inherited on his death. I engaged an estate manager and he found tenants for the house and farm. I haven't been back since the War.' She had a curious expression on her face, a mixture of wistfulness and trepidation. 'Perhaps I will return this year,' she said. 'I should like to look over the place. It has some happy memories.' I hoped I would be able to accompany her. Anything that unravelled the mysteries of Mrs Jameson's life was interesting to me.

Another couple of miles, and Frankie pulled off into a rutted country lane full of puddles. She drove slowly, frowning at every bump.

'It's not designed for these conditions,' she said reproachfully, when Mrs Jameson enquired why we had slowed to a crawl. 'You need a tractor, not a motor car.'

We finally drew up before a fine-looking Georgian house. Frankie parked on the semi-circular driveway in front of the pillared doorway, and we climbed out. I wondered what sort of reception we might receive.

A snooty-looking butler emerged from the house and asked our business.

'Please tell Sir Norman that Mrs Iris Jameson, of Otterling, is here to visit,' said Mrs Jameson. As usual, her regal bearing and air of complete confidence carried the day. The man showed us in to a grand entrance hall with carved oak bannisters sweeping up in a double staircase.

'This way, please.' We were ushered into a lofty library, books lining the shelves from floor to ceiling. Mrs Jameson seated herself comfortably on a green leather sofa and picked up one of the periodicals arranged on the low table before it. I perched on a straight-backed chair and clutched my handbag. No matter how many aristocratic houses I visited with Mrs Jameson, I couldn't get over my anxiety about doing or saying the wrong thing. I summoned up the memory of my formidable day school head teacher. *Shoulders back, head up, and watch your vowels, Marjorie. You're not in Catford now.*

A middle-aged man in colourful tweed plus-fours stumped into the library, walking stick in one hand. He limped towards us, his expression wary. He wore a full moustache and pointed beard, disguising a harelip. I jumped to my feet.

'Mrs Jameson?' He looked at her hard, his bushy brows drawn together in a frown. 'I understood you were living in Italy.'

She smiled and rose slowly. 'I have returned, Sir Norman. I'm staying at Hawkshill Manor. I thought I would come and call on an old neighbour.'

'I see.' He stared at her a moment longer. 'And this young woman?'

74

'May I present my private secretary, Miss Swallow? Marjorie, Sir Norman and I know each other of old. Although it is a very long time since we have met.'

He nodded briskly and sat on a chair beside the sofa. 'Please, ladies, do sit down. Now, Mrs Jameson. Pleasant as this unexpected visit is, I have no doubt you have a purpose beyond the merely social. Especially if you are staying with Constance Hall. I suggest you tell me what it is and save us all some time.'

Mrs Jameson smiled approvingly. 'Most certainly. Sir Norman, I would like to discuss your former under-gardener, Dick Cooper.'

The man's eyebrows lifted. 'The devil you would. He hasn't worked for me since before the War.'

'But his father is still employed at Kingsmead Place?'

'He retired last year. His health is poor.' Sir Norman jutted his jaw at us. 'If that is all, Mrs Jameson?'

She gave a placid smile. 'In January, Dick Cooper was caught committing sabotage of some valuable plants at Hawkshill Manor. The lilies destined for this year's Chelsea Flower Show, at which I believe you propose to show an ornamental garden.'

He groaned. 'Not this again. As I told Walter, if Constance employs incompetent gardeners, she has only herself to blame.'

'Did Cooper prove incompetent when he worked here?' asked Mrs Jameson. 'Is that why you let him go?'

Sir Norman got to his feet and walked to the window. 'He left because he was impatient. Ambitious. I had no need for a plantsman with his own ideas. I thought he might be better suited to the Halls, actually. All this messing around with exotic species and hybridisation. I like gardens, Mrs Jameson.' He turned and looked fiercely at us, as if expecting us to find this controversial. 'Gardens that are restful retreats

75

from the world, with plants that suit the English climate and temperament. Gardens that remind us of the best of our land, our gentle landscape. An English garden should employ soft-edged planting of our native flowers and shrubs, colours which harmonise with the lines of our best classical architecture.

'I abhor the trend for violent colours, hideous rockeries, exotic plants torn from their savage birthplaces and transplanted into the English garden. It's unspeakably vulgar. You may as well put camels on to the race track at Ascot or build a pyramid in the grounds of Buckingham Palace.'

It was a speech he had clearly given before. Indeed, it echoed the article he had written the previous year for the *Journal of the Royal Horticultural Society*, which Mrs Hall had insisted on reading aloud after dinner. Mrs Hall had seen it as a direct attack on her style of gardening, and even on herself. Which, perhaps, it was.

'So, you have had no contact with Dick Cooper since he left your employment?' asked Mrs Jameson, while Sir Norman drew breath.

'What?' He had been so swept up in his rhetoric that he seemed to have forgotten the point of the conversation.

'Dick Cooper. Have you seen him in the past year?' asked Mrs Jameson.

'No, absolutely not.' He seemed to avoid catching her eye, however.

'Does he not visit his family in the village?' I asked. 'Perhaps you might have seen him then.'

He turned to glare at me. 'Perhaps. I don't keep watch over the domestic affairs of my former servants, Miss.'

'Sir Norman, let us cease to beat about the bush. Constance believes you paid Dick Cooper to deliberately over-water her plants, so that her garden at Chelsea would fail and you would have a better chance at the medals this year,' said Mrs Jameson. 'Is there any truth in that accusation?'

Sir Norman's colour looked dangerously high. 'Of course not,' he exploded. 'Constance is intolerable. And you can tell her from me, if she repeats those accusations again, I shall consult my solicitor about a writ for slander. I do not need to stoop to sabotage, Mrs Jameson. I have complete confidence in my display garden.'

'Even with the rain we've been having?' asked Mrs Jameson. 'I understand many of those showing at Chelsea this year are anxious that it is too cool and wet for the flowers to be shown at their best advantage.'

He smiled grimly. 'Many of those showing at Chelsea are incompetent plantsmen, then. Or women. My gardens may be traditional, Mrs Jameson, but my horticulture is completely up-to-date. I have climate-controlled glasshouses, with heating systems for when the temperatures drop too low. My gardening staff are trained to know when a plant needs water and when it needs feeding. And, of course, English plants are used to the English climate. If Mrs Hall's Himalayan lilies cannot stand the English rain, perhaps she should have left them where she found them.'

'I should very much like to see what you have done with your garden, Sir Norman. Would you be kind enough to show me around?' asked Mrs Jameson. She shot me a glance. Before driving over, she had explained that she would try to draw him away in the gardens, giving me the chance to snoop around and ask the staff about Dick Cooper.

Sir Norman seemed torn between desire to boot us off the premises, and desire to show off. The latter impulse won.

He looked at the ornate ormolu clock on the marble mantelpiece. 'I do not have much time. That's one thing all we Chelsea garden designers have in common – a fast-diminishing number of days before we must unveil perfection. Very well, Mrs Jameson. I will give you a quick tour.'

Outside, we strolled across the wet lawn, rain soaking into my shoes yet again. They had barely dried out from the previous day's puddles.

'As you can see, the spring bulbs have been particularly good this year,' began Sir Norman, sweeping his arm towards a colourful border. 'And the beech hedge is just coming into leaf. Beech makes an excellent hedging plant, with colour all the year around. And you can see here I have planted foxgloves, to make use of their height throughout the border. The spires punctuate the mounds of softer plants.'

'Indeed, Sir Norman. Most interesting.' Mrs Jameson shivered theatrically. 'Marjorie, would you be good enough to fetch my shawl? I believe I have left it in the car.'

'Of course, Mrs Jameson.'

I trotted back to the house, grabbed the shawl from the Lagonda and told Frankie what I was up to. She'd tried chatting to the butler, but claimed he was 'too far up his own backside' to speak to a woman who drove a car for a living.

'I saw a chap with a wheelbarrow going around the back of the house,' she said. 'He must be one of the gardening staff. Why don't you try there?'

Chapter 16

I folded the shawl over my arm and dashed around the house into a kitchen garden. A girl in striped uniform and white cap was cutting fresh green spears of asparagus and laying them carefully in a wicker basket.

My mouth watered. She looked up at my approach.

'I say, that asparagus looks good,' I said.

She ducked her head and smiled. 'It's very nice, Miss. Are you looking for someone?'

'I'm looking for the gardeners,' I said. 'Where are the glasshouses located?'

She pointed to a gate in a thick, dark yew hedge at the far end of the garden. 'Just through there, Miss.' She paused and a frown creased her brow. 'We're not supposed to go in, though. That's where the Chelsea flowers are grown.'

I gave what I hoped was a reassuring smile. 'Thank you so much. That's what I'm here about, Sir Norman's Chelsea garden. I'm on the committee.' I hastened away between the rows of lettuces and broad beans, before she could ask any more. I'd noticed that people on committees seemed to get away with a lot, provided they didn't go into any details.

I unlatched the gate. Beyond the impenetrable hedge were rows of glasshouses, more even than at Hawkshill, with hoses and pipes running in and out of them. Each was filled with lines of pots and plants: white night-scented stocks, pink and blue honesty, blowsy magenta peonies. Another glasshouse was devoted to purple and pink sweet peas, their perfume delicate as I passed the open door. Secretly, I rather agreed with Sir Norman. I preferred these homely English flowers to the more spectacular lilies and orchids that Mrs Hall went in for.

At the far end of the rows, I could see men going in and out of a glasshouse which had something blue in it. Delphiniums, maybe, or cornflowers? I hastened my pace along the gravel path. I would ask them quickly about Dick Cooper, whether they knew his father and if they had seen him recently. Then I would dash back to Mrs Jameson, claiming to have had trouble finding the shawl.

The glasshouse flowers were very blue, as bright as a summer sky. Sapphire blue, even. I drew closer, frowning, but there was no mistaking the big spiky petals. Sir Norman Alperton, champion of English flowers and native species, was growing a glasshouse full of Himalayan Sapphire Lilies.

A young man came out, pushing an empty wheelbarrow towards a pile of compost, gently steaming in the sun. He saw me and stopped dead.

'John,' he shouted. 'Someone's here.' A second man followed, older and taller, a canvas apron around his waist and a pair of secateurs held menacingly in one hand. He glared at me.

'Oi! What are you doing? This is private land.' He had a soft country accent, his voice pitched low.

I smiled placatingly. 'I just wanted to ask a question,' I said.

'Well, you can't.' He advanced towards me and grabbed hold of my arm. His grip was firm. 'You can get out of here, whoever you are, Miss.'

'I was looking for Mr Cooper,' I gabbled, trying to pull my arm away. 'I wondered if anyone had seen his son recently. Dick Cooper. Do you know him? He used to work here.'

The two men exchanged worried glances.

'I thought he'd gone to London...' began the younger man.

'Shut your mouth, Simmons,' said John, giving him a fierce look and gripping my arm tighter. 'And who might you be, Miss?' he asked. 'Seeing as how we're asking questions.'

'I'm... I'm on the Chelsea committee,' I said, lamely. 'I'm a friend of Dick. I understood he had been helping Sir Norman with this year's garden.'

The man shook his head, his handsome face set in a scowl. 'What blooming committee? Never heard of such a thing. Right, you can stay here with me, my girl. Simmons, you go and get Sir Norman. I won't have women snooping around his Chelsea glasshouses. Let's see what he has to say.'

I was in a bind. If Simmons fetched Sir Norman, I could hardly claim I'd had to search for the shawl, what with all my nonsense about the Chelsea committee. And he would realise I'd been snooping around and had seen the Sapphire Lilies. It could all get rather unpleasant. On balance, I decided, I'd rather not wait for Sir Norman's arrival.

Simmons set off at a jog-trot towards the house. I turned to my captor.

'I'd be perfectly happy to leave right now,' I said. 'I don't suppose you'd consider letting me go, John?'

'Not a chance,' he snarled. 'We'll get to the bottom of it. I'll call the police, if I have to.'

I sighed. 'Well then, I'm awfully sorry about this.'

'What are you yapping about?' he asked. Then he yelped as

I pinched hard on the fatty area beneath his thumb, twisted his wrist back and forced his arm up his back. Frankie wasn't the only one who'd been learning jiu-jitsu. He let out a shout of pain.

'It's probably best if you kneel down, otherwise your arm might get broken,' I advised.

Sweating and swearing, he did as I suggested. I gave him a gentle push and he toppled over, face down into the heap of compost. I didn't wait to see what happened next.

By the time I was through the kitchen garden and around the house, Frankie had the motor running and Mrs Jameson was waving at me from the back seat. I jumped into the car, and it sped away.

'Golly,' I said, trying to catch my breath. 'That was close.'

'The gardener told Sir Norman there was a strange woman snooping around the glasshouses,' said Mrs Jameson. 'He went through the house to find out what was happening. I thought it might be prudent to prepare for a quick retreat. Now, did you find out anything about Dick Cooper?' She took her shawl from my fist and settled it around her shoulders.

'The gardeners know who he is,' I said. 'He's in London. And someone has sold Sir Norman a stock of Himalayan Sapphire Lilies. I don't suppose Mrs Hall knows about that.'

Chapter 17

We returned to London the next morning, after another uneventful night watching in the glasshouse. As Mrs Jameson said, there was little more we could do until the post-mortem report on Harry Smith came back, and she was keen to track down Dick Cooper.

Sir Norman had telephoned Mrs Hall in a fury, accusing her of sending us to spy on his Chelsea preparations and assault his head gardener. She had retorted that she might not need to spy if he hadn't stooped to sabotage and the suspected murder of *her* head gardener. The situation had become rather heated, and both had threatened the other with the police. Only when Mrs Jameson had reminded Mrs Hall that the police were fully occupied in investigating the death of poor Mr Smith did she calm down a little.

On Mrs Jameson's instructions, I had said nothing about the lilies I had seen at Kingsmead Place. 'We shall investigate further,' she said. 'I would very much like to know how those lilies came to be in Sir Norman's possession before I tell Constance. She's quite agitated enough already.'

We arrived back at Bedford Square in time for lunch. Mrs Jameson had telephoned ahead to warn of our arrival, and our cook had prepared my favourite grilled chicken breast with new potatoes and peas. Listening to the familiar hum of the traffic outside, shouts of tradesmen and delivery boys on bicycles in the square, I relaxed. It was good to be home.

I had barely had time to unpack my suitcase after lunch when Mrs Jameson rang the electric bell in my room to summon me down to the investigations office. This pleasant bright room, looking out on to the trees of the gardens in the middle of the square, housed her library of criminal case books: reference works on gun-shot wounds, poisons, fingerprinting techniques, and anatomy text books. On the centre of Mrs Jameson's rosewood bureau sat an enormous tome, open to a page that showed a line drawing of a plant.

'There you are, Marjorie. Come and look at this,' she said.

I looked over her shoulder. The drawing was of a foxglove, its Latin name written underneath: *Digitalis purpurea*.

'Native of English woodlands, heathlands and popular in gardens,' I read. 'An important source of nectar for bees and other pollinating insects. Common names include Foxglove, Goblin Gloves and Dead Men's Bells.'

'Sir Norman was rather proud of the foxgloves in his garden,' said Mrs Jameson. 'Did you know they are deadly poisonous?'

I didn't. A flaw in the otherwise excellent education I had received as a scholarship student at Sydenham High School for Girls.

'According to Dr James Mackenzie, writing in 1916,' said Mrs Jameson, heaving another book on to her desk and turning the pages, 'extract of digitalis slows the heartbeat. Foxglove leaves have been used for more than a hundred years to treat heart problems, but the use of digitalis is becoming more common among the medical profession. I wonder if Dr Barnes had prescribed it for Harry Smith.'

I sat down and removed Sooty, our little black cat, from the patch of sunshine that fell across my desk. She wasn't really allowed into the office, but usually managed to inveigle her way in. She curled up on my lap as I uncovered my typewriter. I had plenty of notes to write up for our files.

'But if it's poisonous, why is it used to treat heart problems?' I asked.

Mrs Jameson smiled happily. Nothing gave her more pleasure than explaining things to people more ignorant than herself.

'The poison is in the dose, Marjorie. The right amount will correct an abnormal heart rhythm and reduce strain on a damaged heart. Too little will be ineffective. Too much may stop the heart altogether, with fatal results.'

'I see.' I looked up from my typewriter. Sooty tried to bat my hand away from the clattering keys. 'And would that result in signs like a heart attack, such as we saw in Mr Smith?'

Mrs Jameson sighed and closed the book. 'I'm not completely sure. I shall consult an expert. But I don't suppose we should rule it out. I will suggest to the Faversham police that they should request analysis for traces of digitalis.'

'Do you think Sir Norman really did have something to do with it?' I asked. I hadn't liked the man, but it was a big jump from stealing Mrs Hall's lilies to murdering her gardener.

Mrs Jameson looked out of the window, tapping her chin. 'If he did, it was rather foolish of him to show off his foxgloves,' she said. 'Don't you think? And they are common plants which grow in the wild. It would not be necessary to cultivate them in the garden to use them to poison someone. One step at a time, Marjorie.'

She picked up the telephone. After telling the Faversham

police what to do, she placed a call to Scotland Yard.

'Inspector Chadwick, please. Tell him Iris Jameson would like a word.'

A few minutes later she replaced the receiver, smiling. 'Poor Peter never knows what to make of my inquiries,' she said. 'However, he has been most helpful. He has given me the name of a policeman who specialises in horticultural crime. Apparently, there is a thriving black market in smuggled seeds, bulbs and so on. The ingenuity of the criminal world never ceases to amaze me.'

She held out a scrap of paper. 'Detective Sergeant Williams. He belongs to Scotland Yard, but because of the convenient proximity to Covent Garden market, he has an office in Bow Street. Why don't you nip around there this afternoon, Marjorie? It's not five o'clock yet. See if he knows anything about Dick Cooper and his business.'

I tidied away my notes and banished a protesting Sooty to the floor. I'd visited Bow Street police station twice in the past year in Mrs Jameson's service, both times to try to get people out of custody. The desk sergeant was not an admirer of mine. I ran up to my room, brushed cat hair off my skirt and ensured I looked as respectable as possible. I hoped it would do the trick.

Chapter 18

The sergeant folded his arms and leaned on the desk, a mocking smile on his bearded face.

'Well, look who we have here,' he said, making himself comfortable. 'If it isn't Miss Swallow. Go on, then. Who do you want me to release today?'

He shook a bunch of keys at me. 'I've got a full complement of drunks in the tank – none too fragrant, I'd be happy for you to take them off my hands – and an ugly bunch of pickpockets. Some chap who thought it was a good idea to punch a policeman who asked him to move on. A nasty young man who likes to frighten schoolgirls by waving his private equipment around – would he suit you? Oh, and there's a string of ladies of the night upstairs in the women's cells. What'll it be?'

I waited for him to finish, a polite smile pasted on my face. 'I wish to speak to Detective Sergeant Williams. Inspector Chadwick told him I'd be coming,' I said.

He raised his eyebrows. 'Sweet Williams, is it? I'll tell him you're here. If he's not out talking to the flowers.'

I sighed and took a seat on the metal bench, feeling rather sorry for Sergeant Williams. I waited ten minutes, guessing that the delay was caused more by my nemesis the desk sergeant than by Sergeant Williams himself. When he arrived, he had a mackintosh in one hand and an umbrella in the other.

'Inspector Chadwick rang earlier,' he said, tucking the umbrella under his arm and reaching awkwardly for my hand. 'Very pleased to be of service. I was going to take a turn around the market before I go home. Do you want to come? We can talk as we go.'

He was young for a sergeant, with an open, fresh face that I liked immediately. His fair hair was plastered down in a severe centre parting, and he had a smattering of freckles across his nose.

The streets around Covent Garden were quieter in the late afternoon, but there was plenty of evidence of the market which was held there daily, and supplied fruit and vegetables for most of London's shops, restaurants, hotels and cafes. We picked our way through wooden crates and stacked wicker baskets, discarded piles of greenery, cabbage leaves and rotten fruit. A few market porters were attempting to clean up, their enormous brooms creating mountains of waste in front of the portico of St Paul's church.

I explained that I wanted to find out if anybody had been selling stolen bulbs of a new type of lily, without the permission of the company which had paid for the expedition to collect them. Sergeant Williams nodded, his grey-blue eyes alight with interest.

'You've come to the right place. I'm more often looking for smuggled goods. You know, people bringing in tulip bulbs from Amsterdam and selling them without paying import taxes. But this would be the place to find the black market for new species.'

We rounded the stone buildings of the main vegetable

market and headed back towards the enclosed iron and glass flower market, where most of the flowers were sold. Confusingly, the imposing Floral Hall opposite the police station was, Sergeant Williams informed me, now the site of the foreign fruit market.

'I can ask around the flower market myself, but most of the fellows in there know me,' he said. 'I have a few that will tip me off about anything new. You might do better asking yourself, though. Tell 'em you're working for a smart hotel or something, and need something to make the guests sit up and take notice at a special event.'

I smiled. 'Like a gala to celebrate the Chelsea Flower Show?'

He grinned. 'Exactly that. Lord, I'd love to go to the flower show one day. I've been on at my superiors, telling them I should be there to investigate what's happening in the horticultural world. But they say I should stick to the market. Have you ever been?'

I shook my head. 'I think I might be going this year, though,' I said. 'Because of this investigation. One of the garden designers has invited my employer and me.'

'Lucky you,' he said, enviously. 'Come on, let's have a cuppa. There's a stall on Russell Street that'll still be open. It's better than the tea at the station. Friendlier, too.'

We stood by the cart, sipping mugs of hot, strong tea with plenty of sugar, just the way I liked it. Mrs Jameson said if you used good, fresh leaves from China, you didn't need milk or sugar. Graham had been serving up weak-looking amber stuff with an apologetic glance ever since Christmas. I had to go down to the kitchen to get a proper cup.

'Lovely,' I pronounced. 'Sergeant Williams, have you heard of a man called Dick Cooper? Came up to London from Kent a few months ago.'

'Cooper. Cooper. Not that I recollect. I'll keep an ear out, though.' He pointed across the road. 'See that pub?'

It was a down-at-heel looking place with small bulls-eye windows, the peeling sign outside announcing itself as the Lord John Russell Tavern. An old man with a dog that looked even older pushed out through the door and shambled down the street.

'That's where the shady business gets carried out. It opens at four in the morning, same time as the market. They have a special licence. It's a bit rough, mind you. But if you want to find out who's selling what to whom, that's where to go. Take someone with you. Don't go in looking like a lady, for heaven's sake. I'd go with you, but they all know me. You'd get more out of them without me by your side.'

I eyed the building without enthusiasm. The bells of St Paul's rang out, marking six o'clock.

'I'd better go,' I said, thanking him for the tea. 'It looks like I'll have an early start tomorrow.'

Chapter 19

I spent some time in the evening putting together my costume for the early morning expedition. I borrowed our maid Jenny's spare uniform, with my old coat buttoned over it and my most battered black hat, putting into practice Sergeant Williams' suggestion that I should pretend to be from one of the big hotels, looking for unusual flowers for a Chelsea gala. Frankie, on bodyguard duties, was going to wear her chauffeur's uniform, with a false moustache glued on to further disguise her sex.

I admit I did groan when my alarm clock sounded at three o'clock on Thursday morning. This investigation seemed to involve more unsociable hours than my previous undercover job as a nightclub hostess. I rehearsed my patter as we walked through the dark streets from Bloomsbury. Frankie was uncharacteristically quiet, except for the occasional yawn, but I was glad of her company. Although I was more street-wise than I had been when I entered Mrs Jameson's employment, my experiences had made me more, not less, cautious of undercover work. It could all go horribly wrong rather quickly.

We began in the flower market, where bleary-eyed porters were dragging in trolleys and carts laden with flowers. Stall-holders were setting up their stands of lilies, tulips, roses and carnations. No-one took any notice of us as we walked through the aisles, me clutching a basket and Frankie smoking her usual cigarette.

I paused before one stall, crowded with tall galvanised buckets of pink, red and yellow roses. The stallholder had a cheerful round face, brown as a walnut and almost as crinkled.

'What are you after, Missy?' he asked.

'I'm looking for samples of something new,' I told him. 'I work at the Grosvenor Hotel. We're having a Chelsea gala, and they want all the latest varieties.'

His smile faded. 'They do, do they? Blooming toffs. What's wrong with these old-fashioned shrub roses, eh?'

'They look lovely,' I said politely.

'And the damasks smell lovely, too. Go on, have a sniff.'

I complied; the creamy fragrance was every bit as good as he said.

'And that's more than you can say for those hybrid teas everyone is going mad for these days. All lace and no knickers, 'scuse my language. Sorry, Missy. Can't help you. Try Alf over by the door there. He's been trying to produce a blue rose for years. Hasn't done it, mind, but he keeps trying.'

Alf by the door had a long, lugubrious face and a drooping blond moustache. He pressed me to buy a bunch of rather sickly-looking mauve roses, which, as my previous informant had suggested, had no scent whatsoever.

'That's the closest anyone's ever got to blue roses,' he said. 'I showed them at Chelsea two years ago and they won a silver medal. Should have been a gold, but they want the perfume as well, see. You can't have both, that's what I tell them.'

'Maybe I should look for blue lilies,' I said. 'Apparently

there's a new one coming out this year, brought over from China or somewhere.'

He nodded mournfully. 'See, lilies gives themselves to blue. You can get a proper delphinium-blue with lilies. Roses, no. But if you want lilies, try the other side of the hall. They've got all sorts over there.'

We did as he suggested. I approached a stall with a dozen species, each more fantastical than the last. Spiky petals, outlandish oranges and hot pinks, blues of as many shades as a summer sky.

'What's your newest variety?' I asked the stall-holder, a wizened old man drawing heavily on a roll-up cigarette. He was less forthcoming than the others, looking me up and down in an unpleasant manner before expelling the smoke and spitting on the ground.

'Who wants to know?' he wheezed.

Frankie took a step forward. 'She's buying for the Grosvenor Hotel's Chelsea Gala. You should show a bit of respect if you want our custom, my good man.'

He turned his rheumy little eyes from one to the other of us. 'No, she's not. They wouldn't send a maid. They'd send some bloke who knew what he was talking about. And that don't include you.'

'What about those?' I asked, pointing to a bucket at the back of his stand. I couldn't see the flowers properly, but the blue looked like the bright sapphire of the lilies Mrs Hall grew at Hawkshill Manor. 'Are they the new ones from Tibet?'

He jumped up and hurried to cover them with sacking. 'Never you mind. They're for a collector what ordered them specially.'

I smiled, still trying to win him around. 'Could you get some

93

more in? They look like exactly what we need.'

He folded his arms stubbornly and jutted out his chin. 'Nope.'

I could see Frankie was itching to give him a piece of her mind, but I didn't want to draw more attention.

'Never mind, then,' I said, pulling her away. At the next stall, I bought some bright orange star lilies and got chatting to a woman who said she was minding the stall for her husband.

'I'm not really one for lilies myself,' she confessed. 'They make me think of funerals.'

I handed over the money. 'My mum says exactly the same,' I told her. 'Flowers for the dead, that's what she calls them. Won't have them in the house. But the rich folk like them, don't they? Make a proper show.'

'Lord, yes. My Bob, he says there's folk that will pay five pounds or more for just a few corms of the new ones when they come in. He's over at the Tavern now, getting all the gossip about the new varieties. You should ask them in there, Miss.'

She leaned across, glancing over at the stallholder next to her. 'That's where he gets those blue ones from. You ignore him; he's a grumpy old git. But ask around at the Tavern, and someone will know what you're after.'

Chapter 20

My basket laden with ugly orange and mauve flowers, we headed out of the flower market and down Russell Street. It was barely five o'clock, but barrow boys, vans, horses and carts crowded the lightening streets as all the greengrocers of London converged on Covent Garden to buy produce for the day ahead. The Lord John Russell Tavern was squashed into a narrow house opposite the back of the Theatre Royal, but when Frankie pushed through the door, it was as far from the glamour of the stage as you could imagine.

A fug of cheap tobacco and sour beer hung in the air. The small room was crowded with men downing pints and eating anaemic-looking sausages and mashed potato, and noisy with shouted conversation and laughter. I couldn't see any other female customers.

Frankie fought her way to the bar, one arm around my shoulders.

'A pint of best and a half for the lady,' she called across the bar, waving a shilling.

The barmaid winked at her as she pulled the pump handle. 'Look at you in your fancy uniform. Where'd you spring from, the Ritz blooming Hotel?'

Frankie grinned. 'Wouldn't you like to know, sweetheart?'

She passed me the beer. 'Actually, you're not far wrong. We're from the Grosvenor, looking for new species of lily for the Chelsea gala. Who should we talk to?'

The barmaid narrowed her eyes and scanned the crowd. 'Bob over in the corner usually knows. He's big on lilies.' She pointed to a cheerful-looking man wolfing down a plate of sausages. With luck, I thought, that would be the husband of the nice lady from the lily stall in the flower market.

The woman lowered her voice. 'You really want Dick, though. I can't see him. Maybe he's not in today.'

'Dick Cooper?' I asked, hardly believing my luck.

'Shush.' A few of the men at the bar had turned to look at me. 'Ask Bob. But don't use his full name. He don't like it. Just ask if he's seen Dick and tell him you might put some business his way.'

We slipped through the crowd with our drinks, and I squeezed into a spare seat at Bob's table.

'I've been talking to your Missus,' I said with a smile, showing him the orange lilies. 'She said you'd be in here.'

He wiped his mouth with his hand and took a long swallow of beer. 'Don't tell her I only come for the breakfast. She thinks I'm working,' he said with a grin.

'I promise.' I took a gulp of beer for appearance's sake. It was very nasty. I forced myself to swallow it, wishing I could spit it out.

Bob laughed. 'All right then, what did she tell you? Cos I can see you're not here for the beer.'

I lowered my voice. 'I'm looking for new lilies, for a big party to celebrate the Chelsea Flower Show. My mistress wants all the newest, most impressive flowers. She's heard stories about something called the Himalayan Sapphire Lily? I've been told that someone in here called Dick might be able to help, but I don't know him. Can you point him out?'

His face became more serious. 'Right. Well, I shouldn't really say. I don't know that Dick's looking for new clients right now. He has to keep this lily a bit quiet, like. I'm not entirely sure how he got hold of it, if you know what I mean. I'm not touching it. Not until after Chelsea, when it'll be everywhere.'

He looked around the pub, then tugged my sleeve. 'He's just coming in.'

A short young man in a serge jacket with a baker boy cap pulled over his brow was pushing his way through the door. I half-rose, then sank back into my seat. Following him close behind, looking truculent as ever, was Bert Smith, under-gardener at Hawkshill Manor. What should I do now?

'Not so keen to meet him now, eh?' Bob was watching me narrowly. 'Come on, Miss. What's your game?'

'I think we should go,' said Frankie, her voice urgent. I saw the barmaid we'd talked to before gesturing towards us. Dick Cooper was frowning and looking our way, as were several of the men around him. Any second now, Bert Smith would see us, and our cover story would be exposed. To make matters worse, the suspicious old stallholder from the flower market pushed his way through the door and made a bee-line for the two men.

I rose to my feet, clutching the basket and pulling down my hat. 'Excuse me,' I said, pushing through the press with Frankie at my back.

'Oi,' called one of the men at the next table to us. 'I seen you before,' he said, jabbing a finger towards me. 'Having a cosy natter with that copper who's always nosing about. What's his name, Williams?'

The three men at the table rose to their feet, blocking our exit. Their faces darkened with suspicion. The first man rolled up his shirt sleeves and rubbed big, meaty hands together.

'What are you, a copper's nark?'

'We don't like narks in here,' said his companion, spitting on the floor. His grin was wolfish.

The atmosphere was turning ugly. I could no longer see the door. Someone behind me gave me a shove and I staggered into another table laden with beer, which slopped over the sides of the glasses and spilled onto the floor. The drinkers yelled in protest and jumped to their feet.

'Oi! Watch what you're doing.'

'Let us through,' shouted Frankie. 'We're not with the rozzers.' She put an arm around my shoulder and muttered in my ear, 'Don't stop. I don't like the look of this.'

Even with our combined jiu-jitsu skills, Frankie and I were completely outnumbered. I kept pressing towards the door.

'Miss Swallow, ain't it?' Bert Smith appeared through the seething crowd. 'And... is that you, Frankie? What're you doing here?' He looked as shocked to see us as I'd been to see him.

'All right, Bert?' asked Frankie. 'We're in a bit of a spot. Help a couple of ladies in distress?'

'Leave it,' shouted Bert. 'These two are all right. Helped when my old dad died earlier in the week. Come on, let them through.'

The muttering that had been growing in volume around us faltered and died down. The drinkers returned to their pints and people grudgingly moved aside. Bert led the way to the door. When I looked around, I could no longer see Dick Cooper, the man he'd come in with.

We stepped outside. The dank vegetal air of Covent Garden had never seemed so fresh and welcome. I took deep gulps of it, thankful to have escaped the oppressive atmosphere of the tavern.

'Keep moving, Marge,' said Frankie. 'We don't want to hang around here.'

'Wait.' Bert and I spoke simultaneously.

He scowled. 'What the hell were you doing in there?'

'Could ask you the same question,' said Frankie. She unpeeled the fake moustache from under her nose and rubbed spirit gum off her top lip. 'Come on, Bert. I'm all tuckered out. Where can we get a cuppa?'

We stood at the same stand where I'd taken my tea with Sergeant Williams the previous day, although if the woman running it recognised me, she said nothing.

'We're trying to find out how Mrs Hall's Sapphire Lilies have found their way on to the black market,' I said. 'I don't suppose you can shed any light on that, can you?'

He sighed and rubbed his eyes. 'I'm not dobbing in a mate,' he said.

'Course not.' Frankie looked shocked. She handed him a Woodbine and lit a match. 'We ain't even told Mrs Hall about it. We just want to know what's going on. See if it's got something to do with what happened with the sabotage, and your dad.'

He lit the cigarette and took a deep drag, then shook his head. 'You're wasting your time there. Dad had a bad heart. That's the end of it.'

'And the lilies?' I persisted. 'Is Dick selling the bulbs? And are you helping him?'

Before he could speak, Frankie held up her hand. 'Don't be daft, Marge. It's none of our business if Bert decides to go for a drink with an old mate he used to work with. And it's none of our business if that friend has managed to get hold of a few bulbs and sell them on. The way that Mrs Hall had them all working, I wouldn't be surprised if one of the gardeners found he'd got a bulb still in his pocket at the end of the day. And I wouldn't blame him one bit for making some bunce out of it, 'specially if he'd been sacked over some misunderstanding about how often the blooming plants need watering. Ain't that right, Bert?'

Bert grinned. 'Seeds,' he said.

'What?'

'We never managed to grow them on from the bulbs they brought back. We tried for the first year. Not a sausage. Reckon they got damaged on the journey. The seeds from the seed pods took, though. Three years till the seedlings grew into plants ready to flower. Dick was obsessed with those seedlings. Had them growing in all different conditions in the glasshouses. Even took a few home to grow out the back of his dad's cottage, I reckon. You can't blame him if he kept them, once he'd got the sack. He's setting up on his own. Getting a nice little business going. No need to ask about where he came by the first lot of seedlings, is there?'

So that explained where Sir Norman Alperton's Sapphire Lilies had come from – not to mention the blooms being sold on the quiet in Covent Garden market. But did it explain the sabotage? And I wasn't as sure as Bert that his father's death had been from natural causes.

'I completely understand,' I told him. 'I don't blame Dick for keeping them, after all his hard work. And of course, if Sir Norman saw an unusual plant growing in his former gardener's cottage, it's natural that he would ask him to grow a few for his own collection.'

Frankie gave an enormous yawn. 'Well, I reckon that's enough for one morning,' she said. 'My bed's calling. Marge, I'll walk you home, then I'm turning in.'

'What are you going to say?' asked Bert, his eyes wary again. 'Mrs Hall's got us all up here for the garden build now. She's put me in charge of the planting. I don't want to miss the big day. And like Frankie said, I was just having a drink with an old pal.'

I turned the problem over in my mind. It was a bit of a pickle.

'I'll tell Mrs Jameson what we've found out about the lilies being on sale. And I will have to tell her about Dick Cooper,' I said. 'But maybe we don't need to mention that we ran into you.' Not unless the results of Harry's post-mortem examination gave cause for concern, anyway.

He nodded, and we shook hands on it. Frankie and I trailed back to Bedford Square, and I crawled into my bed at just before six o'clock. With luck, I'd get a couple of hours' sleep before Mrs Jameson called me in for a grilling.

Chapter 21

The remainder of the week was uneventful. I paid my usual Sunday afternoon visit to the flat above the draper's shop in Catford, where I presented my mother with the slightly battered mauve roses I'd bought at Covent Garden. She took them with a dubious look and set them in a vase on the mantelpiece next to the framed photograph of my brother.

'Very unusual,' she said.

'They won a silver medal at Chelsea,' I told her. 'That, Mum, is the nearest thing you'll get to a blue rose.'

For once, I was able to talk about my work with my parents. Although they didn't have a garden, my mother loved flowers. Our window boxes were filled to bursting with scarlet geraniums, and she'd planted tubs of fragrant sweet williams and wallflowers outside the shop. She'd even persuaded Dad to give over a corner of his allotment to sweet peas. She was agog with my tales of visiting the famous Constance Hall and the grand gardens at Hawkshill Manor.

'And we're going to see her at Chelsea Flower Show next week,' I told her. 'To admire the garden she's designed for her new lilies. They're very spectacular. They've come all the way from Tibet.'

Mum sighed. 'I would love to go to Chelsea just once before

I die,' she said. My mother had been giving intimations of her imminent demise for the past ten years, although she was in excellent health. 'It sounds like paradise. Will you really see the King and Queen?'

'It won't be paradise unless this rain lets up.' My father set down the musical box he was tinkering with. 'I put in a row of broad beans in March, and they've rotted in the ground. Not a single one's come up. Unless the mice got them.'

'Maybe next year would be better for Chelsea, Mrs Swallow,' said Freddie, my pianist friend. He often came over from his digs in Brixton on Sunday afternoons. My mother had got it into her head that he loved seed cake, so he was manfully munching an enormous slice of it, washed down with tea. 'I'm sure you can find out how to get tickets, can't you, Marjorie? I bet your Mrs Jameson would help.'

I smiled. 'I'll see what I can do, Mum. I don't know about meeting the King, though. Even Mrs Jameson's powers have their limits.'

'Do you want me to take a look at that box?' Freddie asked. Dad had bought it for my mother when they got married, but it had gunged up and stopped working. The little carousel still turned, but no music played. 'My mother used to have one like it. I think I remember how it worked.'

Dad set out the pieces and they sorted through them together, Freddie's fair mop and Dad's sparse grey hairs close together over the table. Mum and I shared a fond glance over their heads. It was good to see Dad taking an interest in something apart from vegetables.

How had that happened? I wondered. One minute, I'd known Freddie as a rather wild young man playing jazz piano in a racy nightclub. The next – although he still played with the

All Stars Jazz Orchestra – he was drinking tea with my parents on a Sunday afternoon, as if he was already the son-in-law they treated him as. And if I rather missed the wild young man he had been... well, perhaps my job provided enough excitement. It was good to see Freddie becoming more confident, steadier in his employment and habits. I was in no hurry to exchange my independence and the job I loved for marriage. Not that Freddie had asked me yet. My mother would have to wait a while longer to wear the fancy hat she'd trimmed and hidden away on top of her wardrobe.

'Did your mother tell you about Samuel Brownlow, Marjorie?' asked Dad, passing Freddie a tiny screwdriver.

I suppressed a sigh. My parents seemed obsessed with telling me news of people I had met once, as a small child, and never seen again.

'One of the shopkeepers?' I hazarded a guess.

'Allotment committee,' said Dad. 'Deputy chairman. Here, Freddie, those cogs should fit together.'

The politics of the allotment committee, I knew from previous occasions, were as bitterly fought as any general election. I braced myself for a litany of complaints about the latest outrages of the allotment holders, discernible only to those directly involved.

'Dropped dead,' my mother chipped in. This was another favourite topic of conversation: news of the ill health or deaths of our elderly friends and neighbours. 'Heart attack.'

'I'm sorry to hear that,' I said politely. 'Was he very old?'

'Pushing seventy,' said Mum. 'But it was his own fault.'

'Now then, May,' said my father. 'He wasn't to know.' He paused to watch as Freddie screwed one piece of metal into another. 'Good lad.'

'What didn't he know?' I helped myself to another slice of cake. It was a bit dry, but quite palatable if you drank enough tea with it.

'About yew,' said Mum.

'About me?'

'No, yew. Yew trees, like they have in graveyards. I mean, you'd think he'd realise. That's why they grow them there. Trees for the dead.'

I was having trouble following my mother's train of thought, but was glad I hadn't brought her the lilies I'd bought at Covent Garden.

'What actually happened to Samuel Brown?' I asked.

'Brownlow, dear. You know, he was married to Muriel who used to work at the shoe shop. She's very upset, especially as he burned out her best pan.'

I sighed, ready to give up on the story all together. The music box emitted a tinkle of notes.

'Oh, well done, lad,' said Dad. He sat back and a big smile spread across his face. 'Samuel Brownlow only tried to make jam out of yew berries,' he said. 'Silly bugger. They found him dead on the kitchen floor. So now there's a vacancy for vice chairman, and I think I might put myself up for it.'

'Dave.' My mother made periodic attempts to restrain my father's language, which he completely ignored.

'Wait.' I set down my cup. 'Yew berries are poisonous? They gave him a heart attack?'

'I thought everyone knew that,' said my mother. 'The outsides of the berries aren't poisonous. The red bit. But the rest of the plant is, including the seeds inside the berries. But Samuel must have not known to take out the seeds.'

Freddie and I exchanged glances and set down our remain-

105

ing crumbs of seed cake.

'That was delicious, Mrs Swallow,' he said. 'I do hope you're not trying to poison me.'

Mum laughed in a way she would not have done if I had made the same joke. But I was too busy thinking about the yew hedge at Hawkshill Manor to join in the hilarity.

Chapter 22

On Wednesday, we had a guest for lunch at Bedford Square. Professor Eileen Power, an historian from the London School of Economics, was a friend and former client of Mrs Jameson. She'd dragged herself away from her desk in nearby Mecklenburgh Square, where she was investigating women's role in the English wool trade of the fourteenth century, at Mrs Jameson's request. Professor Power had recently spent several months in China, where she had met the boy emperor and his Scottish tutor, with whom she corresponded.

Despite her bluestocking credentials, she wore beautiful clothes and jewellery, threw excellent parties and had been instrumental in Mrs Jameson's choice of the rather bohemian Bloomsbury district as our headquarters. I liked Professor Power very much, but her conversation sometimes went a bit over my head.

Once she and Mrs Jameson had dispensed with the gossip about mutual acquaintances at the university, my employer got down to business.

'Have you had any reply from your friend in China, Eileen?'

Professor Power paused, her bright, intelligent eyes regarding her friend with affection. 'About plant-hunting expeditions in the Tibetan Himalayas? You asked some rather specialised questions, I must say. A long way from my usual field of expertise.'

Mrs Jameson smiled and topped up her glass of hock. 'But you are so delightfully well-connected. Who else could I turn to?'

Professor Power moved her glass away. 'No more wine for me. I have to give a lecture this afternoon. I'll be hiccupping all the way through it.' She took a forkful of poached salmon. 'It's far too soon to have a reply to my letter,' she said. 'I doubt it's even arrived yet. The mail takes three weeks, even if all goes smoothly, which it usually doesn't. But fortunately his nephew, who had been out East on a bursary from Edinburgh University, has recently returned from Tibet. He's studying botany, so I thought he'd be the perfect person to ask.'

She pulled a folded letter from her tapestry handbag. 'He tells rather an interesting story. Excuse his slang – he's young.'

She put on reading spectacles and read the relevant passages aloud:

'"You asked about the Buckler expedition. It's caused no end of a kerfuffle. The lamas are very angry about it – and you wouldn't like to come across an angry lama on a Himalayan pass, let me tell you."'

'What's a lama?' I asked. I had in my head the image of a long-necked grazing animal I'd seen in a picture book about south America.

'A sort of senior Buddhist monk. But not as peaceful as that sounds,' said Professor Power. 'Some of them are warriors, and groups of Western travellers have been set upon by them when they don't want foreigners traversing their sacred mountains.'

'Go on,' said Mrs Jameson, her eyes intent on the paper. She didn't like waiting for people to read things to her and would have snatched it, had politeness and respect for our guest not restrained her.

"'The story goes,'" continued Professor Power, "'that Buckler and his partner stayed at a monastery on the sacred mountain – honoured guests and all that, their porters and hangers-on eating the poor old monks out of house and home – for weeks. They had been asked not to venture to the scree slopes on the eastern side of the valley, which are considered holy. They spent weeks hunting, but said they had not found what they were looking for.

"'Then one day, they went out hunting and came back late, packed up their train and left at first light the next day, even though the weather was bad. The monks were surprised and rather angry that they did not thank them properly for their hospitality, as was the usual way of things. Later, the lama in charge of the novices realised that one young lad, who had been sent the previous day to buy grain in the village, was missing. They thought perhaps he had stayed overnight because of the storm, but he did not return when the weather eased. When the monks enquired in the village, they discovered he had never arrived.

"'There was no sign of the missing boy until the spring, when a party of monks went to place prayer flags around the holy mountain. They found a body in a novice's saffron robes, at the foot of a ravine. It was close to a rope bridge, where the monks crossed to the eastern screes.

"'The lamas have said they will no longer allow plant hunters to use their trails, and that the villagers will be punished if they assist the foreigners in any way. Of course, no-one knows what happened to the poor boy, but it does seem suspicious that he disappeared the day before the explorers left in such a hurry.'"

Professor Power folded the letter and replaced it in her handbag. 'That's all the relevant information. Iris, what do you know of the expedition? Why did you ask me about it?'

Mrs Jameson was staring into space, tapping her chin rhythmically with her forefinger. Slowly she blinked, her focus coming back to the present. She turned to Professor Power.

'Thank you, Eileen. That is most interesting.' She sighed and rang for coffee. 'People will go to the most extraordinary lengths to get what they want. We met the explorers, Buckler and Eversholt, down in Kent. I knew there was something wrong when I first heard Tommy Eversholt talk about the expedition.'

Graham Hargreaves arrived. 'Coffee is ready in the drawing room, Mrs Jameson. But I have a gentleman from Faversham Police Station on the telephone for you. Would you like to take the call first, or should I ask him to call back when it is more convenient?'

Mrs Jameson hurried to the telephone in the office, while Professor Power and I made ourselves comfortable in the drawing room. Moments later, she was back, and I recognised the light of battle in her eyes.

'Well, Marjorie, this seems to be a rather bloodthirsty lily. The police surgeon confirms that Harry Smith's death was not from natural causes. No traces of digitalis, but they did follow up on my suggestion about yew.'

I had passed on my mother's words, which Mrs Jameson had appropriated as her own idea. We'd looked up yew in one of her poison books: it flowered in early spring and the berries started to form around the toxic seeds in March or April.

'They found several undigested yew seeds in his stomach,

as well as taxine, the poison that yew produces. It looks as if we have a murder on our hands.'

Another murder, I thought. Perhaps another murder.

Chapter 23

When we arrived at the Chelsea Royal Hospital grounds the next morning, I was glad of the rubber Wellington boots that Mrs Jameson had ordered from Harrods for the pair of us. The rain had barely ceased for the past week and the display gardens, far from looking like paradise, resembled nothing so much as photographs of the battlefields of northern France.

The resemblance went as far as the paths, which were made up of duckboards with old doors and pieces of timber laid over them to try to prevent the wheelbarrows from churning the ground still further. We picked our way along, careful not to slip on the treacherous surface, to where a cart-load of white rocks had been dumped on one side of an unpromising quagmire.

A tall figure in a voluminous waxed canvas cape waved an arm and beckoned us over.

'Welcome to Hell,' said Mrs Hall. 'Have you ever seen anything like it?' Her face was slick with rain and strands of hair had escaped her hat to plaster themselves across her forehead. But despite her words, she was grinning with excitement. Beyond her, three figures in what looked like fishermen's oilskins were laboriously lifting rocks from the pile and shifting them to where Mrs Hall directed. Someone had propped an umbrella over a folding table, where I could just glimpse a soggy piece of graph paper on which was drawn the plan for the garden.

'I'm sure you have it all well in hand,' said Mrs Jameson, nice and dry beneath her big umbrella. I was all too aware of the rain dripping off my hat and on to my nose, while water seemed to have found a direct route from the back of my coat into my rubber boots. 'But you may not have heard the latest from the police.' She glanced around the site. 'Is Bert here?'

Mrs Hall shook her head. 'He's supervising the arrival of the first load of plants. I'm going to keep the lilies at Hawkshill until Monday. But there are less sensitive plants that can go in, once we have the hard landscaping in place. He's taken a truck to meet the train that will bring the primulas and rhododendrons.'

I was relieved. I felt uncomfortable about my promise not to tell Mrs Hall about Bert's presence with Dick Cooper at the Covent Garden tavern last week in the early hours of the morning.

'Is there somewhere we can have a quiet word?' asked Mrs Jameson. 'Preferably under cover?'

Mrs Hall led us towards an enormous canvas tent. 'The stands in the pavilion won't be set up until Saturday,' she said. 'It's empty at the moment.' Inside was dry, although the rain hammering on the canvas meant it was far from quiet.

'The police will want to speak to Bert,' said Mrs Jameson. 'I'm afraid it's bad news. Harry Smith died from poison. I expect they will want to interview everyone again.'

Mrs Hall stared at her in disbelief. 'But there's no time!' she exclaimed. 'We're up against it, Iris. Can't you see how it is?'

'Constance, it's possible that the man was murdered,' said

Mrs Jameson, gently. 'The police tend to take a dim view of such things.'

Mrs Hall took off her hat and wiped her face. The seriousness of the matter seemed finally to get through.

'Yes. Of course. Poor Harry,' she said. 'I do see. It's just...' she glanced around. 'I really am at the end of my tether. Those men outside can shift rocks about, but they have no skill in planting. And we have less than a week until the opening. I really don't know what I shall do without Bert.'

Mrs Jameson tapped her chin thoughtfully. 'I can let you have Marjorie for a few days,' she said, without consulting me. 'And our chauffeur, Miss O'Grady. What about your son, Constance?'

'He's with Bert, but he can supervise the builders when he gets back,' she said. 'Thank you, Iris. But I shall have to find more help from somewhere.'

The canvas doors to the tent parted and Ernest Buckler walked in, rain sluicing off his wide-brimmed leather hat and down his cream-coloured raincoat. Lavinia shivered next to him in a slim navy mackintosh, clutching an umbrella.

'Thank goodness,' said Mrs Hall. 'Ernest, it's going to be all hands on deck. I shall need you to work on the planting, as soon as Bert and Perry get back from the railway station. Marjorie, can you help with that? And Lavinia, I do hope you'll be able to join in.'

The young woman looked rather horrified at the thought of getting her delicate hands dirty – not to mention her pristine coat and the lace-collared frock she wore underneath.

'They're here now,' said Ernest. 'I met them pulling in with the truck over by the garden site. There's something rum going on, though. A couple of policemen are there, and they

114

wanted Bert to go with them.'

Mrs Hall yelped and ran towards the door.

'Well,' said Mrs Jameson, smiling serenely. 'I think I had better consult my friends at Scotland Yard. Marjorie, I'll send Frankie over when I'm finished. The two of you can help here for as long as Constance needs you. I'll see you back in Bedford Square for supper.'

Feeling about as happy as Lavinia, I followed the Bucklers back to the quagmire of the garden. I was even less happy when I was almost knocked down by a man swathed in oilskins trundling a wheelbarrow along the narrow duckboards.

'Watch out, can't you?' he yelled. The more a person is in the wrong, I've noticed, the keener they are to blame the other person for a collision. I was about to make a stinging rejoinder when I saw the man's face. Oh, goodness. It was Sir Norman Alperton's head gardener, last seen pitched headfirst into a pile of manure.

'You.' He set the barrow down. 'What are you doing here?'

Ernest Buckler, who had been stamping up the path ahead of me with his wife, turned and glared. 'I don't know who you are, but this young woman is working with Constance Hall on our garden. I suggest you get back to your own work.'

Sir Norman Alperton, wearing a most extraordinary leather hat like an American cowboy from a film, bustled over.

'John, I need you. What are you dallying for?'

'This was the woman snooping around your Chelsea glasshouses at Kingsmead,' he said, pointing at me. 'She's snooping again.'

Sir Norman glared. 'I remember. You can tell Constance Hall that I have no need of spies or trickery. My English Arcadia Garden will knock her Himalayan nonsense into a cocked hat.'

'You can tell her that yourself. I'll take all the more pleasure from proving you wrong,' said Mrs Hall, who had hastened over on seeing the altercation. She raked her gaze over the muddy plot that Sir Norman was supervising and shook her head. A rustic arbour stood at the centre of the symmetrical design, housing a marble statue of winged Mercury. Men were constructing pergolas and laying crazy paving paths. In John's barrow, a fragrant phalanx of white stocks awaited planting.

'Still stuck on the English cottage garden theme, I see,' said Mrs Hall pityingly. 'I'd never seen a cottage with a garden like that one.

'Still attempting to grow plants utterly unsuited to the English climate, which can't stand a drop of English rain?' taunted Sir Norman. 'I think the Royal Horticultural Society will see past your gimmicks, when it comes to awarding the medals.'

The two designers glared at each other, their respective armies of gardeners standing behind them.

'Come,' said Mrs Hall. 'Let's leave Sir Norman to his patriotic fantasies. We have work to do.'

She swept away and we trailed behind. Glancing over my shoulder, I frowned. A short man wearing a sodden baker boy cap had straightened to watch us go. I'd only caught a glimpse of him in the Lord John Russell Tavern – but it looked to me like Dick Cooper.

Chapter 24

By the time the clouds parted in the afternoon and the sun peeped shyly through the branches of the trees around our garden, all of us were soaked through and exhausted. My back ached from shovelling piles of earth, my stockings were squelching inside my rubber boots and my hands were blistered from wielding a spade. I was also starving hungry. We hadn't stopped for lunch.

'Come on,' said Mrs Hall, stretching upright after hours of stooping. 'I think it's time for a break. The tea-tent is open to serve the gardening crews.'

I looked at my mud-encrusted hands and hoped there was somewhere to wash.

'There's a ladies' wash-room by the tent,' said Mrs Hall. 'You can get the worst of it off there.'

Lavinia, who had been easing plants into the ground under the close supervision of her husband, looked as relieved as I was. Her coat had inches of mud around the hem and cuffs, and her hat had collapsed altogether. We scampered gratefully for the facilities. They were basic enough: lines of enamel bowls with pitchers of cold water, cakes of Lifebuoy soap, and a stack of linen towels. It felt good to get the dirt off my hands and face, though.

'Isn't it awful?' said Lavinia. 'Honestly, I wouldn't have come with Ernest if I'd known we were going to be enslaved like this. I could have gone to Harrods and done some shopping. I only bought this raincoat yesterday, and it's already ruined. Ernest got fed up with me always having to borrow his.'

She presented her pretty china-doll face to me. 'Do I still look hideous?'

'Not a bit of it,' I said, taking the corner of a towel and removing a speck of mud from her forehead. 'But what shall we do about our hair?' My bob went all curly if I didn't brush it firmly after washing it. Lavinia's carefully-arranged coiffure was straggling down her cheeks.

'I know. It's too horrible to contemplate. Do you have a comb in your bag?'

I dug around and found one, and we helped each other get straight. I began to laugh.

'What's funny?'

'I'm sorry. It's just so ridiculous. I was telling my parents on Sunday about my glamorous job, working with Mrs Jameson, visiting famous garden designers and getting tickets to the Chelsea Flower Show. It's a bit of a step-up from serving in the shop. My mother was so jealous. And if she could see me now!'

Tentatively, Lavinia curled her mouth into a smile, then started to giggle. 'I know! All my friends think I live this fascinating life, going to receptions and lectures with Ernest and meeting important people. If only they knew the half of it.'

Something in her voice – a heartfelt wistfulness – caught my attention. I waited, arranging my face into an expression of sympathy.

'It's not just this,' she said, waving her hand to vaguely indicate the washroom, the mud and the whole of the Chelsea site. 'And I don't mind visiting people, or going to lectures and having to look interested at men talking about a whole lot of things I don't understand.'

I nodded feelingly. I spent quite a lot of time listening to people talking about things I didn't understand.

'It's when we're on our own, days and days cooped up in his flat in Knightsbridge without seeing anyone but Ernest,' she said in a little rush. 'He hardly talks to me anymore. And I hardly dare say anything to him, because everything I say seems to annoy him. And then he blows up like a volcano.' Just for a second, she looked truly frightened.

She stopped abruptly and forced a laugh. 'I expect it's because I don't know anything about anything. It's probably my fault for talking nonsense. But we've only been married for six months, and I didn't think it would be... like this.'

I hesitated. The fear in her face had been real, although she'd covered it up quickly. I didn't want to push her too far. I understood the desire to paper over problems in a marriage. My own mother had told me darkly that 'the first year is the worst' and 'they mostly leave you alone after that'.

'I'm sorry you're having a sad time of it,' I said. 'I expect it takes a while to get used to being married. Especially to someone so much older than you.'

She looked up quickly. 'I'm not complaining, really I'm not. But there are days when I – well, I rather wish I was back at home with Mamma and Papa. Or at least that there was someone of my own age around to talk to, who wouldn't expect me to say anything clever. It's all right for someone like Diana. She's intellectual. And she can just take off and do

119

what she wants.'

That was true. However, I remembered, even Diana had been afraid of someone.

'We should go,' said Lavinia. 'He'll be wondering where I've got to. He always says I take too long getting ready.'

She left the washroom at a trot. I walked behind her, mulling over what she'd said.

In the tea tent, I was disappointed to see only a couple of sad-looking rock cakes left on the stall. The sandwiches had long gone. The gossip at our table was all about the police's interrogation of Bert Smith.

'It's a lot of nonsense,' said Peregrine Hall indignantly, seemingly having forgotten that he'd all but accused Bert of murder himself. 'The police are prejudiced. They don't like his political sympathies, that's all it is.'

Mrs Hall shook her head. 'I very much doubt the Metropolitan Police has one whit of an idea of Bert Smith's political inclinations. I imagine they are more exercised by his fight with his father on the day of Harry's death.'

'Perhaps it was an accident,' I said. 'My father knew someone who died after making jam from poisonous berries. Maybe Bert took him over some jam sandwiches for breakfast.'

'Jam?' Mrs Hall fixed me with a withering look. 'What a ridiculous thing to do.'

'Reminds me of something the natives did in Tibet,' said Ernest Buckler, looking up and breaking his silence for the first time. 'Every now and then one of them would collapse after eating wild honey. Rhododendrons, you see. At certain times of year, they're the only forage for bees. But they're poisonous. I once tried drinking nectar from rhododendrons when I lost the path and got separated from my porters for a couple of days. I felt like I'd drunk a bottle of whisky. First it made me delirious, then I was sick as a dog.'

He relapsed into silence. I was beginning to wonder if there were any flowers at all that were not deadly poisonous. Lavinia put down the rock cake she'd been nibbling and looked at her hands. She'd been helping to plant the rhododendrons, I remembered. Thank goodness we had washed properly before tea.

'I don't think Bert took his father anything,' she said, softly. 'I saw him walking over to the glasshouse, the morning it happened. Just before nine o'clock. And I'm sure he didn't have anything in his hands.'

I sat up straight. 'Wait. You saw Bert on the way to the glasshouse just before nine? And he came to the house just after nine, while we were all eating breakfast.'

She coloured. 'I was having a stroll in the flower garden before I joined you. That's when I saw him.'

Out of the corner of my eye, I noticed Peregrine's colour had heightened too. He picked up a sugar lump and stirred it vigorously into his tea, slopping it around the edges.

'Harry was dead when we arrived,' I said, slowly. 'And if Bert got to the glasshouse only a few minutes before that, he wouldn't have had time to do anything suspicious. Lavinia, I think we should tell the police. Especially if they really do suspect Bert Smith.' I appealed to Mrs Hall. 'Don't you think so?'

She picked up her handbag. 'If it means Bert is released and can get back here more quickly to supervise the planting, I'm all for it. Come on, ladies. Miss O'Grady, you can drive us to Scotland Yard.'

'No need.' Peregrine was on his feet before Frankie could

put down her teacup. 'I'll take Mrs Buckler in a taxi-cab. You can all carry on here, where you're most needed.'

Chapter 25

In the end I went with Peregrine and Lavinia, at her urging. She appeared more relaxed the further away from Chelsea we got. Peregrine Hall seemed to revel in his role as her protector, flagging down a taxi and ushering her inside as if he was escorting her through a jungle.

I wasn't sure which police station we should go to, so I suggested we see Sergeant Williams at Bow Street. Fortunately, he was crossing the piazza as our taxi drew up, so I didn't need to endure the jokes of the desk sergeant. Sergeant Williams ushered us straight through to his office, a cubby-hole of a room with no window, a desk and two upright wooden chairs. It was illuminated with a harsh electric lamp hanging from the ceiling. The bookshelf was stacked with cardboard files and several used tea mugs sat on the desk. He pushed them out of the way and offered the chairs to me and Lavinia, while he perched on the desk. Peregrine stood like a soldier behind Lavinia's chair.

'I hear you had a lively time of it at the Lord John Russell last week, Miss Swallow,' he said. 'Did you discover anything of interest?'

I smiled. 'Nothing definitive. However, Mrs Buckler here has information which your colleagues should know. The trouble is, I don't know which police station will be holding Bert Smith. I hoped you could help us to find out.'

He arranged his face into an expression of seriousness and took out his notebook. 'Of course. Please go ahead, Mrs Buckler.' He frowned and looked up. 'Would that be any relation to Mr Ernest Buckler, the plant hunter?'

'My husband,' she said with a faint smile. I saw him look surprised and glance from her to Peregrine, who was scowling at Buckler's name. 'We were staying with Mrs Constance Hall down in Kent,' she explained. 'And the poor gardener died. Mr Smith, was it? But now they've arrested his son, and I told Marjorie that it couldn't have been anything to do with him because I saw him leave the gardener's cottage just before it happened.'

Sergeant Williams noted down what she said and asked various pertinent questions. Then he looked up.

'And did anyone else see the young man?' he asked.

Lavinia blushed and looked awkward. 'Well, yes.'

'I did,' said Peregrine, defiantly. 'We were both walking in the gardens, see. Taking an early-morning stroll.' He was brick red. It was his embarrassment, more than the mere fact of their having walked in the gardens together, that alerted me that something other than innocent coincidence might be at play.

Sergeant Williams nodded briskly. 'And your name, Sir?'

'Peregrine Hall. Hawkshill Manor is my home,' he explained stiffly.

'Give me a few minutes,' said Sergeant Williams. 'I'll find out where Mr Smith is being questioned. As you say, your information may be of assistance. I'll pass it on and let you know if they need you to attend.'

We waited in his office.

Lavinia turned to me straight away. 'It's so awful, having to talk to the police,' she said in a hushed voice. 'I never thought I would be inside a police station. But I suppose you come here all the time.'

I smiled. 'I seem too, lately,' I said. 'But only since I started working for Mrs Jameson. Policemen aren't so different from other men. Some are nice – like Sergeant Williams here – and others less so.' Like the Bow Street desk sergeant, and the police who had been in the pay of the Limehouse gangsters during our last investigation.

'I say,' blurted Peregrine. 'No need to tell anyone that I was in the gardens at the same time, is there?'

I turned to look at him, surprised. 'It may be helpful to have both of your testimonies,' I said.

He nodded, moodily. 'Yes, I see that. But there's no need to talk about it at home, is there? With Mater and Pa. Or... or any of the others.'

Lavinia was looking busily in her handbag for a pocket handkerchief. Her cheeks were spots of pink, bright as the roses in the flower market.

'Such as Mr Buckler?' I asked.

Neither of them answered, thereby giving me all the answer I needed.

Sergeant Williams reappeared. 'It seems they're interviewing Mr Smith at Pimlico,' he said. 'It would be most helpful if you would pop along there and repeat your statement formally, Mrs Buckler. And you too, Mr Hall.'

They rose to go. 'Might I detain you for a moment, Miss Swallow?' asked the sergeant.

'You two go ahead,' I told them. 'I'll see you back at the

garden.'

They departed at once. I had the impression that Lavinia was annoyed with Peregrine for making such a point of his wish to keep their early-morning garden stroll from her husband. After all, why should they not both take a turn around the garden before breakfast?

Although... I remembered that Peregrine had been one of the late-night watchers. One would have supposed him to have slept late the following morning, not be up before breakfast and wandering the flowerbeds. My mind flitted back to that Sunday night. Could it have been Peregrine I'd seen prowling around, just before midnight? Ernest Buckler had announced his intention to go to bed early, before his four o'clock shift, but perhaps his wife had stayed up late.

Something else occurred to me. The hedge that divided the garden from the yard was of yew. And that was where I'd seen the figure in white.

'Miss Swallow?' Sergeant Williams recalled me to myself.

'I'm sorry. Of course. What did you want to ask me about?'

He raised his eyebrows. 'This business of yours last week, about the lilies. Does it have anything to do with the suspicious death in Kent?'

'To be perfectly honest, Sergeant Williams, I don't know. But...' I hesitated. 'Dick Cooper, who used to work at Hawkshill Manor, was in the tavern. I spoke to someone who said he had been supplying lilies to specialist collectors. And...' Perhaps, I realised, I should have mentioned this before.

'And?' he prompted.

'And Cooper was with Bert Smith, the son of the gardener who died. The one they're talking to at Pimlico. So, I don't know if the two investigations are connected, but it is something of a coincidence.'

Sergeant Williams wasn't smiling any more. 'If there's one thing that seven years in the police force has taught me,' he said, 'it's to be extremely suspicious of coincidences.'

'Yes,' I said. 'That's what Inspector Chadwick says.'

Sergeant Williams let me use his telephone to report the latest developments to Mrs Jameson in Bedford Square. She suggested I return to Chelsea for Frankie, and that the two of us should drive to Pimlico to collect Bert Smith.

'I'd very much like a word with that young man,' she said. 'And if he goes straight back to Chelsea, Constance will have him hard at work again and we shan't get the chance.'

Chapter 26

Mrs Jameson's plan worked up to a point. Bert, on his release from Pimlico police station, was furious. He refused to go back to Chelsea, but he also refused to go with us to Bedford Square.

'I've had enough of being told what to do,' he said. 'They're all against the working man – the toffs, the government, the police. You have to look after yourself in this life. No-one's going to do it for you.'

'Too blooming right,' said Frankie. 'I'll drink to that. Tell you what, why don't we? It's gone five o'clock and there's a pub around the corner. I could murder a pint after all the graft I've put in for your Missus today, Bert. None of which comes under the usual duties of a chauffeur, I might point out.'

I was surprised. Frankie wasn't usually one for drinking during the daytime, especially if she had to drive. She grinned at me and winked.

'You won't tell, will you, Marge? Come and have a lemonade with us. Digging trenches isn't part of what a secretary usually does, either, is it? You can drive us back later. They won't know what time Bert got out, will they?'

That was true. Peregrine and Lavinia had disappeared by the time Frankie and I got to Pimlico police station, having given their statements and left. And I hardly ever got the chance to get behind the wheel of Mrs Jameson's Lagonda. It was much more fun to drive than the ambulances I'd learned on during the War. And if Bert wouldn't talk to Mrs Jameson, he might just talk to Frankie and me.

The Pelham Arms was a rather inviting public house. It was bright with flowers – wallflowers in window boxes, purple and yellow pansies making a mass of colour in hanging baskets around the door. The three of us, on the other hand, were not the most attractive customers the pub had ever welcomed. Frankie and I were mired from the knee down. Bert was unshaven, having got up early to meet the train with the plants and then spent the day being questioned in a police station. However, the proprietor did no more than eye us curiously and recommend we sit in the snug.

'The saloon bar gets a bit rowdy for ladies on an evening,' he said, his glance returning to Frankie, clearly unsure whether she was to be included in this category or not. She smiled cheerily, ordered two pints of best bitter and a lemonade 'for the lady', then sat in an armchair in the snug with her knees wide, leaning her forearms on her thighs. Her trousers were filthy, and her boots caked in mud.

Bert took a long swallow of his beer and leaned back, eyes closed. 'Needed that.'

'You've had a rotten day,' observed Frankie.

'I've had better,' he agreed. 'This stuff about Dad being poisoned. Who would do such a thing? My mum's going to be so upset. At least they've stopped accusing me. She couldn't have borne that.'

Poor Mrs Smith. 'I'm so sorry,' I told him. 'Do pass on my best wishes to your mother when you see her next.'

He opened his eyes. 'I'll do that. She was very grateful for what you did for my dad, Miss.' He took another mouthful of beer and glowered into the small fire. 'I can't believe the coppers thought I had something to do with it. What sort of bloke would bump off his own father, eh?'

Frankie shook her head sympathetically. 'It's not right, Bert. I don't wonder you're fed up.'

Since entering Mrs Jameson's service, I'd seen enough of the way some family members behaved towards each other to know that blood ties did not preclude murder. Indeed, Mrs Jameson said that most murders were committed by someone related to the victim. However, now was not the time to make that point.

'But someone gave him poison,' said Bert, his expression grim. 'That blooming lily is poisonous, ain't it? What if the bloke who'd been on the watch before him – what's his name, that posh bloke? What if he'd given him sandwiches with a lily leaf inside or something?'

Frankie raised her eyebrows at me. 'Who was on the last shift, Marjorie?'

I thought back. 'It was Tommy Eversholt, Diana's husband. But why would Mr Eversholt want to hurt your dad, Bert?'

Bert shrugged. 'Who knows? Maybe it was him that was doing the sabotage. Maybe Dad had found out and was going to tell Mrs Hall. So, he bumped him off before he could say anything. He knew all about the lily being poisonous, didn't he?'

We lapsed into silence. I didn't think Bert's explanation was very likely, even leaving aside the fact that the lily had not been used as the poison. Nor did I truly believe Bert himself had been involved in his father's death. But the awkward fact remained that he seemed to be the only one who had a motive. Bert had argued with his father about going to Chelsea, and Harry Smith's demise meant Bert got his wish. I supposed that, as a gardener, he would be aware of the poisonous properties of yew trees.

'Why do you want to be here so much?' I asked him.

'Here?'

'At Chelsea. I mean, the flower show is all about high society and rich people showing off, isn't it? What's the attraction?'

He shrugged again and kicked the fender. 'It's where it all happens, ain't it? You work all year, then you get to see what the result looks like, and what everyone else is doing. And I've had enough of being buried in the countryside, seeing nobody.'

I nodded. 'I can see that. So, why didn't your father want you to come?'

He pushed back his chair. 'Who says he didn't?' He looked at me belligerently.

'Well, I heard him say so himself,' I said. 'When Mrs Jameson and I came over to your cottage and talked to your mum. He shouted it as he walked out of the cottage. Then you went out the back door.'

He continued to stare at me, his face twisting with suspicion. 'So, you were snooping around. Like last week in the Lord John Russell.'

'Not at all,' I said. 'We came to talk to your dad about the lilies. We could hardly help hearing what he said. Half the estate must have heard him.' However, I had been snooping when I'd found Bert's copy of the *Manifesto of the Communist Party*, and the note within it. The note that had given the date of the Royal visit to Chelsea: Tuesday May 22. Today was Thursday the 17th.

I had a sudden prickle of fear. What had Mrs Hall said to Peregrine when he expressed sympathies for the communist cause – do you want to see the King and Queen murdered?

'Is it about the King's visit?' I asked. 'Are you planning something for that, Bert?'

He flushed dark red. For a moment, his face was as angry as any Bolshevik assassin. He got to his feet and pulled his jacket back on.

'I'm off,' he said. 'I've had about enough of this. First the police, then you.' He leaned towards me. 'You want to mind your own business.'

He slammed his way out of the door. Frankie, who had been holding herself ready to intervene if he'd turned nasty, let out a whistle.

'I reckon you hit a nerve there, Marge. He's up to something, ain't he?'

I sipped my lemonade, thinking rapidly. 'I should warn Inspector Chadwick,' I said. 'What if Bert and his communist friends are planning to attack the King?'

Frankie shrugged. 'What if they are?'

I was shocked. 'We must stop them! Don't you care about the Royal family?'

She set down her pint glass and laughed. 'Do you think the Royal family care about me? Come on, Marge. You've got a head on your shoulders. Bert's right. It's the toffs at the top that keep the whole system in place.'

'But look what's happened in Russia.' Frankie and I had never talked about politics before.

'Exactly. It shows there's another way to run a country.' She relented. 'Look, I'm not a revolutionary. I've got nothing against the Royals. I just want to be left alone to earn a decent crust, save up enough to lease a motor garage and run the place myself. But seriously, Marge. Do you really think Bert's going to murder the King?'

Chapter 27

I put the Lagonda into gear and drove slowly around the side streets, getting the feel of it. The engine purred nicely, and the walnut steering wheel was smooth under my hands. I preferred driving to sitting in the back seat; I was less likely to feel travel-sick and you got a better view.

'That's it. You're a natural,' said Frankie, sitting beside me. Gaining confidence, I took us over Ebury Bridge where the trains puffed their way into Victoria Station. I braced myself to join the traffic that choked the streets between the station and Buckingham Palace.

'There's a short cut through that way,' called Frankie, pointing. 'Ebury Street. Then go right up Buckingham Gate past the Palace.' She grinned. 'We could stop off so you can wave a union jack at the King and Queen if you like.'

'Very funny.' I manoeuvred along the narrow street. 'Wait. Isn't that Lavinia Buckler?'

I pulled in sharply behind a laundry van and we peeped out. Lavinia and Peregrine Hall were getting out of a taxi-cab. She appeared to be distressed, dabbing at her eyes with a pocket handkerchief. We watched as Peregrine paid the driver, then took her arm and escorted her up the grey stone steps and through the elegant portico of The Goring hotel.

'That's where the Halls are staying,' I said. 'Mrs Hall says she always stays at The Goring when she's in town. But Lavinia and Ernest have a flat in Knightsbridge.' If Peregrine was escorting her home, he'd brought her to the wrong place.

Frankie raised an eyebrow. 'I don't suppose they've dropped by for afternoon tea,' she said.

I looked at her, crossly. 'Well, they might have done. After everything that's happened today, that might be exactly what they feel like doing.' Personally, the thought of scones, tea and cake made me quite weak with desire. I wished I could follow and find out, but I doubted the hotel doorman would let my muddy boots and coat over the threshold.

'She wants to be careful,' said Frankie. 'That bloke she's married to doesn't look like the understanding sort.'

I remembered Ernest Buckler's cold expression as he'd watched Lavinia playing cards with Peregrine in the drawing room at Hawkshill Manor.

'No,' I said. 'I don't think he is.' So, what was Lavinia playing at, gadding around with Peregrine Hall in such a public fashion? He was clearly a smitten puppy, but I wasn't sure Lavinia was quite so keen on the callow young man. She had said she wished she had someone of her own age to talk to, but Peregrine's conversation as demonstrated so far had not been electrifying.

I put the car back into gear and drove to Bedford Square, giving my full attention to the busy traffic. I hopped out of the car in front of the house and handed it over to Frankie to take back to the garage.

'Evening, Miss Marjorie. Let me take those muddy boots for you.' Graham Hargreaves, our kindly butler, was never taken aback by the state of my clothes when I returned from an investigation. 'Shall I send Jenny up to help you get changed?'

I smiled and shook my head. 'No need, Graham. Is Mrs Jameson in the office?'

'She's having cocktails in the drawing room. Inspector Chadwick is visiting. She asked if you would join them when you returned.'

Good. Despite Frankie's mockery, I remained concerned about the possibility of harm to His Majesty at the Flower Show.

'I'll get changed and be right down.'

I wished I had time for a hot bath, but made do with a quick rinse at the basin, thankful once again that Mrs Jameson had insisted on central heating and hot water on tap. I was glad to get out of my damp clothes. I changed into one of the two evening dresses I possessed, pulled a shawl over the light lilac-print voile and tried to tame my frizzy hair.

'There you are, Marjorie,' said Mrs Jameson as I arrived, slightly out of breath, in the drawing room. From the glint in her eye, the French 75 in her hand was not her first.

'Miss Swallow.' Inspector Chadwick rose to greet me. 'I hear you have had a busy day.' There was a whisky and soda on the table by his armchair, so he wasn't on duty. I liked Inspector Chadwick, with his solemn moustache and the twinkle in his eye when he was amused. He looked like the debonair detective in an American film, well-built and solid in his evening clothes.

Graham brought me a cocktail and I sipped cautiously at the bubbles. A solitary rock cake in the afternoon had not been sufficient to line my stomach after my day's labour.

'What happened to Bert? I understand that he was released at five o'clock,' said Mrs Jameson. I might have guessed that she would know from her contacts the precise time of his release.

'He was,' I admitted. 'But he refused to come here. Frankie and I did our best. We took him to a public house, and he did talk, a bit. He was very angry about being accused of his father's murder. He talked about the lilies being poisonous, so I don't think he knew what had actually been used.'

Mrs Jameson nodded. 'Or knew better than to say so.'

'He suggested that Tommy Eversholt might have given Harry poison in a sandwich. Because Tommy was the last one on the watch, and he handed over to Harry Smith before Mrs Hall arrived,' I added.

'Where is this Eversholt fellow?' asked Inspector Chadwick. 'It's not my investigation, but I'd certainly have a few questions for him.'

'In Scotland, I believe,' said Mrs Jameson. 'Marjorie, you took the address from Diana Eversholt, didn't you? They made a very sudden departure, almost as soon as Harry Smith's body was discovered, on what sounded like a rather flimsy premise. It certainly merits investigation.'

I went to find the notebook with the address in Scotland. My stomach rumbled and I hoped it wouldn't be too long until dinner. I thought back to breakfast time. Thank goodness I'd had bacon and eggs, which had been almost as good as that served at Hawkshill Manor.

I had a sudden flash of memory: Tommy Eversholt tucking into a heaped plate of bacon, eggs, mushrooms and kidneys the morning after our watch.

I rushed back to the drawing room. 'He didn't eat his sandwiches!' I burst out.

Inspector Chadwick raised his eyebrows. 'A little more

context, if you wouldn't mind, Marjorie?'

I thrust the notebook with the address at him. 'Tommy Eversholt. The morning after we'd been watching overnight, we all had breakfast together. Tommy had done the shift from six until eight and he said he was starving. He ate an enormous breakfast. But he wouldn't have been hungry if he'd eaten his sandwiches immediately beforehand.'

Mrs Jameson was ahead of me. 'And yet there were no sandwiches left in the wrappers when we arrived at the glasshouse,' she said. 'So, Bert's right about one thing. Harry Smith must have eaten the last lot of sandwiches left out for the watchers.'

'Which makes sense,' I added, 'because he'd missed his own breakfast. Bert said he'd gone off without it because he slept in late. They argued about it. But why would Tommy Eversholt want to kill the gardener?'

Mrs Jameson frowned. 'What? Oh, I see. You're looking at it the wrong way around, Marjorie. Don't you see?'

I didn't, but I was too tired to argue. Inspector Chadwick scribbled the address from my notebook into his.

'I'll have a word with the chap in charge and suggest they speak to Tommy Eversholt as soon as possible. Well done, Marjorie.'

I sat back down, flushed with his praise, and picked up my French 75. 'There's one other thing you should probably know. I rather think someone may be planning an attack on the King.'

Chapter 28

Inspector Chadwick almost dropped his whisky.

'What's this, Marjorie?' asked Mrs Jameson, her voice sharp. I began to wish I'd talked my suspicions through with her first.

I told them about the note I'd found inside Bert's copy of the *Manifesto of the Communist Party,* and his response when I'd challenged him about the Royal visit.

'Is that it?' Mrs Jameson did not look impressed.

'We heard Mr Smith shouting at Bert that he could forget about going to Chelsea,' I reminded her. 'And you said perhaps it was something to do with his political beliefs. Mrs Smith said they argued about politics.'

Inspector Chadwick leaned back in his chair. 'It's a bit flimsy,' he said. 'There's no law against having a copy of a book, and the Communist manifesto hasn't been banned here, even if some people think it should be. And anyone might find out the date of the Royal visit to the flower show.' He made a note. 'All the same, I'll have a word with the chaps in the Royal Protection Service. It doesn't hurt to be prepared. And if anything did happen and I'd not told them, there'd be the most almighty row.'

Mrs Jameson still looked disapproving. 'That cocktail's gone to your head, Marjorie. We had better go through to dinner.

And you can explain what kept you out so late this evening.'

Rack of lamb and plenty of roast potatoes soon had me feeling myself again. After her earlier disapproval of my theories, I decided to stick to the facts when reporting to Mrs Jameson what I'd seen of Peregrine and Lavinia's movements at The Goring hotel.

'Hmm. The boy's a bit of a fool, but the girl is positively reckless,' said Mrs Jameson. 'Does she think her husband won't mind that sort of display?'

I relayed my conversation with Lavinia in the washroom. 'She told me everything she said annoyed Mr Buckler, and that she sometimes wished she was home with her mother. She talks like she's younger than she is.' Lavinia was twenty-five, the same age as me. Although I wasn't married, I felt I knew a lot more of the world.

Mrs Jameson looked thoughtful. 'I was married at her age,' she said. 'The first year can be very hard. You don't realise what you've got yourself into until after the wedding. By which time it's a bit late.'

I held my breath, hoping she would give more information about her mysterious late husband, the artist Julian Jameson.

'But there it is. These days, men and women seem to swap their partners around like hats.' She wiped away her wistful expression with a conventional social smile. 'I wonder how Ernest Buckler's first wife managed to extricate herself from the marriage. Perhaps I should ask her.'

How would Ernest Buckler take it, I wondered, if his second wife also wanted to leave him for another man? Diana Eversholt had said they were all 'terribly modern' about the divorce and remarriage, but I didn't really believe her. It must have been humiliating for him to see Diana – brave, bold Diana

140

– reject him for his junior partner. And he'd spoken about jealousy and spite, when asked about who would sabotage the lilies. I rather doubted that his feelings towards Tommy Eversholt were as benign as he'd pretended.

Perhaps he had seen in Lavinia someone he could dominate completely, who would be no threat to him. A pretty child, compliant, wealthy and highly presentable. Someone he could parade around on his arm, so that people would think the split from Diana had been his decision. How awful, then, to be rejected a second time, and for a boy barely out of university.

I remembered the look of fear in Lavinia's face when she spoke of her husband, and shivered. She and Peregrine seemed to be playing a very dangerous game.

Chapter 29

I was back on gardening duty at Chelsea on Saturday afternoon. To my surprise, in the two days since I had last been there, Mrs Hall's garden had transformed from a quagmire with heaps of stone lying around into a fair representation of a valley with a stream running through it.

Rhododendron bushes in full flower masked the edges of the garden and softened the starkness of the white rocks that represented the mountains. The rocks gave way to blue-grey gravel, raked to look like mountain scree. A terrace stood ready to receive the Sapphire Lilies on Monday. Primulas, poppies and other flowers I didn't recognise were planted close to the stream bed.

The stream itself was causing Mrs Hall trouble when I arrived.

'The blasted thing!' she exclaimed. Walter Hall, who had arrived from Kent that morning, was fiddling around with what he told me was a hydraulic pump.

'Go back up and try it again, Perry,' called Mrs Hall. Peregrine, whose Oxford bags and sweater were already rather damp, turned on a tap at the top of the pile of rocks. It sprayed all over him, flowing everywhere except into the channel prepared for it.

'Oh dear,' I murmured to Frankie, who was leaning on her spade to watch.

'They've been at it for ages,' she said with a grin. 'They should have asked me. I can see what the problem is. That spigot needs rethreading. But I'm just a woman, so I don't know anything. Shame, isn't it?'

'Frankie!' I shot her a reproachful glance. 'You should offer to help. It's not fair.'

She shrugged. 'I'm not a gardener, am I? I work under direction, and this is what I've been told to do.' She resumed shovelling compost on to the terrace.

Fortunately, at that point, Walter Hall took over from his son and presumably did whatever Frankie had said needed doing to the spigot, whatever that was. The water flowed down the channel into the artificial stream, disappeared into a reservoir at the bottom and was pumped back to the top. We all cheered.

My voice died away as Bert Smith arrived with another cartload of plants. He glanced at me, his face impassive.

'This lot needs to go in above the terrace,' he told Mrs Hall.

'Splendid. Thank you, Bert. Lavinia and Marjorie, can you see to that?' she asked. 'Plant the colours in drifts, so they overlap at the edges. No straight lines. It's not a municipal park.'

Lavinia and I exchanged meaningful glances, but picked up our trowels and did as she said.

'Have you been here long?' I asked.

'Ernest dropped me off mid-morning,' she said. 'He's gone down to Hawkshill Manor to supervise the packing of the lilies. He's coming up with them in the train on Monday morning.'

Lavinia seemed to breathe more freely without her husband.

143

She laughed more at Peregrine's feeble jokes, didn't complain when the drizzle started up again and worked with a zeal that surprised me.

'Have you heard about the gardener?' she whispered, after checking that Bert was out of sight.

'Heard what?' I wasn't sure how much she knew.

'They say he was poisoned. Isn't it awful?'

I glanced up at her face, expecting to see fear. But she looked excited, as if it was a game, not a matter of life and death.

'It's very sad for poor Bert and Mrs Smith,' I said. I tried to keep the reproof out of my voice.

'Oh, of course.' A moment later, she was whispering again. 'How do you suppose it was done? Do you think they used the poison in the lilies? It could have been an accident, I suppose. I mean, the gardener was in those glasshouses with the lilies all day. He could easily have touched them too often or something. Maybe that's what the police will conclude.'

'Perhaps,' I said. I wondered if it was possible that Harry had poisoned himself accidentally. But I rather feared the sandwiches were to blame. I'd thought over what Mrs Jameson had said about looking at it the wrong way around, but I didn't understand. I wasn't going to ask her until I'd puzzled it out.

Lavinia rested back on her heels. 'Have you come across many cases of poisoning, working with Mrs Jameson?'

I considered. 'One of cyanide. Another using morphia. And this, of course.'

She shivered, but her eyes were bright. 'How dreadful. How do the police know when it's poison? I mean, people thought the gardener had a heart attack at first, didn't they?'

I pushed my damp hair out of my eyes. 'Some poisons act on the heart. But when there's a suspicious death, the police surgeon carries out a post-mortem examination of the body. There are lots of ways to detect poisons nowadays. They analyse the body tissues – the liver and the stomach contents and so on. Chemical tests can find out if someone's ingested poison. They even use frogs' hearts to test for poisons like digitalis.'

Between cases, Mrs Jameson had set me to read the latest reports of evidence submitted to coroner's courts and at murder trials. I was becoming quite an expert on the Marsh test for arsenic and its interpretation. I'd also learned that one should be very wary of unsolicited boxes of liqueur chocolates, cups of cocoa, coffee, and opened bottles of wine.

Lavinia looked wistful. 'Aren't there undetectable poisons, though?'

I laughed. 'You mean the sort of thing that south American tribes use to poison their arrows, which baffles Scotland Yard? I think that's just in Sherlock Holmes.'

Lavinia stood up and stretched. 'If you wanted to poison someone,' she asked, her voice bright and interested, 'how would you go about it?'

I rose to my feet and looked at her with a prickle of foreboding. 'I wouldn't,' I said, shortly. 'It's a horrible way to die. Don't even joke about it.'

The smile faded from her doll-like face. 'Of course. I was just being silly,' she said. She strolled over to talk to Peregrine, who was supervising the workmen arranging slate gravel around the artificial stream. He held his umbrella solicitously over her golden head.

Where had Lavinia's sudden interest in fatal poison come from? Was she worried for her own wellbeing – or was she considering the use of poison herself? I did hope not. She

145

didn't seem intelligent enough to get away with murder.

By the time I'd finished planting the drifts of flowers to Mrs Hall's satisfaction, she had decreed it was time for tea. I headed to the wash tent. Lavinia had disappeared in that direction half an hour before and was no doubt taking the opportunity to stay out of the rain for a while. I surveyed my ingrained hands and wondered if I would manage to get the muck out from under my nails before the Royal visit on Tuesday.

As I pushed aside the canvas flap, I could hear Lavinia's voice. I paused. Contrary to her earlier good humour, she was sobbing. I slipped silently between the canvas folds and listened hard.

'No, please don't cry.' Peregrine Hall, sounding panicked.

More incoherent sobbing from Lavinia.

'I'll do anything for you. You know that. But be sensible, my darling, please.' His voice wobbled.

'You say that,' she burst out, passionately. 'But you don't mean it. I can't bear it any more, Perry. I really can't. You said you'd help me. Well, now's your chance.'

My heart was thudding so loud I was surprised they couldn't hear it. What had Lavinia asked the boy to do?

'I do wish you wouldn't blub,' said Peregrine. 'Look, I should go back out. They'll notice I've gone, and they'll all be stopping for tea soon. I'll think about it, I promise. But please stop crying.'

Hastily I backed out and retreated around the corner. A moment later I was able to give a reasonable impression of someone walking briskly towards the wash tent, as Peregrine mooched past, hands in his pockets and a look of thunder on his face.

'Is everything all right?' I called, trying to keep my voice normal.

He glanced around at me. 'What? What do you mean?'

I forced a smile. 'You don't look very happy.'

He shrugged. 'It's pouring with rain, and I'm soaked through. Isn't that reason enough?'

'Oh well,' I said. 'It's time for tea, anyway. That always cheers me up.'

He scowled and stalked off in the direction of the garden. I pushed into the wash tent, making enough noise that Lavinia would hear me coming.

'Tea time,' I called, gaily. 'Are you coming out, Lavinia?'

She had dried her eyes and was looking remarkably cool for someone who had been sobbing her heart out a moment ago.

'Just fixing my hair. Marjorie, would you be a love and help me to pin it back up?' Her eyes fell on my grubby hands. 'Well, when you've had a wash. You look like Lady Macbeth.'

The words hung between us as I picked up a nail brush and poured cold water into a bowl.

Chapter 30

I rose early on the morning of Tuesday 22 May. Despite Frankie's teasing, I was beyond excited at the prospect of seeing His Majesty King George V and Queen Mary at the Chelsea Flower Show. I had a bath, dried off briskly and stood in anxious contemplation of my wardrobe.

I had picked out fabric for my best day dress back in February – sky-blue chiffon with a white polka dot – and my mother had made it up in the latest style, with a dropped waist, white sailor collar and sash. I remembered thinking how lovely it would be on a warm spring day. It should have been perfect for the opening of the Chelsea Flower Show. But a glance out of the window showed that the weather persisted wet and chilly. Should I risk it? I supposed I could layer on woollen undergarments and a cambric petticoat, belt my raincoat over the top and take it off at the last minute.

Then there was the question of shoes. The paths at Chelsea were still muddy, despite the attempts of the grounds staff. Wellington boots were really the only sensible footwear, but they would look ridiculous with my dress. My favourite white T-strap pumps were out of the question – they would be ruined in seconds. I would compromise, I decided, with winter lace-up shoes. No-one was going to look at my feet.

I fastened my string of seed pearls at my neck and tied a blue-and-white polka-dot ribbon around my hat. I hoped an umbrella would protect it from the worst of the elements.

Graham smiled as I walked into the breakfast room. 'You look very smart, Miss Marjorie. Quite fit to meet the King. Do tell us all about him, won't you? Jenny and Mrs Smithson will be particularly interested to know what Queen Mary is wearing.'

For once I was almost too nervous to eat breakfast. 'I shan't get to talk to Their Majesties,' I said. 'But tell them I'll report back as best I can.'

'Here. I made it in the kitchen for you.' Graham handed over a cup of mahogany-brown tea. 'Milk and two sugars.'

I took it gratefully. 'You are kind.' Maybe I could manage a slice or two of toast.

Mrs Jameson's tobacco-brown silk moiré with black frogging was old-fashioned by her standards – she didn't often restrict herself with corsets – but made her look as regal as Queen Mary. She had pinned her grey hair back with jet clips and had a new, rather becoming silk hat in place of her usual turban.

'You look lovely,' I told her, feeling a bit silly in my flimsy frock. She cast a critical view over me.

'Very pretty, but you do realise it's pouring with rain? I'm wearing my new coat and taking an umbrella. What have you got on your feet?'

I showed her. 'And I'll wear a raincoat over the top.' My excitement bubbled over, despite the inclement weather. 'Isn't it thrilling, Mrs Jameson? I never thought I'd get anywhere near the King.'

Her face softened. 'I hope he lives up to your expectations,

Marjorie. And, for Constance's sake, I hope he enjoys the garden. She was there until dark last night, planting out those wretched lilies. I expect she's there already, polishing the petals.'

By the time we arrived at the garden at half past nine, it was pristine. Peregrine Hall, looking tense, was testing the workings of the mountain stream.

'It wouldn't do to drench the Royal party, what?' Walter Hall rubbed his hands together and chuckled. He looked very smart in a dark overcoat with a fur collar, holding a top hat under his arm. 'They will be wet enough with this rain.'

I realised he was trying to jolly everyone up. His wife, pacing from one end of the garden to the other in a smart ankle-length coat in burgundy wool, couldn't stand still. Ernest Buckler and Lavinia stood by the lilies, her arm clutched firmly in his. Mr Buckler's face was grim. Lavinia's eyelids were pink and puffy, as if she'd been crying again. She kept her eyes downcast.

'Constance, it looks marvellous,' said Mrs Jameson, soothingly. 'The lilies are perfect. Such an amazing colour.'

Mrs Hall turned to greet us, her face distracted. 'If only it was dry. They look so much brighter in the sunshine.'

Actually, despite the heavy grey clouds, the garden looked wonderful. The rain trickling down the rocks into the stream made it seem even more realistic, and the drops glittered on the lily petals. The yellow primulas and poppies that Lavinia and I had spent so many hours planting looked as if they had grown there naturally, and the white rhododendron flowers nodded their heavy heads like weary dowagers.

I couldn't see Bert Smith. Perhaps Mrs Hall had decided he wasn't needed today. Or, I thought guiltily, perhaps the police had called him back for questioning to keep him out of the way of the King.

'Where's Bert?' I asked.

'He went to get some boards to lay down over the path,' said Mrs Hall. 'He should be back any minute. We want to be sure the Royal party can step into the garden and look at the lilies properly. They won't want to if they're going to get muddy.'

'Here he is,' called Mr Hall, all joviality. 'Perry, go and help him, there's a good boy.'

Mrs Jameson checked her wristwatch. 'Constance, there's over an hour before they are expected. Why don't we go and have a cup of coffee in the tea tent, or a look inside the flower pavilion? You're fretting yourself to pieces here and it's perfection.'

'I can't,' she began.

'You jolly well can,' said Mr Hall. 'I think coffee is a splendid idea. I'll come with you. Perry, you can join us when you've helped Bert lay those planks down. Ernest, Lavinia?'

'I'm all right out here,' said Mr Buckler. 'I'll have a stroll around the gardens. Lavinia will come with me.'

'Oh, but I would so like a cup of coffee to warm up,' she said. She turned her forget-me-not eyes on her husband. 'Please, Ernest. I'm freezing.'

Like me, Lavinia had opted for style over warmth. Her pale pink silk was very becoming, but she was shivering with cold.

He sighed and relinquished her arm. 'Go with Constance and Walter,' he commanded. 'And make sure you're back here in plenty of time.' Lavinia darted to Mrs Hall's side like a bedraggled butterfly escaping a spider.

'Everyone should be back here at a quarter to eleven promptly,' said Mrs Hall. 'The Royal party is expected at eleven.'

With a last lingering glance at the garden, she swept us off to the shelter of the tea tent, which was busy with nervous gardeners and their guests.

'I say,' said Mr Hall. 'Isn't that the Eversholts?' We approached their table. 'I didn't know you were back from Scotland,' he said. 'How jolly that you could make it.'

Tommy got to his feet and pumped Mr Hall's hand. 'Wouldn't miss it for anything, eh, Diana? Quick bite in here, then we're going to check out the competition. You just missed that Alperton chap. Gone back to his garden, I suppose.'

Diana smiled, her eyes jumping from one to another. She looked stylish as ever – her dark red coat and shiny black boots both appropriate for the weather and elegant. But she was nervous as a cat.

'Tommy was very keen to be here. And my editor would be delighted if I could include a line about the King's reaction to the garden, Constance. Would you mind awfully if we came with you? If it won't be too much of a crowd, I mean.'

Mrs Hall had been scanning the room, presumably for her nemesis Sir Norman. 'What? Oh, yes, of course. Where did you see him, Tommy?'

'Going out as we came in, with an elderly chap with a big white moustache and top hat, his chest covered in medals. Deep in conversation.'

Mrs Hall wrung her hands. 'Lord Lambourne, the president of the Royal Horticultural Society. He'll be showing the Royal party around. Alperton is up to something, I know it. I should go to find Lord Lambourne at once.'

'Sit down, Connie,' Mr Hall snapped. 'Drink your coffee and leave the man alone. He has enough to do without your

152

feuding.'

She looked mutinous, but sat.

'Are the Bucklers here?' asked Diana casually.

'Lavinia... where is Lavinia? She was with us a moment ago. Perhaps she went to wash her hands,' said Mr Hall. 'Ernest is around somewhere. He said he was going to look around the gardens. And Perry will be joining us soon. Can I get you anything else, Diana? Another cup of coffee?'

She shook her head and rose. 'Thank you, no. To be honest, it's pretty terrible. I'm going to investigate the flower pavilion. Tommy, will you come with me?'

The coffee was as bad as Diana had said, and the tension in our little group became almost unbearable. The minutes ticked past, and I began to wonder if I should go to find Lavinia. She'd been an awfully long time washing her hands. Then I remembered that Peregrine was due to join us after he'd finished covering the path. I sighed. I had no wish to interrupt another tryst in the washroom.

Eventually, Mrs Hall looked at her wristwatch and rose. 'Twenty to eleven. I'd rather wait in the garden,' she said. 'Even if it does mean getting wet through.'

Chapter 31

We trooped after her. As we reached the exit, Lavinia arrived, out of breath and with her hair disarrayed.

'Whatever is the matter?' asked Mrs Hall. 'I thought you were coming for coffee.'

'I'm sorry,' she said. 'I… I just had to do something. I'll come back with you now.' Her cheeks were flushed peony-pink, and her hat had slipped sideways.

'Let me straighten that for you,' I said.

She gave me a grateful smile. 'It got caught up,' she said vaguely. 'Thank you, Marjorie.'

'Have you seen Peregrine?' Mrs Jameson asked. 'I thought he was to join us.'

'Oh… no. No, I don't know where he is,' Lavinia said. Her expression was unconvincing.

Mr Hall looked troubled, but kept up the bonhomie. 'It probably took longer than expected to sort out the path,' he said. 'Come under my umbrella, Lavinia dear. You're getting quite damp.' He offered her his arm, leaving his wife to stalk off to the garden with Mrs Jameson.

The planks had been laid neatly along the path inside the garden, giving a platform for viewers to stand and observe the lilies without getting their feet muddy. As we arrived, Bert came puffing around the corner with a wheelbarrow of gravel.

'I thought we could cover the planks over,' he said. 'Make it look more natural, like.' He'd pulled his cap down over his forehead, but his face was still slick with rain and his hands covered in mud.

'Good idea,' said Mrs Hall. She seized a spade.

'Don't be ridiculous, Connie,' said Mr Hall. 'Leave it to Bert. Ah, here's Perry. Where have you been, my boy? Help Bert cover over the wood. Make it snappy; they're due in ten minutes.'

The two young men worked quickly and in silence. Soon the Himalayan Valley Garden looked as if it could have been dropped by aeroplane from Tibet, complete with bubbling brook. Constance Hall breathed.

'I do believe we're ready,' she said. 'Now, where is everyone?'

Diana strode over, her umbrella shading her berry-red hat. She looked perfectly composed. 'It's wonderful,' she said. 'Well done, Constance. Have you seen my husband anywhere? I lost him in the pavilion.'

Tommy was next to arrive, puffing and out of breath. 'Thank goodness you're here, Di,' he said heartily. 'Everything all right, old girl?'

'They're coming,' hissed Constance Hall. 'Where on earth is Ernest? He was going to explain about how you found the lilies.'

I craned my neck to see. A group of people with big black umbrellas was moving slowly along the path. I strained my eyes. There was an older man with a big white moustache and medals, as Tommy had described, gesturing and making introductions. Lord Lambourne, I presumed, guiding the Royal party. And there was a very upright lady in a long purple brocade coat and big old-fashioned hat, holding an umbrella. Was that really Queen Mary? Just ahead of her walked a bearded man in a black coat with a white carnation in his buttonhole. I squealed with excitement. That must be the King.

'They're spending a very long time talking to Alperton,' said Mrs Hall, grimly. 'I suppose he's telling them they should dig up the Buckingham Palace gardens and replant them with hollyhocks and rows of runner beans. Oh, this is too bad of Ernest. I was relying on him. Tommy, you will have to explain about finding the lilies.'

'Me?' He looked startled.

'Obviously. No-one else was there. Hush, now. Here they come.'

We all stood up straight as soldiers, Constance Hall flanked by Tommy Eversholt and Mr Hall at the front, while the rest of us tried to keep out of the way behind them. The Royal party arrived, and we sank into low bows and curtsies. Flash-bulbs popped as the newspaper photographers took pictures. Goodness. Would I be in the *Daily Mail*? I wondered. My mother might never get over the excitement.

The moustachioed chap smiled. 'Your Majesties, may I present Mr and Mrs Hall, who have created the Himalayan Valley Garden. And Mr… Eversholt, isn't it? Mrs Hall, I understand you are unveiling a most unusual lily today?'

Mrs Hall rose from her curtsey and welcomed them into the garden, explaining about the Sapphire Lilies.

'Mr Eversholt found them in the mountains of Tibet and brought them back for us to cultivate.'

'I say,' remarked the King. 'That must have been quite an adventure.' His face was lively and interested, his eyes kind.

'Rather,' agreed Tommy, who was very red in the face. 'Extraordinary place, Tibet. Remarkable flora and fauna. And the chaps who live there, of course. Monks, you know. Very hardy. Like the plants, what?'

'Your lilies are exquisite,' said Queen Mary. 'That blue… did you ever see such a colour? "Solomon in all his glory…"'

She leaned towards the plants, white-gloved hand outstretched, and there were more flashes as the photographers moved in. There was a nasty moment when I saw Mrs Hall start forward as if to snatch the Queen's hand away. Mr Hall grabbed his wife's arm firmly.

'They are rather poisonous, I'm afraid,' he said. 'I'd advise against touching them.'

The Queen raised an imperious eyebrow. 'Beautiful and deadly,' she said. 'Quite a bouquet.'

I had half an eye on Bert Smith all this time, ready to spring into action should he threaten Their Majesties. However, he stood silently to one side of the garden, cap in his hands. Whatever he'd planned to do, his courage had clearly abandoned him. Perhaps he'd simply thought better of it, or maybe the actual presence of the monarch had overwhelmed him.

The King expressed interest in the workings of the artificial stream. I saw Lord Lambourne glance at his pocket watch as Walter Hall launched into an explanation of the hydraulic pump.

'So, it goes back up to the top there by the rhododendrons?' said the King, pointing. He paused and frowned. 'I say. Whatever's that sticking out of the bushes?'

We all turned to look. For a moment, I fought an impulse to laugh; it looked so incongruous. Then I realised.

'Please step back, Your Majesty.' Several burly-looking

157

men in dark overcoats materialised and formed a tight group around the King and Queen. The photographers started their barrage of flashes again.

Lord Lambourne and Walter Hall scrambled up the rocks, heedless of their smart clothes. Lord Lambourne looked around, his face pale as milk.

'Please take Their Majesties somewhere safe,' he said, his voice sounding high and strange. 'Call a doctor. And contact the police at once.'

The Royal party was hastily bustled away, with half of the photographers in pursuit. The rest of us stood and stared. At the top of the rocks, a boot stuck out of a rhododendron bush.

Chapter 32

'Let me see.' Mrs Jameson climbed to the top of the rocks, with me close behind. Lord Lambourne and Walter Hall held the rhododendron bushes aside, crouching by the figure on the ground.

'Dear God,' murmured Mrs Jameson.

I pressed my fingers over my mouth to prevent myself from crying out. The boot belonged to Ernest Buckler. He was still wearing it. He lay on his front, half-covered with branches, his left cheek pressed into the earth. His eyes were open, but he looked very dead. The back of his skull was shattered, the ground around him soaked in blood.

'Marjorie?' said Mrs Jameson.

I swallowed hard, removed my gloves, then reached out and laid my fingers against Mr Buckler's neck. Cold, wet. No pulse. I looked up and shook my head.

'He's gone.'

'Constance, take Lavinia and the others away from here,' called Walter Hall, his voice unsteady.

'What is it? Not more poison?' asked Mrs Hall.

'No. Not poison.' Lord Lambourne straightened up. 'Please return to the foot of the garden, everybody, and await the arrival of the police. You, man. Get back, for God's sake. This is the scene of a crime.'

This last was aimed at a photographer who was scaling the rocks. Walter Hall, moving surprisingly fast for a man of his years, pushed him back down.

'Keep away from there,' he warned.

'It's my job,' the man protested.

'And you will disturb the evidence the police need to do theirs,' said Mrs Jameson sternly. 'Lord Lambourne, we should all return to the path as carefully as possible. This place needs to be guarded until the police arrive.'

We picked our way down the rocks.

'What's happened?' asked Lavinia, clutching Mr Hall's arm. 'Where's Ernest? Is that… is he up there?' She'd lost her umbrella somewhere and the rain had soaked through her pink frock. She was pale as death. A photographer thrust his lens at her, and she cried out, turning her face away.

'Lord Lambourne, where can we take the ladies?' asked Mr Hall. He took Lavinia's arm and shielded her with his umbrella. 'We cannot leave them out here in the rain with the press.'

The older man wiped his face. 'Of course. Take them to the tea tent… no, that will be crowded with people. To the Governor's House, then.' He saw a group of red-coated Chelsea Pensioners hovering nearby, their wrinkled faces full of concern. 'Thank goodness. You chaps, please form a cordon across this garden. No one is to go inside until the police arrive, do you hear me? Especially not that lot,' he said, indicating the photographers with disdain.

The pensioners formed a line across the foot of the garden. Although their combined ages might reach six hundred, the glint in their eyes suggested that the young photographers would be foolish to try to breach it.

'I will escort Mr and Mrs Hall, Mrs Buckler and their guests to the Governor's residence. No-one is to leave until the police say so,' Lord Lambourne said, his upright bearing and air of instant command speaking of years of military service.

I turned to Mrs Jameson with a wordless question. Were we to stay and investigate, or go with the others?

'Lord Lambourne,' she said, quietly. 'My assistant and I have some experience in these matters. I will accompany the others to the house, but may Miss Swallow stay here and record the facts of the scene? She has previously provided very useful information to Inspector Chadwick of Scotland Yard, who I suggest is summoned as soon as possible.'

He looked doubtful, but at the mention of the inspector's name, he nodded. 'All right.' He turned to me. 'I'm sure you know your business, Miss Swallow. Please ensure you do not disturb any evidence. And join us as soon as you can. One of these pensioner chaps will show you where to come.'

The party was escorted away: Lord Lambourne leading with Mrs Jameson, Walter Hall following with Lavinia, his wife and son. Tommy and Diana Eversholt, who had barely spoken since the discovery of the body, walked behind them with heads bowed. Bert Smith, twisting his cap in his hand, brought up the rear.

I felt somewhat overwhelmed. This was the first time that Mrs Jameson had left me in charge of recording a crime scene without her supervision. I reached into my handbag and took out my notepad and pencil.

'I need to record everything I can see,' I said, as much for my own benefit as for the pensioners. 'Methodically, so I don't miss anything.' They parted to let me through.

I looked at the plants, the earth, shingle and gravel. The

161

previous crime scenes I had inspected had all been indoors, in the dry. They had seemed more manageable, somehow. I stood under my umbrella, listening to the rain beating down, and tried to steady my mind.

I began by drawing a plan of the garden, from the rocks to the stream, indicating where the plants were grouped. The shingle had been raked over that morning, as had the small patches of bare earth around the plants. I couldn't see anything in the way of footprints.

I narrowed my eyes. Shouldn't Ernest Buckler's footprints be visible, at least? But if he had walked on the shingle, the rain would have washed away any sign of mud.

Keeping well to one side, I walked up the slope with my eyes trained on the ground. I went slowly, looking for disturbed gravel, mud out of place, dropped matches or cigarette ends, even broken twigs or trampled leaves. Nothing.

At the top of the slope, I paused again. The murder weapon was not hard to discern. A lump of white rock, its pointed end covered in blood, had been discarded by the top of the stream. It was about the size of a large house-brick. The blunt end would fit into a hand – a large hand, at least. A man's hand, I thought. I sketched it quickly, drew out the tape measure from my handbag, measured and recorded its dimensions.

I paused and took a breath of the cool air. I did not relish the next phase of my recording of the scene.

The earth around the base of the bushes had been disturbed, even before Lord Lambourne and Mr Hall trampled it. There were gouges made by Ernest Buckler's boots. Did he make them himself? Or was he dragged there, in an attempt to hide his body? I tracked them back.

There was more blood – washing away fast – on the rocks

at the top of the slope where the water outlet was located. The tap was propped up with rocks, the water still running. I frowned. When Frankie and I had watched Mr Hall and Peregrine fixing it last week, it had been half-buried in the earth. I made a note. Perhaps it had been moved since, to give a better flow of water. Or perhaps it had been knocked out of position and quickly propped back in place.

Mr Buckler was wearing a dark suit smarter than any I had seen him in before: fine black wool with black boots that had been recently polished, although they were now caked in mud. His white shirt front was streaked with mud and blood. His jacket was torn slightly where one sleeve was set in. I crouched to examine it more closely. The stitches attaching the sleeve had held, but the woollen fabric had ripped. I imagined someone pulling his body by the jacket.

I quickly sketched the outline of the body, and the tracks made by his boots, indicated the tear on his jacket and the wound on his head. I forced myself to look at it properly; I'd seen worse in the hospital, I reminded myself. Although not much. Fragments of white bone showed through his sandy hair, clots of blood and worse. I closed my eyes for a moment, fighting nausea.

'Hey! What are you doing up there?'

I stood and saw a brace of policemen standing at the foot of the garden by the crimson line of pensioners. One was waving angrily. Oh dear. Perhaps Inspector Chadwick had not been available. A doctor stood to one side, clutching his bag. There was not much for him to do here, except confirm the cause of death.

I picked my way carefully down the garden and tried to seem professional.

'I'm Miss Swallow, assistant to the private detective Mrs Jameson,' I said. The elder of the two policemen looked furious.

'I don't care if you're the assistant to the Queen of Sheba,' he said. 'You keep away from that body. D'you hear me?'

I smiled politely. 'I've finished my inspection,' I told him. 'It looks to me as if Mr Buckler was hit on the back of the head with a sharp rock, while crouching over the water outlet. His assailant dropped the rock, dragged the body under the bushes to conceal it as best he could, then propped up the tap, which had been knocked over by the falling body. I can't give you a time of death, but Mr Buckler was here, alive and well, when we went to the tea tent at a quarter to ten. His body was found just after eleven o'clock. I'm afraid that's all I can tell you at present.'

I left him standing open-mouthed and turned to one of the pensioners. 'Would you be a dear and show me where the Governor's House is, please?

Chapter 33

The governor of the Royal Hospital, General Sir Neville Lyttelton, had installed the Halls, Eversholts and Lavinia Buckler in his drawing room. Servants were dispensing hot coffee and brandy.

General Lyttelton, an upright old man with a frizz of curly hair around the sides of his bald head, stood with his back to the windows, an understandable expression of bewilderment on his face. Lord Lambourne was with him, although he looked anxious to get away. I understood why when I was close enough to hear Constance Hall.

'I do understand, but I need to know that the garden won't be penalised when it comes to the medals,' she was saying. 'The committee will have plenty of time to view it once the police have finished, and the Royal visit had almost concluded when… when the unfortunate discovery was made. As you saw yourself, the design is most original, and I think you will agree that the plants are in perfect condition…'

'Mrs Hall, I have more important things to think of right now than the medals,' said Lord Lambourne, making no attempt to hide his exasperation. 'Such as the safety of the Royal family and all our exhibitors and visitors. Now, if you will excuse me…' He shook hands with General Lyttelton and made good his escape.

I crossed the room to the fireplace, in the hope of warming up a bit. Lavinia Buckler was wrapped in a blanket by the fire, her face hidden in her hands. She was sobbing quietly. Diana Eversholt sat on the sofa by her side staring into space, her face blank with shock. She was patting Lavinia's back mechanically, but barely seemed aware that she was doing so.

Beyond them, a great marble fireplace, carved with ornate swags of vines and acanthus leaves, set the tone for the grandeur of the room. Huge paintings of posturing aristocrats sneered down from the walls, as lush as if they had been painted by Van Dyck. I took a closer look at the labels. They were by Van Dyck.

Mrs Jameson, who had been talking to Walter Hall and his son at the table, hurried over and drew me aside.

'There you are, Marjorie. What's been happening? Is Peter Chadwick here yet?'

I brought her up to date with my inspection of the scene, the arrival of the police and my banishment from the site.

'Oh, that is a nuisance. Maybe he's on his way,' said Mrs Jameson.

'Would you like some coffee?' asked a gracious-looking lady, pausing on her way to the door.

'Thank you so much,' I said. I was shivering almost as much as Lavinia. 'That would be lovely. I'm afraid I'm getting mud on the floor.'

She glanced down at my claggy footwear. 'Please don't mention it,' she said politely, and I rather wished I hadn't. 'I'm Lady Lyttelton. My husband and I are at your disposal while the police investigate this horrid affair. Perhaps you would like to clean up a little?'

'You are very kind, My Lady.'

One of the servants led me to a bathroom where I washed my face and hands and dried my hair as well as I could. My stockings were wet, and I rubbed my feet dry on a towel. I thought with disquiet of the police investigation. Inspector Chadwick would not be pleased that any fugitive murderer had been politely invited to wash the evidence from their hands and tidy themselves up before the police interviewed them.

'Have you seen the body?' asked the young maid who had escorted me, her round eyes stretched wide.

I took a last look in the mirror. My poor blue-and-white frock drooped sadly, and my hair was going frizzy, but it was the best I could do.

'I have,' I said, keeping my voice neutral.

'What's it like? Go on, Miss. I've never seen a real murder before.'

I sighed. Another detective story fan, no doubt, thrilled by the idea of murder.

'Lucky you. I wouldn't recommend it,' I said briskly. 'Is there somewhere I can clean off these shoes?'

She led me through to the servants' quarters and I used the boot scraper at the back door to remove the worst of the mud. Bert was in the corner of the kitchen, drinking tea. I hesitated, then dropped into the chair next to his and propped my wet shoes on the fender by the fire.

'How are you feeling, Bert?' I asked. 'You are having a hard time of it. First your dad, then this.' I knew how violence could trigger distress in former soldiers, sparking off unwanted memories of the horrible conflict they had lived through.

He glanced up, his face sombre. 'I'm all right.' But his hands

167

shook as he set down his cup.

'And you didn't see anything of what happened to Mr Buckler?'

'No.' He looked up. 'Me and Perry – Mr Peregrine – fixed the planks, then I went off to get the gravel.' I remembered Bert coming back with the wheelbarrow, just as we returned from the tea tent.

His use of Peregrine's pet name hadn't escaped me. 'You are friendly with Peregrine Hall, aren't you? Did you know each other as children?'

'We grew up together,' he acknowledged. 'I was a bit older, like, and he was lonely during the school holidays. Neither of us had brothers or sisters. He used to tag along when I went fishing. I taught him to ride a bicycle. Then I went off to the War, and he stayed in the school room.' There was a touch of scorn in his voice. But Peregrine hadn't been old enough to fight.

'Does he still confide in you about things?' I asked, thinking of Peregrine's dog-like devotion to Lavinia. If anyone had a motive to murder Ernest Buckler, he did. And he hadn't joined us in the tea tent or explained his whereabouts.

'You mean politics?' asked Bert, unexpectedly.

'Well, yes. Or anything else.'

He shrugged. 'He wanted to know about communism. We talked about it. I'd met this bloke in the army who was in the Party, see. It made sense to me then, the class struggle. I mean, you could see it. All of us poor sods in the trenches and the generals safely behind the lines in their cushy billets, sending us out to die.'

I nodded sadly. 'I know. I lost my brother. It was a terrible time.' I remembered how I had loathed the colonel who had sent James into that last pointless battle.

'Perry said there was a society at his university, and he was going to join,' said Bert, breaking into my reverie. 'But he knew Mrs Hall wouldn't hear of it. He was the one that said I should do something when the King came to Chelsea.'

Ah. Did that explain the note about the Royal visit in the Communist Manifesto?

'And did you? I mean, I know you didn't do anything. But did you plan to?'

He sighed. 'I was going to shout something. Down with the King, time for a republic. But when it came to it, it all seemed a bit... a bit stupid, really. Childish, like. I'd have lost my job, and then where would my mum go? We'd lose the cottage.'

I nodded in sympathy. 'It's easier for people like Peregrine Hall to take a political stance. They don't have as much to lose,' I said.

He turned to look at me, and his face relaxed. 'You're all right, you are,' he said. 'When you're not poking your nose into things that are none of your business.'

I smiled. 'Unfortunately, that is my job,' I said. 'And I'd better get back to it.'

Chapter 34

To my relief, the first person I bumped into on my return to the drawing room was Inspector Peter Chadwick from Scotland Yard. The two uniformed policemen I'd met at the garden stood behind him with their helmets in their hands, the elder one looking slightly resentful.

'Good afternoon, Miss Swallow. I might have known that you and Iris would be up to your ears in this business.' Inspector Chadwick gave me one of his rare smiles.

I beamed. The inspector had first met Mrs Jameson in France during the War and made our lives easier by respecting her experience and methods. At times, he took advantage of the fact that she was not constrained by police procedure.

'So, do you have a solution for me yet?' he asked, eyes twinkling. 'General Lyttelton is arranging to put an office at our disposal. I understand you have already met my colleagues.' He indicated the two policemen. 'Sergeant Morris and Constable Parker, from Pimlico police station. They will be working with me on the case.'

Constable Parker, who had a round face and red hair, favoured me with a boyish grin. Sergeant Morris nodded stiffly. He was a thin, rather ratty-looking man with pinched nostrils that were pink with cold. I could see he intended to be as obstructive as he could manage without incurring Inspector Chadwick's wrath.

I glanced around the room. Ernest Buckler's widow and former wife were still sitting in silence on the sofa. Tommy Eversholt was pacing in front of the window. He'd pulled off his tie and was looking distraught. Walter Hall and Mrs Jameson were trying to calm an increasingly shrill Constance Hall, while Peregrine sat alone in the corner, staring at the carpet. So many people, so many interlocking relationships and possible motives.

'It's rather a complicated case,' I said. 'And it seems to keep getting more so. We began with an accusation of sabotage against Mrs Hall's lilies. Then there was the poisoning of the gardener, and now we have Mr Buckler's murder. But I can't understand who would want both Harry Smith and Ernest Buckler dead.'

Inspector Chadwick nodded gravely. 'An escalation of criminality. Well, if this chap has gone from killing lilies to killing people in a matter of weeks, he needs to be stopped before he targets anyone else.'

'You believe it's a male, Inspector?' asked Sergeant Morris.

The inspector shook his head. 'Too early to say. I was speaking generally. Although… what do you think, Miss Swallow?'

I thought of the bloodstained rock and the force that would be needed to bring it down hard enough to crush a man's skull. Could a woman do that?

'A man or a strong woman, with big hands,' I said. I found my eyes straying to Constance Hall, and then Diana Eversholt. Both were tall and used to hard outdoor work. Mrs Hall had been with us the whole time, of course. Diana… she was a formidable woman. But surely not a killer?

I passed over Lavinia, then turned my eyes back. Her hands were small, delicate. But Lavinia's weapons might not be her own hands. What was it that she'd been pleading with Peregrine to do?

Mrs Jameson excused herself and came over to join us. 'Peter. So good to see you. Has Marjorie been bringing you up to date? We have much to discuss.'

His hazel eyes crinkled as he smiled at her. 'I'm disappointed, Iris. I'd expected you to have the whole thing wrapped up by the time I got here. I thought I could just whip out the handcuffs and escort your prisoner to the cells, then take you and Miss Swallow out to lunch to celebrate.'

'Stuff and nonsense.' She looked pleased, nonetheless. 'Now, who are these gentlemen?'

Inspector Chadwick made the introductions. 'Mrs Jameson is an experienced investigator who is already working on matters related to this case. I intend her to be an expert consultant for the murder inquiry. If we work together, we are likely to reach a conclusion more quickly.'

Sergeant Morris sniffed. 'As you wish, Sir.'

'I read about that murder you had in Bloomsbury,' said Constable Parker. 'Nasty business. Glad they got the right person in the end.'

Mrs Jameson smiled generously. 'That was most gratifying. Now, is our office ready? We need to construct a timeline and consider the evidence of the crime scene.'

Inspector Chadwick sent the sergeant to speak to General Lyttelton. Morris didn't look amused to be ordered around by a woman. As usual, Mrs Jameson had assumed she was in charge.

The office was less distractingly grand than the drawing room. It was obviously General Lyttelton's own office, furnished in a military style with regimental regalia on the mantelpiece, paintings of battlefields, an enormous leather-topped desk with brass corners and leather club chairs.

'What else will you need?' asked the general.

'May we use your telephone?' asked Inspector Chadwick. 'And please bring the largest sheets of paper you can find. Can we use your chart stand?'

'Of course, Inspector.' He gave the big globe in the window a gentle spin. 'And ring for any refreshments you require. The bell is under the desk. There's whisky and brandy on the bureau by the door.' He withdrew.

'Very nice,' said Sergeant Morris, looking around with disapproval. 'I suppose this is what you expect at Scotland Yard, do you?'

Inspector Chadwick regarded him with mild exasperation. 'I'm grateful for whatever facilities are available,' he said. 'Now, Sergeant. Let us get to work. What did the doctor report? Constable, please take notes as we go.'

I'd already pulled out my notebook and pencil from my handbag. Note-taking was usually my role. It looked as if we would be doubling up.

'I've made a map of the garden, and where the body was found,' I said.

'I've done that too,' said Constable Parker.

Mrs Jameson rolled her eyes. 'Perhaps you can compare your notes afterwards,' she suggested. 'Two sets of eyes are always better than one, after all.'

'Indeed,' said the inspector. He was beginning to look like a harassed school teacher with an unruly class. 'Now, Sergeant

173

Morris. The doctor's report.'

Chapter 35

As expected, the doctor had found life extinct due to a heavy blow to the head. 'He said it would have been more or less instantaneous,' said Sergeant Morris, taking his time over pronunciation of the word. 'No time to cry out. Dead when he hit the ground, as they say.'

'And the murder weapon?' asked the inspector.

'Almost certainly a large rock, with a pointed end,' said the sergeant. 'It was found at the scene, with blood stains on it.'

I looked up. 'I drew it. And I've got the measurements. I think it would fit into a man's hand.'

'Me, too,' said Constable Parker. He showed me his drawing and we compared our measurements. They were identical to within an eighth of an inch.

'And how has the crime scene been preserved?' asked Mrs Jameson. 'It's raining hard. We need to know that the evidence is not all washing away.'

Sergeant Morris spoke reluctantly. 'It has been preserved according to our usual procedure, madam.'

'Don't call me madam,' snapped Mrs Jameson. This form of address was a particular dislike of hers, and I'd spent my first months in her employment trying to remember not to use it.

'We put a canvas tent over it, Mrs Jameson,' volunteered

Constable Parker. 'Borrowed from the Royal Horticultural Society. They were going to use it for ticket sales.'

I supposed the whole show would have to be closed for the day. I wondered whether the Royal party had been able to view the exhibits in the big canvas pavilion, or if they had been whisked off to their next engagement. What a lot of trouble the murder had caused. I thought with renewed respect of Lord Lambourne, who would have to reorganise everything.

'Good work,' said Inspector Chadwick. 'I will view it later. But Marjorie, would you like to share your observations about the scene?'

I repeated what I had told the police officers earlier, with my conjecture that Mr Buckler had been at the water outlet when the fatal blow was struck.

'They'd had trouble with it last week. I wondered if it had stopped flowing, and Mr Buckler had gone to see what was wrong with it,' I said.

Mrs Jameson was quick to get the inference. 'The murderer might have turned off the pump or blocked the pipe, knowing that Mr Buckler would go to see what had happened. Then he or she waits, concealed in the rhododendrons, until Mr Buckler is crouching or bending over it. They cosh him over the head and drag his body hastily into the bushes, as indicated by the marks from his boots.'

'They knocked over the tap, so they had to prop it up again and set it going,' I added.

Inspector Chadwick nodded and raised his eyebrows. 'Sergeant Morris? Does that accord with your reading of the scene?'

'It's possible,' said the man. 'But I prefer to work from facts, rather than conjecture.' He folded his mouth primly.

'Now, what about the timeline?' said Mrs Jameson, ignoring the sergeant. 'We arrived at the garden at half past nine, didn't we, Marjorie?' She wrote on the large sheet of paper that General Lyttelton had set up on the chart stand for us. 'Present on our arrival: Walter and Constance Hall, Peregrine Hall – wasn't he fiddling about with the pump this morning, Marjorie? – Ernest and Lavinia Buckler.' She wrote their names down.

'And Bert arrived with the planks for the path,' I said. 'You suggested we went for coffee, Mrs Jameson. That was about a quarter to ten.'

'Walter, Constance and Lavinia went with us. Peregrine and Bert started work on the path. Ernest stayed behind to look at the other gardens,' she added.

Inspector Chadwick stared at the chart. 'So, the murder happened between a quarter to ten and eleven o'clock, when the Royal party visited?'

'Earlier than that,' said Mrs Jameson. 'We reassembled at the garden before a quarter to eleven, at Constance's request. I think we would have noticed someone being bludgeoned to death behind us. We were away from the garden for just under an hour.'

Inspector Chadwick took the pen from Mrs Jameson's hand. 'So, we can rule out Constance Hall, Walter Hall and Lavinia Buckler,' he said. 'As they were with you in the tea tent.'

'Actually, no,' I volunteered. 'Lavinia disappeared as we walked to get our coffee. We thought she'd gone to the wash tent, but she didn't join us until we were leaving again. She looked… flustered. Her hat was crooked, and she was out of breath, as if she'd been running.'

'Is that the young lady on the sofa what was married to

the deceased?' asked Constable Parker, his cheeks colouring. 'Because I wouldn't say a young lady like that could have done the murder.'

'Too delicate and pretty?' asked Mrs Jameson, her feline smile stretching across her face, ready to pounce.

'Too small,' said the constable, stoutly. 'It's a big bit of rock and you'd have to bring it down hard.' He demonstrated with the general's brass paperweight. 'I wouldn't have said she could lift it with one hand.'

'The thing is,' I said, 'Peregrine Hall was missing, too. He was supposed to meet us in the tea tent after he'd laid the planks. But he didn't, and he ran back to the garden just before the Royal party arrived. Also, I think something had been going on between him and Lavinia.'

I repeated the words I'd heard pass between them on Saturday.

'She was begging him to help her. She said she couldn't bear it any longer and that he'd offered to help, and now was his chance. He told her to be sensible, then he said he'd think about it.'

Sergeant Morris cracked his knuckles, making Mrs Jameson wince with distaste.

'There you go, then. Cherchez la femme, as they say, and findez le guilty homme. Shall I bring him in for questioning, Sir?'

'In a minute,' said the inspector, looking surprised at the man's display of rudimentary French. 'We'll talk to them separately. See if they can explain where they were, or if they have an alibi. But before that, I think we should consider the wider case. We don't just have one murder to investigate, Sergeant. There are two – not to mention a case of sabotage.'

Possibly three, I thought, remembering Diana Eversholt's words in the glasshouse at Hawkshill Manor.

'I'll recap for the new members of the team,' said Mrs Jameson briskly. 'We were called in to investigate sabotage of Mrs Hall's lilies. The morning after a night watch to try to catch the saboteur, the gardener Mr Smith was found dead, seemingly of a heart attack. The post-mortem examination discovered that he had been poisoned with taxine, one of the cardiac glycosides, a substance found in the yew tree. Initially, his son Bert was suspected, because they had rowed on the morning of the death, and then the man who watched before the gardener's arrival, Tommy Eversholt. But I have reason to believe Mr Smith may not have been the intended victim.'

Of course… I began to understand why Mrs Jameson had said I was looking at the murder from the wrong perspective. But if the gardener had not been the target, who had?

Sergeant Morris was not impressed. 'And have you solved any of these cases?' he asked.

'Not yet,' Mrs Jameson admitted. 'But all these crimes are tied together. And they all have their roots in the wretched lilies that Buckler and Eversholt brought back from Tibet.'

'So,' said Constable Parker, 'we're looking for someone who wanted to kill some lilies, who then killed the gardener looking after them, and murdered the bloke what found the lilies in foreign parts. A sort of horticultural maniac.'

Inspector Chadwick snorted with laughter. 'That's about the size of it, lad.'

'Perhaps,' said Mrs Jameson, her eyes narrowed. She tapped her fingers rhythmically on her chin, always with her a sign of deep thought. 'Why don't we call Lavinia Buckler in for a chat?'

Chapter 36

'Please have a seat, Mrs Buckler. May I offer you my sincere condolences? I'm sorry to intrude at this difficult time, but I do have to ask some questions. I'm sure you understand.'

Inspector Chadwick was all fatherly concern as he settled Lavinia in a chair by the fire. Lavinia's gaze flickered around the room, lingering over me and Mrs Jameson. Her eyelids were swollen, her face pale. She had borrowed a paisley cashmere shawl and clutched it around her shoulders. She did not look much like a femme fatale whose plans had come to a successful fruition.

'I will make this as painless as I can, Mrs Buckler. Firstly, can you think of anyone who might have had a reason to want your husband dead?'

She gave a little gasp and flushed pink. 'Oh! No, of course not.'

'Think a little, Mrs Buckler. Any rivals in the field, anyone he might have crossed on his travels?'

Relief flickered over her face. 'Well, I suppose there might have been. I don't really know much about his work. But who knows what sort of characters he'd met over in China and India? Do you think that was it?' she asked, hopefully.

'And how about his former wife and her husband? Was Mr

Buckler on good terms with the Eversholts?' pressed Inspector Chadwick.

'Oh, it couldn't have been Diana or Tommy,' said Lavinia quickly. 'They're ever so nice. Diana and Ernest… they had already divorced by the time Ernest and I met. There was never any jealousy or anything of that sort.' She looked up through her eyelashes at the inspector. 'You don't suspect Diana, do you? What possible reason would she have?'

Mrs Jameson interjected. 'You were all house guests at Hawkshill Manor, Lavinia. Did you often socialise with the Eversholts? Was it not awkward?'

She shook her head. 'I only met them at Hawkshill, Mrs Jameson. Two weeks ago, when you were there, and before then at Christmas. I did worry that it might be awkward at Christmas, but Ernest said not to be silly.' Her face fell. 'And Diana was kind to me. She knows what it's like, you see.'

'She knows what it's like to be married to Ernest Buckler?' suggested Mrs Jameson, her voice silky. She was at her most dangerous when she sounded like that.

'Oh, yes.' Lavinia nodded, then looked up quickly. 'I mean… Just that it was not always easy. He's away a lot, and of course he's quite definite about what he likes and what he doesn't like.'

'You told Marjorie that you wished you were back at home with your family,' Mrs Jameson said. 'And that everything you said seemed to annoy him, until he erupted like a volcano. Did Ernest Buckler have a temper, Lavinia? Did he get angry and shout at you?'

Lavinia threw me a reproachful look. I felt rather mean for breaching her confidence. She pressed her handkerchief to her eyes and looked up at Inspector Chadwick.

'It's not fair to ask me things like that,' she said. 'It's been such a horrible shock. I still can't believe it. I can't believe that poor Ernest is dead.'

Inspector Chadwick patted her hand. 'I'm sorry, Mrs Buckler. We are simply trying to get a full picture of your husband and his world. Let's move on to more practical things. When did you last see your husband?'

She looked puzzled. 'Well, when everyone else did. We went to get a cup of coffee and he stayed at the garden. You were there with us,' she said to Mrs Jameson.

'I was. You said you were frozen and desperate for coffee. You pleaded with Mr Buckler to allow you to go. But you didn't come to the tea tent with us, did you? Where did you go, Lavinia?'

She licked her lips and looked around us. 'I went to wash my hands.'

'For fifty minutes?' asked Mrs Jameson.

'I washed my hands, then I thought I would go into the pavilion and look at the floral displays. I didn't know if I'd have another chance to see them,' she said.

'And which exhibits did you visit? Do you remember any flowers that caught your eye?'

She looked towards me, with a slight expression of panic. 'Roses. There were some very pretty roses. And... and sweet peas.'

Mrs Jameson nodded to me. 'Make a note of that, Marjorie. We can ask the rose and sweet pea exhibitors if they saw Mrs Buckler.'

She sagged a little, but forced out a small smile and nodded. 'It was rather busy. I don't suppose anyone would notice just one person.'

'And did you meet anyone in the floral pavilion? Mr Peregrine Hall, for example?' asked the Inspector.

Lavinia paused, as if calculating which was the better answer. 'No. I mean… I might have seen him, but not to talk to.'

'You might have seen Mr Hall?' interjected Inspector Chadwick. 'We will need to confirm as best we can the movements of the whole party. Did you see Peregrine Hall in the pavilion, or not?'

She hesitated, her gaze flickering between us. 'I don't know,' she said. 'It might have been him, but it was very busy. I might have been mistaken.' She looked down again, wringing her handkerchief in her hands. 'This is all very difficult. I don't want to have to talk anymore.'

'Of course,' said Inspector Chadwick, his voice soothing again. 'Just tell us what happened after you'd been in the floral pavilion. Did you return to the garden?'

'No, I… I went to the refreshments tent. I thought I'd just have time for a cup of coffee, but you were leaving,' she said, looking at me. 'You do remember, don't you, Marjorie? I joined you all in the tea tent.'

I nodded. I also remembered how she'd told Mrs Hall that she had to do something before joining us. And that she'd denied knowing where Peregrine was. No mention then that she might have seen him in the floral pavilion. No mention of the floral pavilion at all.

'Thank you so much, Mrs Buckler. I'm sorry to have added to your distress. If I might ask you to wait with the others in the drawing room for a short while longer?'

Inspector Chadwick turned to Constable Parker. 'Would you ask Mr Peregrine Hall to join us, Constable?'

Chapter 37

Peregrine Hall didn't look much like a murderer. He looked more like a frightened schoolboy summoned to the headmaster's office after being caught cheating in an exam. His long face was gloomy, his tie awry and his pale auburn hair stuck up at the back like a fluffy chick. I could well imagine him tagging along behind Bert Smith, climbing trees and learning to ride a bicycle.

He took his seat without a word, clasped his hands together and fixed his gaze on the floor.

'Mr Hall, please describe to us your movements after your parents left for the tea tent this morning,' said Inspector Chadwick, adopting a business-like tone.

Peregrine shuffled in his seat. 'I helped Bert set out the planks over the path in the garden. He was worried about the way they looked, and I suggested we should cover them with gravel. He said he'd go to get some.'

He stopped. Eventually it became apparent he was not planning to say anything more.

'But when we returned to the garden, you weren't there,' said Mrs Jameson. 'Where were you?'

He shrugged. 'I wandered around a bit. Thought I'd have a look at the other gardens. And... and I needed to use the facilities, so I went to the wash tent.' He stopped again. Perhaps experience with headmasters' inquisitions had taught him to cease talking when he felt he'd said enough.

'What time would you say Bert went to fetch the gravel, Mr Hall?' asked Inspector Chadwick.

He looked up then, the same indecision on his face that I'd seen in Lavinia. 'Not sure. I suppose about a quarter of an hour after they'd all gone for coffee.'

'And that was when you wandered off to look at the gardens and use the facilities?'

He nodded. 'Yeah. I suppose so.' He looked at the ground, and colour began to mount in his cheeks. Was he lying?

'Did you go into the flower pavilion?'

That pause again, the calculation as to the best answer.

'It's a straightforward question, Mr Hall.' Inspector Chadwick's tone was much sharper than he'd used with Lavinia Buckler.

'No. I went... I went past it. Might have stuck my head in.'

Mrs Jameson sighed. 'Perry, did you see Lavinia Buckler in the flower pavilion?'

He shook his head.

'Did you see Lavinia Buckler anywhere else?'

He returned his gaze to the carpet and muttered that he didn't think so, but it had been very crowded. His face had flushed dark red.

'I can't hear you, Mr Hall. Please answer directly, remembering that this is a murder investigation, and your evidence may be relied on in court. Did you see Lavinia Buckler at any point between her departure from the garden at a quarter to ten and her return at quarter to eleven?' Inspector Chadwick's voice cut like a whip through the ambiguity that Peregrine Hall was trying to construct.

'No, I... I...' he looked up at us, his face anguished. 'Look, I did see Lavinia. But she said not to tell anyone. She was worried about how it would look. But I don't know what happened to Buckler, I swear it.'

Mrs Jameson smiled. 'Now, that's more sensible, Perry. Please tell us what really happened.'

Strands of sandy hair stuck to his sweating face. 'I can't. Really, Mrs Jameson, I can't tell you. I did go to the wash tent. And it's true that we were together, for about twenty minutes. She'll tell you, if you say I said so.'

'In the wash tent?' Inspector Chadwick exclaimed. Peregrine said nothing. 'Would it surprise you if I said that Mrs Buckler has denied seeing you during that time, except for a glimpse in the flower pavilion?' asked the inspector.

Peregrine pushed his hair out of his face. 'Well, she would say that. She's scared of him. She needed someone to protect her.'

The words hung in the air. Mrs Jameson stepped into the breach.

'Are you saying Mrs Buckler was scared of her husband, Perry? And that she needed someone to protect her from him?'

He nodded.

'And did you see that as your role?'

He swallowed and dropped his eyes, unable to hold her gaze. 'Maybe. I tried to look after her. It's rotten, an old man like that marrying someone like Lavinia.'

'What did Lavinia Buckler ask you to do for her on Saturday morning in the wash tent?' Mrs Jameson slid the question in as smoothly as a knife into warm butter.

186

He looked up then, his gaze locking with mine. 'You heard.'
'I'm afraid so,' I told him.

'Please answer the question, Mr Hall,' said Inspector Chadwick.

He shook his head. 'She didn't mean it. She was just scared. It's been awful for her. You don't know what she's been through with that brute.'

'What did Mrs Buckler ask you to do?' repeated the inspector.

Peregrine swallowed and rubbed his face. 'She wanted me to get rid of him,' he said, his voice cracking. 'She said she was too scared to do it herself. But I didn't do it, Inspector. I promise. It was all just talk.'

Inspector Chadwick nodded slowly. 'But you understood Mrs Buckler was asking you to kill her husband. What method did she suggest you used?'

I remembered Lavinia's questions about poison, her interest in my knowledge.

He looked wretched. 'She suggested we use a poisonous plant. Maybe because of what happened to Harry. I don't know. I thought she was joking.'

A cold thought struck me. What if the poisoned sandwiches had been intended for Ernest Buckler? I believed I'd seen a white figure going into the garden at midnight, before Harry's death. Collecting yew berries, perhaps? Peregrine had taken the shift before Ernest, of course. Maybe he'd intended to poison Ernest's sandwiches, but somehow Ernest had eaten the wrong ones. And Peregrine finished the job at Chelsea, using more direct means. Although... the conversation I'd overheard between Peregrine and Lavinia had come after Harry Smith's death. That didn't work.

187

'What preparations did you make for this, Mr Hall?' The inspector pressed on.

'Well, none. I wasn't going to do it, was I?'

'Mr Hall, I put it to you that you had plotted with Mrs Buckler to murder her husband by poison. But you saw a more direct opportunity. This morning, after Bert Smith had gone to get gravel, you were left alone with Mr Buckler. He was crouched over the water tap, which you had disabled. And you took a rock and brought it down on his head, crushing his skull and killing him.' Inspector Chadwick fixed the boy with a steady gaze.

'I didn't do it! I have no idea what happened to him.' Peregrine pulled off his tie, looked desperately from the inspector to Mrs Jameson and me. 'I was with Lavinia. Ask her, please.'

'Thank you, Mr Hall. I have no more questions for the present.' Inspector Chadwick turned to the policemen. 'Sergeant? Do you have an empty cell at Pimlico?'

'Certainly, Inspector.' There was a ferrety grin on the man's narrow face.

'No!' Peregrine jumped to his feet. 'I told you, I didn't do it.'

'Peregrine Hall, I am arresting you on suspicion of the murder of Ernest Buckler. Sergeant Morris, please escort Mr Hall to Pimlico and book him into custody. Mr Hall, I will arrange a further interview with you in due course. You will need to speak to your solicitor. Would you like me to ask your father to arrange that?'

Peregrine struggled half-heartedly as Sergeant Morris fixed the handcuffs on his wrists. 'For God's sake, man! This is all a mistake.' He looked at Mrs Jameson, his eyes beseeching. 'Don't tell Mater. She'll go mad.'

Mrs Jameson sighed as the two uniformed officers marched Peregrine Hall out of the Governor's House and into a black police car parked outside.

'Marjorie, would you pop into the drawing room and ask Walter Hall to come in? I suppose we'd better break the news to him first.'

Chapter 38

'I'm sure this is all a mistake,' said Mr Hall, wiping his forehead with a handkerchief. 'Iris, you can't really think that Perry is involved?'

Mrs Jameson looked at him kindly. 'I'm sorry, Walter. Really I am. But Perry strongly implicated himself. Whatever the truth of it, he needs to be questioned and he needs a solicitor.'

'I'll call my man,' he said. 'And I want to be there when he's questioned. The boy's innocent. That's the trouble. Too innocent.'

'He is twenty years of age, Walter. Old enough to be questioned as an adult, and old enough to answer for his actions.'

Mr Hall threw her a strange look as he hurried from the room. 'You made some odd decisions yourself when you were young, Iris. Infatuation does things to a person's judgement. Don't think I don't remember.'

Mrs Jameson pressed her lips together until they were thin white lines, her hooded grey eyes cast down. I had come to dread this expression, which indicated extreme irritation. She turned to look out of the window. Her anger rarely lasted more than a few minutes, but she was best left to herself to simmer down quietly.

'What will you do about Lavinia?' I asked the inspector. If Peregrine had been arrested because she asked him to help her murder Ernest, surely she was the more guilty party. 'Are you going to arrest her, too?'

Inspector Chadwick struck a match to light his pipe and puffed until it was drawing.

'Oh, I think we will leave her where she is for the time being,' he said. 'She's not going anywhere. She'll hear about Peregrine's arrest, of course. It might prompt a reaction. We shall see.'

Mrs Jameson turned back into the room, her expression once more serene. 'Leave her to stew a bit, you mean? Excellent idea. Let's have Diana in next, don't you think? She's a sensible woman. I'd like to hear her opinion of Ernest Buckler.'

Diana Eversholt was poised, but pale. 'Do you mind if I smoke?' she asked, holding up her Turkish cigarette. Inspector Chadwick held a match for her, and she inhaled greedily. 'Thank you.'

She took a seat, crossed one knee over the other and gazed around the military-style room. 'What a den. I feel like I've been asked to devise a strategy to relieve Mafeking.' She gave her ironic smile, but a muscle was jumping around her left eye.

'We'll begin with your relationship with the deceased, Mrs Eversholt. Would you be kind enough to explain how you met Mr Buckler, tell us a little about your marriage, and how you would describe your subsequent relations?'

She exhaled a cloud of fragrant smoke. 'Goodness. How long do you have?' She composed herself. 'Well, I met Ernest in Tibet in... let's see. Fifteen years ago, the spring of 1908.

191

I was twenty-four, on assignment for a magazine, writing about the mountain people and doing some climbing. He and his caravan rolled into the next village along the valley, so of course I had to go and visit. It had been a while since I'd spoken to an Englishman. He was rather surprised to see me, I think. Not many Englishmen in the mountains, but even fewer Englishwomen.

'We ate tinned bully beef and compared notes. He had a case of half-bottles of champagne, supposedly for medicinal purposes, so we cracked one open. I liked his adventurous spirit, and his admiration for the Tibetan people, which I very much shared. I went back to London soon afterwards, and he looked me up when he was home the following year. We married in 1910.'

She paused and looked at Mrs Jameson, her eyebrows raised. 'Do you want a full account of the honeymoon looking for orchids in Bhutan, or the drab little flat we rented in Knightsbridge? It turned out that we agreed perfectly well on expeditions, but were horribly on each other's nerves when cooped up in London. There was a baby, but it didn't live.'

She blew smoke at the ceiling. 'The War came as something of a relief, frankly. Ernest was all right – he was posted to various locations around the Far East, barely saw a shot fired in anger. I reported from the frontline in France and Belgium.'

She paused, and I saw the reflection of the horrors she must have witnessed in her warm brown eyes.

'I think he felt a little ashamed afterwards that I'd seen more action than he had. Anyway, he came home full of plans for an expedition to Tibet to find these lilies someone had told him about. The Halls agreed to put up the money, and he roped in his old school friend Tommy, who was looking for a job after he got back from France. I liked Tommy. He's easy-going, funny and lively. The opposite of Ernest. The three of us travelled together to Tibet, but I got sick in Lhasa, so they left me behind.'

'They left you there alone?' asked Inspector Chadwick, looking horrified at this unchivalrous behaviour.

She shrugged. 'I felt terrible. I collapsed in the street, then spent two days throwing up. There was a Red Cross nurse staying at our hostel and she said she'd look after me. Ernest was impatient to get going, and he was no use at all when one was sick. So, I told them to go. I felt better within the week and rather fed up to have missed the fun.'

Mrs Jameson was listening intently. 'Do you know what caused your illness?'

Diana took a drag on her cigarette, then stubbed it out. 'No,' she said, exhaling. The room was filling up with smoke, a blue haze misting the air. 'At the time, I assumed it was food poisoning. But recently, I've been wondering. Ernest used to laugh at me for how much I hated butter tea. It's all they drink in Tibet – disgusting stuff; blocks of the worst quality black tea boiled up with water, and then they whisk in yak's butter, usually with a bit of yak hair and general crud attached. Vile. Ernest bought a pot of honey to sweeten it. I tried it a few times, but it didn't really help with the taste.'

'Rhododendron honey?' I broke in.

She smiled. 'You're ahead of me, Marjorie. Anyhow, whatever the cause, I stayed in Lhasa for a couple of months. I recovered from my illness, wrote some articles, and did some climbing. Then Tommy and Ernest got back, and we went home.'

She looked apologetically at the Inspector. 'I've been going on too long. The concise version is, Tommy and I fell in love on the journey back. Ernest… he wasn't thrilled, as you can imagine, but he knew we weren't suited. He agreed to a divorce and once it had come through, I married Tommy. By that time, Ernest had met Lavinia, so he was happy too. We've been on friendly terms with both of them since. End of story.'

'Until you rushed away from Hawkshill Manor the day that Harry Smith was found dead,' observed Mrs Jameson. 'On a sudden assignment from a newspaper editor. Although no-one in the household remembered a 'phone call coming through.'

Diana shook her head and answered briskly. 'There was no assignment, Mrs Jameson, as you doubtless realised. I invented it to get us away.'

'Thank you for your candour,' said Mrs Jameson. 'It does so simplify matters. Did you suspect that Harry Smith had been poisoned? Was your suspicion linked to your experience in Lhasa?'

Diana sighed. 'I knew that seemingly natural illness could be the result of poison. But if it was poison, it made no sense that the gardener was the target. If those sandwiches were poisoned, they were intended for my husband.'

Of course. I kicked myself for being so dense. Mrs Jameson, watching intently, gave no sign of surprise.

'Let me be clear. You suspected someone of attempting to murder Mr Eversholt?' asked Inspector Chadwick.

She shrugged. 'I wasn't sure what to think then, but I was taking no chances. I decided to get Tommy away from there. I had to keep him safe. It was possible that Harry had died of natural causes, of course, but also possible he'd been poisoned. Tommy was the last of the watchers, so there was only one packet of sandwiches and one thermos of coffee left for him.'

I broke in. 'But he didn't eat his sandwiches!'

'Precisely,' said Mrs Jameson. 'As you noticed, Marjorie, Mr Eversholt had a hearty appetite at breakfast on Monday morning.'

Diana sighed. 'Thank goodness. He said he'd rather have a good pile of hot eggs and bacon than some mouldy old sandwiches that had been sitting around all night. It was rotten luck on poor old Harry Smith, though. He must have decided not to let them go to waste.'

Especially as he'd gone to work without his breakfast. Whoever had poisoned the sandwiches had not wanted to kill Harry at all. So, Bert's quarrel with his father, Dick Cooper's grudge over being sacked, Sir Norman Alperton's desire to prevent Mrs Hall from winning gold were all completely irrelevant.

But then...

There was a pause, the only sound the ticking of the clock on the mantelpiece. A log shifted in the fire, sending up a shower of sparks. The inspector knocked out his pipe.

'And who do you think wanted to kill your husband?' he asked.

Diana looked into the fire. 'I think my husband knows something that was rather dangerous for Ernest,' she said. 'Something that happened in Tibet, when they found the lilies. I was worried that Ernest had decided it would be better if Tommy wasn't able to tell anyone else. And at Hawkshill, Ernest deliberately took the shift before Tommy. I think he poisoned Tommy's sandwiches.'

The pieces of the puzzle shifted again and started to form a coherent picture. The white shape heading out of the gate through the yew hedge on the first night's watch. Lavinia, wearing a big cream-coloured mackintosh that she'd borrowed from her husband. Her husband, in the same coat, collecting yew seeds at midnight before his shift. I felt sick. What if I'd blown my whistle, brought the grooms running and frightened Ernest Buckler away? Would Harry Smith still be alive?

Mrs Jameson leaned forward. 'And what is the secret that your husband knows about Mr Buckler?'

'You will have to ask Tommy. I don't know the details myself. I decided not to ask.'

Mrs Jameson nodded slowly. 'You are very wise, Mrs Eversholt,' she said. 'It is powerful knowledge, I take it. Enough, perhaps, to persuade a husband to give up his wife?'

Diana returned her gaze with her eyes level and no trace of embarrassment.

'Women have few enough weapons when it comes to securing a divorce, Mrs Jameson. I was not going to pass up any that came my way, even if I didn't fully understand them.'

As soon as one question seemed to have been answered, another arose. If Ernest Buckler had attempted to murder Tommy Eversholt, then who on earth had murdered Ernest Buckler?

Inspector Chadwick set down his pipe and looked at the clock over the mantel.

'This has been most helpful, but let us return to the events of this morning,' he said. 'When did you arrive at the Royal Hospital grounds?'

'Ten o'clock,' said Diana promptly. 'We strolled around the gardens, but it was so wet. I suggested a cup of coffee and we sat for a while in the tea tent. We were about to leave when

Mr and Mrs Hall arrived, with Mrs Jameson and Marjorie.'

She stretched, rolling her elegant shoulders. 'Then we went to the floral pavilion and somehow lost each other. It was crowded, and I supposed Tommy had got chatting to someone. But we'd agreed to be at the garden by a quarter to eleven, so I made my way back and he arrived soon after. I have no idea what happened to Ernest. Except that it looks rather like divine justice.'

'And do you have any evidence to corroborate that you were in the pavilion?' asked the inspector.

She looked startled for a moment, then laughed, a harsh, cynical sound. 'Oh, well. It makes no difference now, does it? Poor old Ernest wasn't poisoned, after all.'

She dipped into her handbag and held up a book. 'I chatted to a most interesting man at one of the specialist stands,' she said. 'I expect he will remember my questions.'

The book's title was *Poisonous Plants In the English Garden*. 'He sold me this book. I thought perhaps I should find out a bit about poisons,' said Diana. 'For defensive purposes, you understand.'

Chapter 39

There was a tap on the door and Constable Parker, returned from Pimlico, looked in.

'Mrs Buckler would like another word with you, Sir. And Mrs Hall is asking to speak to you too.'

Inspector Chadwick sighed. 'No doubt. Tell them I'll be with them as soon as I can.'

Diana looked up, alert. 'You can't think Lavinia is involved? She's practically a child.'

'That will be all for now, Mrs Eversholt. Would you be so good as to return to the drawing room?'

She got up and stretched her long limbs. 'I know you must do your job. But it is most frightfully dreary in there. Can't Tommy and I go back to our hotel?'

'Constable Parker, please ask Mr Eversholt to join us.' Inspector Chadwick turned to Diana. 'I'll reconsider the situation after I've interviewed your husband, Mrs Eversholt. Until then, I'd appreciate your patience.'

Moments later, Constable Parker marched back in, holding Mr Eversholt by the arm. Tommy's boyish face was almost comical in its dismay as he stepped into the study and reached for his wife's hand.

'Diana, are you all right? Have you heard about Perry?

Constance is frantic.'

Diana turned quickly to the inspector. 'What about Perry?'

'Please return to the drawing room, Mrs Eversholt. Mr Eversholt, take a seat. You can go now, Constable.'

Reluctantly, Diana left the room. Tommy sat down and blew out his cheeks.

'Right, then. How can I help you chaps?'

Before the inspector could begin, Mrs Jameson stepped in. 'Did you know that your wife believed Ernest Buckler had tried to kill you, Tommy?'

His jaw fell open. 'She... Diana told you that?'

We waited. Beads of sweat appeared on Tommy's forehead. The clock ticked.

'I mean... I thought she was being overly dramatic. Ernest was a bit of a rum fellow. But we'd known each other a long time. Since school, actually. I didn't take it seriously. Dashed inconvenient, all that rushing up to Scotland. No shooting, no hunting at this time of year. What's a fellow to do?'

'Yet Diana was willing to put you through that in order to protect you from her former husband,' said Mrs Jameson. 'What else do you think she might do to protect you?'

'Eh?' He wiped his face with his handkerchief and looked from Mrs Jameson to the Inspector. 'Don't catch your drift, Mrs J.'

She smiled and picked up the book that Diana had left on the desk. 'Do you recognise this book, Tommy? Your wife had it in her handbag. Have you any idea why she might have bought it?'

'Don't know it. Not much of a reader, myself,' he said, stoutly. 'Look here, if you're insinuating that Diana bumped off old Ernest, you're barking up the wrong tree. She might get some

199

ideas in her head, but she's a good egg. You can forget about all that rot. Anyway, Ernest wasn't poisoned, was he?' He forced a laugh and mopped his face again.

Inspector Chadwick stepped in. 'Thank you, Mr Eversholt. Perhaps you could tell us why Mrs Eversholt thought you might be in danger from your old school friend? Was it because he was angry with you for taking his wife?'

A brick-red flush mounted from Tommy's unbuttoned collar and into his face. 'That's a rotten way to put it. Diana said it was all over with Ernest before anything happened between us. Ernest was decent about it, actually. He agreed to the divorce.'

'I'm curious,' said Mrs Jameson. 'Your wife said her former husband was a jealous man, and I have seen myself that he can be short-tempered. Why did he agree to a divorce? It seems out of character.'

'I suppose he knew there was nothing to be gained from making difficulties.'

'And this was on your return from the trip to Tibet on which you discovered the Sapphire Lily?'

He nodded. 'It was.'

Mrs Jameson held up her hand as Inspector Chadwick leaned in to ask another question.

'I have heard a curious account of that expedition, Tommy. It makes me wonder whether something happened on that trip that gave you… shall we say some bargaining power over Mr Buckler? Something that made it sensible for Mr Buckler to agree to divorce his wife, so that she could marry you.'

Tommy wriggled like a fidgety schoolboy. 'How do you mean? I don't see what my marriage has to do with anything.' He hunched his shoulders and looked at the floor.

Inspector Chadwick pulled up a chair and sat down opposite

Tommy, leaning his forearms on his knees.

'Look at me, Mr Eversholt. I'm investigating two murders. I want to ensure there is not another one. Do you hear?'

Reluctantly, Tommy raised his head and nodded.

'So please tell me what happened in Tibet, and how that affected your partnership with Mr Buckler. It's important I understand everything. Will you do that?'

The clock ticked. Tommy Eversholt held the inspector's gaze. Finally, he nodded again.

'All right,' he said. 'Not a pretty story, I'm afraid. Dashed nasty business. But it can't hurt to tell you now.'

He repeated what we had already heard about the expedition so far – the trek up the valley, the frustrations he and Ernest had faced trying to get information from the villagers. The directions, eventually, to the monastery high on the slopes of the mountain, where the monks made them welcome and shared their frugal ways.

'They were clear from the start,' said Tommy. 'They would host us, but they would not help us to find the lilies. They said the lilies were sacred to the slopes of the holy mountain, and could not be cut, dug up or in any way harmed. I think Ernest thought they would come around.'

'And someone did come around?' asked Mrs Jameson.

'One of the young lads. Tenzin. The novices are just schoolboys, you know. I'd been teaching them to play cricket.' Tommy's face relaxed into a smile for a moment.

'Tenzin said he knew where the blue lilies grew, and he would show us. But that we weren't to touch them, because that would make the monks angry. Ernest said they wouldn't know, but the lad was very solemn. He said the mountain would tell them. He made us promise.'

Tommy's head dropped and he seemed to struggle to find the words to continue. One day the boy, who was around twelve years old, had been asked to go down to the village to buy food. He came to Tommy and Ernest early in the morning, woke them and said he would take them to see the lilies, but then he would need to rush back down to the village.

'The going was tough,' said Tommy. 'Rocky ground, narrow paths that crept around the side of the mountain. The weather was worsening; driving rain and the wind was relentless. There were fissures in the rock, fifty feet across over mountain streams. We had to cross by rope bridge. It's pretty hairy, I can tell you. They sway like mad in the wind and it's a dashed long way down.' He swallowed hard.

'After a couple of hours, we came to the last rope bridge. On the far side, we could see the eastern scree slope, practically covered in blue. There was a break in the clouds, the sun made it over the mountain and the lilies just glowed. Never seen anything so beautiful in my life.'

A shudder ran over him. His eyes were unfocused, as if he was somewhere else entirely.

'The boy said we could go across to look at them more closely, but mustn't touch them. He starts across. I'm adjusting my pack – you need to balance your luggage carefully before you step out on a rope bridge.' He looked down at his hands. 'And then Tenzin screams.'

Silence hung heavy for a moment.

'It only lasts a few seconds, I suppose. But I can still hear it in my head, going on and on. I look up, and he's falling. Ernest... Ernest has his hand on the rope.'

'You think he deliberately jerked the rope to throw the boy off?' asked Inspector Chadwick.

The clock ticked. 'I don't know.' Tommy looked up, his eyes suddenly much older in his boyish face. 'I just don't know. I said we should climb down after him, or at least go back and get help. Ernest told me not to be idiotic. He said there was no way the boy had survived. And then he went across the bridge.

'I tried to climb down, but it was hopeless without someone to belay. So, I stood and watched as Ernest wandered among the flowers and took samples. He cut off seed heads and dug up bulbs and packed whole plants in cotton. After we got back, he said we should leave the monastery at once. I wanted to tell the monks what had happened.'

'But you didn't,' said Mrs Jameson.

He shook his head and sat in silence for a moment, his eyes clouded with shame.

'When we got back to Lhasa, I told Diana that I was breaking with Buckler. I said she should too, if she had any sense. I told her... I didn't say exactly what had happened. But I told her about how Ernest just left Tenzin there and went to get the plants and didn't tell anyone about it.

'I knew by then I wanted to marry Diana. I mean, who wouldn't? She's an amazing woman. But Buckler didn't love her. He just wanted her as one of his specimens. I said that I'd tell the authorities what I'd seen before we left Tibet, unless he agreed to a divorce.'

Mrs Jameson nodded slowly. 'And did Ernest Buckler know whether you saw him jerk the rope?'

Tommy shook his head. 'I let him think that I did. But I only saw his hand on the rope. I didn't see him do it.'

Chapter 40

'Sorry to interrupt, Sir,' Constable Parker put his head around the door again, 'but there's a bit of a disturbance.'

We could hear shouting from the hallway – Mrs Hall bellowing at the general, who was trying to placate her – and hysterical weeping from Lavinia.

'Mr Eversholt, please remain here. I'd better see what's happening,' said Inspector Chadwick.

In the marble hallway, Constance Hall had donned her waxed canvas overcoat and was heading for the door, furled umbrella raised in her hand.

'I will not have my boy in custody, when the police have not even spoken to the most likely suspect,' she shouted. 'If you aren't going to arrest him, I shall bally well confront him myself!'

'Madam, I must insist,' said General Lyttelton. 'The police have asked me to ensure everyone stays here. I cannot let you leave.' He stood stoutly before the front door as if prepared to defend it from enemy hordes.

'Mrs Hall, if you attempt to leave, I shall arrest you and tell the constable to take you to Pimlico police station in handcuffs,' said Inspector Chadwick.

Constance Hall turned her ire on him. 'Why are you so

insistent on arresting members of my family, Inspector, when the most likely culprit is making good his escape?'

Walter Hall, on whose shoulder Lavinia Buckler was now weeping, appealed to the inspector.

'Won't you just talk to my wife for a moment, Inspector? It is hard for us to understand what is going on. She's very worried about Perry.'

'And about what is going to happen to the garden,' his wife added. 'Unless you arrest Norman Alperton immediately. He's probably out there now, destroying the plants. He is the only one with a clear motive for all these crimes, Inspector.'

'Now, Connie,' her husband began. 'You don't know that.'

She slammed the tip of the umbrella on the marble floor. 'Number one: he had every incentive to pay my under-gardener to sabotage the lilies. Number two: when his plans were thwarted by Harry Smith, he took his revenge on my head gardener, assuming that we would be unable to produce the garden without him. Number three: when I confounded all his expectations and unveiled the best garden in the show, he arranged the murder of Mr Buckler to ensure nobody would present me with the gold medal it deserves.'

'Connie, my dear…' Walter Hall was staring at her in something approaching horror. 'That's absolute nonsense. Madness.'

Mrs Hall ignored him. 'Well, Inspector? Is that not the clearest account of these crimes that anyone has yet come up with? Why do you not act?'

Inspector Chadwick's face gave nothing away. 'I will consider your suggestions, Mrs Hall, and act accordingly. In the meantime, please return to the drawing room. There are policemen stationed at your garden. I can assure you nobody will be able to destroy it.'

'And I suppose they are trampling all over my delicate alpine plants with their enormous boots.' Mrs Hall looked accusingly at Constable Parker's feet. He shuffled uncomfortably. His boots were indeed rather large.

Inspector Chadwick strode across the hall and stood squarely in front of her.

'Mrs Hall, I don't think you have fully understood the situation. Your garden is no longer a garden. It is a crime scene. It is the site of a murder investigation. And unless you co-operate fully with that murder investigation, I will have no hesitation in placing you under arrest.'

They stared at each other for a moment. Mrs Hall was tall, but he was taller. Mrs Hall was strong, but he was stronger. Each had a formidable will, but Mrs Hall stepped back first.

We all breathed a sigh of relief as she stalked haughtily to the drawing room.

'Oh, Inspector Chadwick,' breathed Lavinia, detaching herself from Mr Hall, who rather reluctantly followed his wife. 'I thought I should clear something up. Only it's rather delicate.' She bit her lip and looked down, allowing a tear to track down her cheek. For the first time, I was unmoved by her pretty show of emotion. The way she tried to charm every man into doing her bidding was starting to become irritating. Especially as she'd landed Peregrine Hall in a cell.

The inspector gave her a brisk nod. 'In due course, Mrs Buckler. I will send for you when I'm free to speak.' I covered my mouth with my hand to disguise my smile. The man who was proof against Mrs Hall's anger was not going to fall for Lavinia's tears.

We retreated to the study, victorious. Mrs Jameson, who

had been sitting in the chair next to Tommy Eversholt, got to her feet. Her eyes were glittering, and she too wore a look of triumph.

'Peter, Mr Eversholt has something to tell you. I think it might explain things rather well. Tommy, will you tell the inspector what you've just told me?'

He looked up, his face miserable. 'Diana doesn't know about any of this. She'll be so angry with me when she finds out. She thinks I'm a fool anyway.'

'Go on,' said Inspector Chadwick.

'It was me.'

Chapter 41

I gasped. Surely not. Tommy was so nice, so friendly. I couldn't imagine him doing anything brutal. My mind flashed forward – the arrest, the trial, the judge placing a black square on his wig and pronouncing the death sentence for murder. Diana was going to be devastated.

'It was the thought of that boy, Tenzin,' said Tommy. 'His body lying down in the ravine, and Buckler just carrying on, collecting the lilies as if Tenzin wasn't there, counted for nothing. And then Buckler getting all the plaudits for them, getting the blasted lilies named after him, even. He had a profit-sharing arrangement with the Halls, you know. Those lilies could have made him a fortune.'

He thumped one fist into the other hand, and I jumped at the force of it. His face was dark with anger.

'And they were stolen. We didn't have permission to take them. We wouldn't even have found them without Tenzin. And Buckler let him die, or worse, caused his death. Stole the lilies. I couldn't stand it. The thought of him meeting the King getting all the glory.'

Inspector Chadwick's eyebrows had shot up his head. He looked incredulous.

'Are you telling me that you murdered Ernest Buckler, M

Eversholt?'

Tommy gave himself a little shake, as if returning to us from whatever landscape his memory had conjured up.

'What? No, of course not. But I tried to kill off the lilies.'

I let out a great sigh of relief. Thank goodness.

'Mr and Mrs Eversholt were at Hawkshill Manor at Christmas,' said Mrs Jameson. 'I was struck that the sabotage had begun then, and that after Mr Cooper's dismissal, it stopped. Until a few weeks ago, when the Eversholts were once again house guests with the Halls.'

Tommy looked up. 'Did you guess when we met you there?' he asked. 'Was it that obvious?'

She smiled, rather patronisingly. 'I had my suspicions. You paid Dick Cooper at Christmas, didn't you?'

Tommy nodded. 'He wanted to leave, anyway. He was going to set up in business for himself. Wanted to start his own nursery. Needed a bit of capital to get going. I didn't object to helping him along.'

'He's growing the lilies at his dad's cottage,' I said. 'He took some of the seedlings when he left Hawkshill Manor. He sold some to Sir Norman, and he's selling the flowers to specialist dealers at Covent Garden market. Frankie and I saw him in a pub there.'

Tommy let out a bark of laughter. 'I don't blame him,' he said. 'I felt badly for him when Constance gave him the push, but he said he had plans. I went to see him in London earlier this month, to find out how to do the job myself. But then, of course, I only managed it a couple of times before you set up the watch system, Mrs Jameson. And then Diana dragged me off to Scotland. So here we are.'

'Here we are indeed,' said Inspector Chadwick, dryly.

'Why did you come back?' asked Mrs Jameson. 'Would it not have been safer to stay in Scotland until after Chelsea?'

He looked uncomfortable. 'I wanted to say something about it to the King. Show up Buckler for the cold fish he is. I had this rather mad idea of telling His Majesty about the lilies being stolen and Tenzin being abandoned. But when it came to it...'

Mrs Jameson leaned closer. 'But you had the perfect opportunity, Tommy. Buckler wasn't there. You talked to the King yourself, didn't you? Constance asked you to tell His Majesty about finding the lilies. Why didn't you tell him about Ernest Buckler's appalling act?'

He looked at her, stricken. 'I suppose I lost my nerve.'

What was it about royalty that caused grown men to crumple? I wondered. I remembered Bert's aborted plans to protest against the King, and how he'd changed from communist firebrand to humble tongue-tied gardener in the Royal presence. I supposed that was why England didn't seem likely to have a revolution any time soon.

Mrs Jameson's feline smile spread across her face. 'You didn't lose your nerve. I think you have quite a lot of nerve, Mr Eversholt. You didn't say anything about Ernest Buckler, because there was no need.' She leaned forward and tapped him on the knee. 'Because you already knew he was dead.'

I gasped and saw Inspector Chadwick start forward in surprise.

'Didn't you?' pressed Mrs Jameson.

'Oh, Lord,' said Tommy.

Chapter 42

'Go on,' said Inspector Chadwick.

Tommy dug a handkerchief out of his pocket and mopped the sweat from his forehead. He took a deep breath and I saw something in his face change, harden. He'd taken a decision, and he was going to stick to it.

'I'm not saying anything more,' said Tommy. He closed his mouth, tilted his chin up, looked from the inspector to Mrs Jameson to me. He seemed almost relieved, his brow clear and his expression content.

'I should warn you, Mr Eversholt, that any failure to pass on important evidence will go very hard against you,' said the inspector. Tommy nodded and folded his arms.

I exchanged glances with Mrs Jameson. She looked confident in her assertion. Tommy had known Ernest Buckler was dead, before the King had made the grisly discovery in the garden. The question was, why had he said nothing about it at the time, and why was he refusing to tell us anything about it now?

'Peter, I rather think that Mr Eversholt has made up his mind,' said Mrs Jameson. 'I'm sure he thinks he is doing the right thing. Perhaps he can be persuaded later that he is mistaken, but we should not waste our time now.'

The inspector frowned. 'I'll have to put him under arrest, too,' he said. 'Obstructing the course of justice, at the very least. Possibly aiding and abetting an offender. And I'm not ruling out murder.'

Mrs Jameson nodded. 'As you wish. It would be nice to have him somewhere close to hand, rather than having to go all the way to Pimlico to talk to him again, however. Mr Eversholt, would you be amenable to being locked into a storeroom for a short period?'

Despite Inspector Chadwick's mutterings about unorthodox methods and his head being on the block if anything went wrong, that was exactly what happened. General Lyttelton put a small cloakroom at our disposal and Tommy allowed himself to be led there and the key turned in the lock. He didn't look happy about it, but he did not speak. Indeed, he had not spoken since his declaration in the study.

'What now?' asked Inspector Chadwick. 'Come on, Iris. You must have a plan.'

My employer had seated herself at the General's desk. Her gaze was veiled, her hooded grey eyes unseeing as she tapped her fingers on her chin.

'We should leave her for a while,' I said quietly. 'She needs to think. I'm sure she'll come up with something.'

We tiptoed out of the study and into the kitchen. I rather hoped we might find some food.

'Will you be joining the rest of the party for luncheon?' asked the cook. 'Lady Lyttelton asked us to prepare a cold collation in the dining room. Most of the guests are there now.'

I glanced at the kitchen clock over the fireplace. It was almost two o'clock. My stomach gave a mighty gurgle, much to my embarrassment.

'Would you be kind enough to make up a plate for us here?' asked the inspector. 'I think we should leave the guests to themselves for now.' He grinned at me. 'I'm starving, too. I'll think better when I've eaten.'

We sat at the kitchen table and chomped on big wedges of pork pie with pickle and hardboiled eggs.

'What are your thoughts, Miss Swallow?'

I chewed and swallowed. 'Tommy saw something. Either he saw Mr Buckler's body, or he saw someone attacking him. But he didn't raise the alarm or tell anyone later. So, he's protecting someone,' I said.

'His wife.'

I sighed and nodded. 'I still can't see Diana Eversholt murdering anyone. But...'

'But it's easier to imagine her doing it than her husband, isn't it? Psychologically, I mean.'

It was true. Diana Eversholt was courageous, bold and fiercely protective of her husband. She knew that Ernest was dangerous. She would not hesitate to act to protect Tommy.

'We should talk to Diana again,' I said. 'Find out what Tommy saw. He might have been mistaken. Maybe if he knows she's going to be in trouble...'

The inspector shook his head. 'A man can't be forced to give evidence against his wife,' he said. 'I don't know whether Mr Eversholt knows that, but I bet Mrs Eversholt does. We will have nothing to hold over him.'

He took another bite of pie and chewed thoughtfully. 'You got on all right with Sergeant Williams at Covent Garden, then? He's a decent fellow.'

'Oh, yes. I liked him,' I said. 'He suggested that we went to this pub near the market. That's where Frankie and I found

213

Dick Cooper and heard about him selling the lilies to Sir Norman Alperton. We almost got into trouble, but then…'

I stared at the empty chair by the fire. 'Oh dear. Inspector Chadwick?'

'Hmm?'

'Where's Bert gone?'

The inspector frowned at me. 'What do you mean?'

'Bert Smith, the under-gardener. He was there with us today at the garden. When I got back earlier, he was sitting by the fireplace, but he's gone.'

Inspector Chadwick got to his feet and rang the bell. 'That's a nuisance. Chap shouldn't have gone without asking permission. I didn't know he was here. Did you talk to him earlier?'

I nodded. 'I found something out. You know I was worried he might be planning an attack of some sort, against the King? Well, it was a protest. He was going to shout out "Time for a republic". But he said when it came to it, he decided it was all rather silly. He was worried about losing his job, and his mother having nowhere to live.'

The inspector grunted. 'Sensible man.'

'So, he didn't say anything. He seemed a bit shaken up by the whole business, coming so close on his father's death.'

The scullery maid ran into the room, her face round and shiny as ever. 'Oh! I'm sorry, Sir. I'll get the housekeeper for you,' she said.

'No need, Miss. Do you know where the man who was sitting by the fire has got to? Mr Smith. He was supposed to stay here.'

She fidgeted with her apron strings. 'I'm sorry, Sir. I think he went a couple of hours ago. He was there one minute, gone the next.'

The inspector sighed. 'Tell one of the policemen to come here, will you? We'll have to track him down again. Why the devil can't people just stay where they are?'

Constable Parker was recalled from the dining room, where he had been ensuring none of the other guests made a bid for escape. He was embarrassed about Bert Smith's disappearance.

'I am sorry, Sir. I think the sergeant clean forgot about the man. We were rather taken up with the other parties, Sir.'

'Well, you'd better put the word out. I want him back here.' Inspector Chadwick turned to me. 'Where do you think he might go, Miss Swallow?'

'I don't know where he was staying. I suppose Mr and Mrs Hall would know.' I thought it unlikely they had put him up in The Goring hotel. 'But there's a pub around the corner from Pimlico police station. Frankie and I took him there after he'd been in for questioning. The Pelham Arms. You could try that.'

The constable nodded briskly and turned on his heel. 'I know it. Decent place. I'll run along there myself, Sir, once I've talked to Mr and Mrs Hall. And if he's not in the pub or at his lodgings, I'll go into the station and get the word out.'

Chapter 43

'I'd better check up on the others,' said Inspector Chadwick. 'Don't want anyone else going AWOL.' He strode down the corridor to the dining room, with me hurrying along behind.

A long table of gleaming mahogany was laid for luncheon in a dark-panelled room with paintings of yet more battles. Various cold meats, salads and savouries were set out on the sideboard for people to help themselves. The Halls sat at the far end of the table. Walter Hall was eating stoically. Constance Hall was staring listlessly at her empty plate. I felt a pang of sympathy. It must be rotten, to put so much effort and passion into making something beautiful, then to have it all ruined.

Diana Eversholt and Lavinia Buckler were at the end of the table closest to the door. Lavinia looked up nervously as we came into the room.

'Oh, Inspector. Are you free now?'

Diana carried on eating, looking quite composed. She glanced up and smiled at me, but her smile was rather brittle

'Are you finished with Tommy, then?'

'Not quite.' Inspector Chadwick answered both questions together.

'It won't take a moment,' said Lavinia. 'Only I think there may have been a misunderstanding.'

He sighed. 'Come through, then, Mrs Buckler. Mrs Eversholt, we will need to speak to you again shortly.'

She nodded, her eyes uneasy. 'Of course.'

Walter Hall rose. 'How long are we likely to be needed here, Inspector? My wife is very tired. I think it would be best for her to return to the hotel and lie down.'

'Not much longer, I hope.'

The inspector turned to General and Lady Lyttelton, who sat in the window seat and were no doubt anxious to be rid of their troublesome guests, although they were far too well-bred to say so.

'General, I hope we will be able to leave you to your privacy before long. I am most grateful for your hospitality and forbearance. In the meantime, I would like to ask everyone to remain here.'

When we returned to the study, Mrs Jameson was on her feet, her eyes bright. 'There you are, Peter. I think our course is clear...' she broke off as Lavinia Buckler tripped into the room. 'What is this?' she asked, as if we were cats who had dragged in something half-eaten.

'I'm so glad to be able to talk to you,' said Lavinia. She twisted her wedding ring around on her finger. 'I think that Peregrine may have made a mistake about something I said. And it would be so awful if the poor boy was to get into trouble for it.'

'Sit down.' Inspector Chadwick indicated the low chair by the fire. 'Please explain what you mean.'

'Well – I think he's rather fond of me. In that silly way that boys sometimes are, when they are young.' She tried a tinkling laugh. It fell like broken glass on a marble floor.

'Lavinia, what did you ask Peregrine to do?' asked Mrs Jameson.

217

'Well... I told him I wasn't always happy with Ernest. I can be honest, can't I? It wasn't easy, living with him. I said the same to you, Marjorie, didn't I?'

I nodded. 'You did.' I'd felt sorry for her, back then. I wasn't sure I still did.

'And perhaps I said that my life would be easier without him. It's very shocking, isn't it? But you can see I didn't mean anything by it. And if dear Perry has done anything silly, it wouldn't be because of me. It was just the sort of thing that anyone might say.' She gazed up at Inspector Chadwick with her big blue eyes.

'What words did you use, exactly?' he asked.

She looked down and twisted her ring again. 'I don't remember. I didn't mean anything.'

'Did you, in Mr Hall's words, ask him to get rid of Mr Buckler, because you were too scared to do it yourself?'

She gave a little gasp. 'No! I mean... it's true I was afraid of Ernest. He had such a temper. But to get rid of him... That wasn't what I meant.'

Mrs Jameson picked up the notebook I'd left on the desk. 'On Thursday May 17, you were seen going into The Goring hotel with Peregrine Hall at 6pm, without your husband or any other chaperone. On Saturday May 19, at 3.30pm in the wash tent, you were overheard begging Mr Hall to do something for you. Mr Hall expressed reluctance and you pressed him to carry out your wishes. You told him that he said he'd "do anything for you" and "wanted to help" and you said that "now is your chance".'

Lavinia's mouth was open in shock. She turned on me.

'You were listening outside! That's a rotten trick. What a nasty mind you must have, Marjorie. I suppose it's to be expected, with your background. Shop girls are so vulgar.'

That stung, I admit. I looked away, my cheeks hot. I couldn't trust myself to speak. And what would I say, anyhow? I had listened. I remembered how I'd defended Lavinia when Frankie had made insinuations about her at the hotel. I wished I hadn't bothered.

'That's very silly, Lavinia,' said Mrs Jameson, briskly. 'Now, why did you buy this book?'

She held up the copy of *Poisonous Plants In The English Garden* that Diana Eversholt had shown us earlier.

'I... I didn't. I haven't seen it before.'

'Even sillier. The stallholder will remember you, and the questions you asked. You can thank Mrs Eversholt for trying to protect you. But your desire to learn about poisons accords with your questions to Marjorie on Saturday, and with what Mr Hall has admitted to us.'

Lavinia opened and shut her mouth a few times, without anything coming out.

'Well?'

Tears began to trickle from her sapphire eyes. 'I was just interested,' she said. 'It was all talk. I can ask questions, can't I? I haven't done anything. I haven't done anything wrong at all.'

Inspector Chadwick sighed. 'Entering into a conspiracy to murder. Incitement to commit murder. And making plans to murder by administration of poison. Serious crimes, all of them. Very serious indeed.'

She pulled the shawl around her shoulders, looking small and scared. 'Are you going to arrest me?'

'Not yet. Perhaps it is fortunate for you, Mrs Buckler, that someone else seems to have got there first.'

Chapter 44

Inspector Chadwick marched Lavinia back to the dining room. Mrs Jameson patted the chair next to her, which was also next to the fire.

'Come,' she said.

I sat, waiting for instructions. What a horrible day this was turning out to be. I remembered how excited I'd been in the morning, putting on my pretty new frock and wondering if I would get to meet the King.

'You mustn't mind it when ignorant people make unkind remarks,' she said. 'There's nothing vulgar about intelligence, whatever type of people one comes from.'

I looked up, surprised. Her voice was kinder than usual.

'I know I have been out of sorts in recent weeks,' she said. 'Being back at Hawkshill Manor has brought up many memories. I apologise for being crabby, Marjorie. You have done very well in this investigation. As you always do.'

I almost fell off my chair. Not only an apology, but praise!

'Thank you. That's very nice to hear.' It was. Rare praise seemed more meaningful when it finally came. 'But there's nothing to apologise for, honestly. I'm very happy in my employment.'

That was the truth. My previous positions – as an assistant

in my father's drapery business and a VAD nurse during the War – had been much less exciting and glamorous than my work as Mrs Jameson's private secretary. It was important to remember that, rather than feeling sorry for myself.

'Good.' Mrs Jameson smiled and rose. 'Ah, here's Peter back. Now, I have a plan. It should wrap things up rather nicely, I think.'

She explained what she needed us to do. I went to get Diana, while Inspector Chadwick retrieved Tommy from the cloakroom.

'Marjorie, do tell me what's going on,' begged Diana as I beckoned her out of the dining room. 'Lavinia came back with the inspector looking like she'd shrunk in the wash. I gather from Mr Hall that poor Perry's in custody, and you've had Tommy for ages.'

Despite my suspicions of the woman's capacity for murder, I still found myself warming to her. I liked her much better than Lavinia, at any rate.

'Mrs Jameson hasn't told me what her theory is yet. I can't help you. Sorry,' I said, truthfully enough.

The study was empty. Diana eyed the bottles of spirits lined up on the shelf. 'I don't suppose I could have a whisky, could I? It's been a hell of a day.'

'Better wait a bit,' I said. 'You don't want to get muddled.'

She laughed. 'You're sweet, Marjorie. I'm already muddled. What I want to get is drunk, horribly and disgracefully. I suppose that'll have to wait till we get home.'

She took an upright chair in front of the desk. 'Is this where I sit for my interrogation?' she asked. Her joking was wearing a little thin. I sensed she was more nervous than she wanted me to know.

The door opened and Inspector Chadwick entered with his hand on Tommy Eversholt's shoulder, pushing him into the room. Tommy's hands were cuffed before him and his eyes downcast. Mrs Jameson followed them in, her face solemn.

'No!' cried Diana, leaping to her feet. 'What are you doing?'

Tommy looked at her like a sick calf. 'Sorry, old girl. I thought it was for the best. You'll be all right, won't you?'

'I'm taking Mr Eversholt into custody,' said Inspector Chadwick. 'You should inform your solicitor and arrange for a criminal barrister to be engaged to defend the charge of murder. I expect the committal hearing will come before the magistrates next week, once the coroner has registered his verdict of unlawful killing.'

All her poise deserted her. 'Tommy, I don't know what you've told them, but for God's sake stop playing games. Inspector, something is horribly wrong. Whatever it is, you must stop this. I know Tommy didn't kill Ernest. I can prove it.' Her face was pale beneath her sun-tan.

'Don't say it, Diana,' said her husband, his voice frantic. 'Please, don't say it. I'm all right. It doesn't matter about me.'

She stared at him, open mouthed. 'My God. Tommy... you think it was me?' She sat down abruptly. 'You really think I killed Ernest. Good grief.' She started to laugh, on the edge of hysteria. 'And you were prepared to hang for me... oh Tommy. You are ridiculous. But we must untangle this at once. Inspector, what has he told you?'

'It's more what he hasn't told us,' said Inspector Chadwick, his voice dry. 'Mr Eversholt, shall we pick up where we left off? Please explain how you knew that Ernest Buckler was dead, before the discovery of the body during the Royal visit.'

He unlocked the handcuffs and gently pushed Tommy

towards a chair next to his wife. They clung together for a moment, and she gave a little sob that belied her casual manner.

'You're sure?' Tommy asked Diana. 'I don't want to mess this up.'

'Ridiculous man,' said Diana, her eyes soft. 'Sit down. Tell them what you saw.'

Tommy had lost track of his wife in the floral pavilion, as she'd said. He had wandered out to look at Sir Norman Alperton's garden, knowing it would be impolitic to do so when Mrs Hall was back.

'I saw Diana standing by the rocks in the Himalayan Valley garden. Then she turned and walked quickly away, almost running back towards the flower pavilion. I was going to run after her, but Dick Cooper came up and started talking to me. He was working for Sir Norman for a couple of days, getting everything shipshape. He showed me all around the garden, and I asked him how he was getting on with the business. Then I saw Sir Norman coming back, and I didn't want to get into a long discussion with him, so I wandered over to our garden.'

He looked at Diana again. She was composed now, drawing a cigarette from her case. She nodded.

'Go on.'

'I saw Ernest's body, sprawled on the ground by the rocks. And... and I could see he was dead. I couldn't think what to do. There was no-one else there. I knew everyone would be back at any minute, so I pulled him under the bushes. The tap had got dislodged and the water was running the wrong way. I knew if I didn't fix it, someone would come and have a look, so I set it up again. Then I washed my hands in the stream and ran towards the floral tent, in the hope of finding Diana.'

She patted his hand. 'You should have told me, darling.'

Tommy looked down. 'I couldn't find you, and then I noticed the time and realised everyone would be returning to the garden. So, I tried to pull myself together and went back. I was terrified someone would have found Ernest's body already, but they hadn't. And Constance asked me to talk to the King, and I could hardly get any words out.' He paused and gave a great shuddering breath. 'And then the King saw Ernest's foot. I hadn't dragged him far enough into the bushes.'

He squeezed his wife's hand. 'I was so worried that someone else would have seen you. I knew that, whatever you'd done, it was only to protect me.'

My heart was beating almost as fast as the clock's relentless tick. I wondered if Freddie would have been prepared to hide a body and take the blame for me, then shook off the silly thought. But if Tommy had thought it was Diana, and Diana said it wasn't, then who had killed Ernest Buckler?

'Diana,' purred Mrs Jameson, 'perhaps it's time for you to tell us what you were doing in the garden when Tommy saw you.'

She disentangled her hand from his and lit her cigarette. 'I suppose I better had,' she said. 'Although I do feel rather rotten. One doesn't like to land people in it. There is such a thing as natural justice, after all.'

'I think you'll find the court will decide about that,' said Inspector Chadwick.

Mrs Jameson and Diana Eversholt exchanged a sad smile. 'I daresay they will. But I wonder if they will come to the right conclusion,' said Mrs Jameson.

Chapter 45

Diana leaned back in her chair. 'Well, then. After I lost Tommy in the flower tent, I went out to look at Mrs Hall's garden. It was looking splendid, despite the rain. Ernest was there, crouched over the top of the stream. He said the tap had got blocked up with mud and started to spray water about.'

She took a deep drag of cigarette smoke and began to cough. 'Sorry. I should cut down on these things, only my doctor says they are good for the throat. I suppose that was why you didn't see Ernest with me, Tommy. He was sitting on his heels, looking at the tap.'

She balanced her cigarette on the ashtray.

'Anyway. Ernest was being – well, being Ernest. He asked about Scotland, in a way that made it clear he didn't believe I'd really been there. He can be horribly sarcastic. So that got my back up, rather. I was quite tempted to push him into the mud. I told him it was none of his business where I went, and he said it was if I didn't keep my husband under control.' She looked apologetically at Tommy. 'I don't know what he meant by that, darling.'

Tommy sighed. 'I do. I think he knew about the lilies.'

Diana raised her eyebrows. 'The lilies?'

'Later,' suggested Mrs Jameson. 'Carry on with your story,

225

Diana.'

'Hmm.' She gave her husband an appraising look. 'All right. I was pretty angry by then. I said it was about time he got over me and left the two of us alone. And that I would make sure he never got the chance to do to Tommy what... what he'd done to the gardener.'

Inspector Chadwick whistled. 'You accused your former husband of poisoning Mr Smith?'

'He pretended he didn't know what I meant. But he knew, all right. Ernest was always fascinated by plant poisons. I told him that I knew he'd poisoned Tommy's sandwiches. That he'd been the one on watch before Tommy, and there was only one packet of sandwiches left by the time Tommy arrived for his watch. Ernest was in the perfect position to add the poison.'

Diana took another drag of her cigarette. 'I told Ernest he had Harry Smith's blood on his hands. He laughed and said I'd always had an over-active imagination. He said I had no proof, that anyone could have picked yew berries.'

Inspector Chadwick leaned forward. 'He knew Mr Smith had been poisoned by yew berry seeds?'

The police had been careful to keep that knowledge quiet. Only Mrs Jameson and I had been made privy to the particular poison that had been found in Mr Smith's body. So only one other person would know what had been used. The murderer.

Diana nodded. 'He did. I suppose he sprinkled the seeds into the chutney or something. They'd have been easy enough to disguise.'

'And what did you do after this exchange, Mrs Eversholt?'

She exhaled, looking at the ceiling. 'I stormed off. I'd had enough of my ex-husband for one day. I went back to the flower tent. On my way, I saw Lavinia and Peregrine slipping out of the wash tent together. She looked rather dishevelled. Oh, I didn't blame her, although I thought she should be more discreet. I went into the pavilion, browsed for a while and looked around for Tommy.

'Then I spotted Lavinia again at the Royal Horticultural Society book stall. I wandered over and she jumped like a mountain goat, trying to hide the book she'd just bought. She stuffed it in her handbag and almost ran away, saying she needed to get back to Ernest. I asked the man what she'd bought, and he showed me the poisonous plants book. He made a joke of it – said she'd been asking all sorts of questions and he hoped she wasn't going to murder her husband.' Diana gave a rather brittle laugh. None of us joined in.

'I must admit, it struck me as rather funny that the wife of a man who poisoned others seemed to be planning to poison him. After Ernest's body had been found, Lavinia was in a tizzy about the book. While we were in the drawing room, she asked what to do about it. I took it from her and put it in my bag.'

'But what happened to Ernest?' burst out Tommy. 'It was only – I don't know – must have been ten minutes between you dashing off and me finding the man's body.'

Inspector Chadwick was looking concerned. 'Is that all you can tell us? Nothing else that might help us to identify the killer of your former husband? You see, that does rather mean you were the last person to see him alive. And you had been arguing. It doesn't look good for you, Mrs Eversholt.'

Diana exchanged glances with Mrs Jameson. 'Must I really?' she asked.

Mrs Jameson nodded, kindly. 'I think you better had.'

She sighed. 'I'd thought Ernest and I were alone in the garden. But as I stormed off, I almost ran into Bert Smith on the other side of the bushes. He must have been listening the whole time. He heard me accuse Ernest of poisoning his father, and Ernest laughing in response. The look on his face...' She shuddered. 'I've never seen anyone look so terrible in all my life. I'm afraid I simply ran away.'

Inspector Chadwick was on his feet before she had finished speaking. He snatched up the telephone and asked to be put through to Pimlico police station.

'Peter?' called Mrs Jameson. 'Aren't you going to fetch Bert?'

'Oh dear,' I said. 'The trouble is, Mrs Jameson, we don't know where Bert is.'

Chapter 46

'Oh, fiddlesticks!' Mrs Jameson exclaimed. 'Why not? Didn't he come here with us?'

I explained how I had realised Bert was missing when Inspector Chadwick and I had tea in the kitchen. 'The inspector told Constable Parker to find him. Perhaps he has done so already,' I said. 'He was going to check his lodgings, and a pub we went to.'

But if I was Bert and I'd coshed Ernest Buckler over the head, I wouldn't head for the Pelham Arms for a pint of bitter. I'd get away from Chelsea as fast as my feet would take me, as soon as I could slip out of the kitchen unobserved.

'Where would he go?' asked Mrs Jameson.

'Back to Hawkshill Manor?' suggested Tommy Eversholt. 'Perhaps he'd want to see his mother.'

Diana shook her head. 'I'd ship out on the next boat,' she said. 'Take the train down to Dover or Portsmouth and hop over to France. They should put the word out to the ports, if they want to catch him.'

Tommy sighed. 'You would, yes. But Bert won't have any money. Not enough money, anyway. And I don't suppose he's in a rush to get back to France, after what happened to him there in the War. Does he speak French, even?'

I got to my feet. 'He'll need help. Money, like you said. Mr Eversholt, you talked to Dick Cooper earlier. Bert and Dick were drinking together at Covent Garden the other week. And Dick's got plenty of cash, from what I heard at the market.'

Inspector Chadwick replaced the telephone mouthpiece. His thunderous looks told all.

'They haven't found him. He's cleared out his room at the hostel where he was staying.'

Mrs Jameson took the inspector's place at the telephone. 'Marjorie, didn't you say Frankie was friendly with Bert? I'll get her to bring the car over. Mr Eversholt, please go with Marjorie and see if you can find Dick Cooper at Sir Norman's garden.'

After hours of sitting and talking, it felt good to be on the move. Tommy and I ran through the puddles back to the Royal Hospital grounds. Members of the public and journalists had been excluded. Only a few scarlet-suited Chelsea pensioners and some rather damp gardeners were still wandering the paths.

Two stoic-looking policemen stood in the drizzle by the Himalayan Valley garden. They'd rigged up a white canvas tent over the crime scene. I wondered if Mr Buckler's body was still inside it. Along the path, the English Arcadia garden was deserted. I supposed it would have been too much to expect Dick Cooper to be still working there.

'Blast. What now?' asked Tommy.

I considered. 'Where did you meet Dick Cooper before? You said you'd been in touch with him to learn what to do to the lilies.'

He nodded. 'We went to this rather disreputable public house near Covent Garden,' he said.

230

I groaned. 'The Lord John Russell Tavern?' It would be. The last place in London that I wanted to go back to.

'That's the one. I say, you haven't been there, have you? It's not the sort of place I'd take a lady.'

Back at the house, Walter and Constance Hall were closeted with Inspector Chadwick and Mrs Jameson.

'I'm sorry, Mrs Jameson. Dick Cooper doesn't seem to be here anymore,' I said.

'Blast. We've called Hawkshill Manor,' she said. 'The staff will inform us immediately if Bert returns. The local police have been asked to keep a watch at Faversham railway station. And the inspector has spoken to Sir Norman to try to find out where Dick Cooper is staying. Unfortunately, he doesn't know, although he says he believes he has lodgings in the East End.'

Mrs Hall shook her head. 'After all we've done for Bert Smith. But there you have it. The working classes have become so ungrateful. That's what Bolshevism does, I suppose. Unleashes the brutality in a man. If it takes hold, none of us will be safe in our beds.'

Mr Hall sighed. 'I'm sure it won't come to that, Constance. Now, Inspector. I take it you will be releasing my son from custody?'

'In due course,' said Inspector Chadwick.

'Weren't Peregrine and Bert friends when they were younger?' I asked.

Mrs Hall frowned. 'Perry did tag along with him when he was little,' she said. 'I didn't see any harm in it at that age. Why do you ask? You can't think that Perry has helped him escape? He's been in a cell since lunchtime.'

'Of course not,' said Mrs Jameson, picking up on my meaning

231

immediately. 'But if they were friendly as children, perhaps Perry might know something to help us discover where Bert might go?'

Inspector Chadwick rose. 'Good idea. I'll go over to Pimlico and talk to him now. Mrs Hall, can you think of anywhere else that Bert might be?'

'We do have one possible lead,' I volunteered. 'Covent Garden market, and the Lord John Russell Tavern. Frankie and I saw Bert and Dick drinking in there together.'

'That's where I met Cooper,' said Tommy Eversholt. He was standing well back, avoiding looking at the Halls. I supposed they didn't know yet that he had been the saboteur. 'Why don't I go with Miss Swallow and see if we can find him?'

We all jumped at a prolonged toot of a motor car horn. Mrs Jameson's dark green Lagonda sat on the gravel drive outside the window, Frankie at the wheel. She leaned out of the window and waved her jaunty chauffeur's hat.

'Oh, really,' muttered Mrs Hall.

I jumped up. 'Shall we go, Mrs Jameson? Even if we don't find them, we might get a lead.'

She waved her hand. 'If Peter has no objection.'

'Call Sergeant Williams over from Bow Street if you need any help,' said Inspector Chadwick. 'No heroics, Marjorie. Bert Smith is clearly a dangerous man. Don't try to bring him in on your own.'

Chapter 47

'Blimey, Miss. You're a glutton for punishment, ain't you? Didn't think we'd see you back.'

The barmaid at the Lord John Russell Tavern put down the cloth with which she'd been wiping the tables. The pub was quiet, a few old boys supping their pints of bitter in silence, dogs at their feet. No Bert, no Dick Cooper. The stench of beer, sweat, cooking fat and stale tobacco still hung around the place.

'It's quiet now, but it'll fill up soon,' she warned. 'What do you want?'

'To ask about someone I saw in here last time,' I said.

The barmaid pursed her lips and began to shake her head. Then she saw Tommy and broke into a wide smile.

'I remember you. You tipped me half a crown when you were in last month. Got any more of those burning a hole in your pocket?'

Tommy winked. 'Might have, if you're a good girl. D'you remember who I was meeting that night?'

'Same bloke that she was after,' she said, jerking her thumb in my direction. 'Dick. Popular, ain't he? Well, I ain't seen him today. Can't help you there.'

'Pity.' Tommy took out a shiny gold sovereign and turned it

in his fingers. 'Must be a lot of people come looking for Dick. Wonder how they get messages to him. Say, for example, if I wanted to write him a note.'

She shrugged. 'I'm always happy to oblige a regular customer,' she said, eyes on the coin. 'I could take a message for next time he comes in.'

'And if I wanted to talk to him urgently?'

She hesitated.

Tommy shrugged and pocketed the coin. 'Never mind. Just wondered,' he said. 'Expect someone else can tell us.'

'Wait.' She glanced around the pub. The regulars seemed sunk in gloom, staring into the bottom of their glasses. She slipped behind the bar, shuffled a few bottles around and pulled out a battered envelope hidden behind them. 'I keep messages for him in this,' she said. 'It's got an address on it.'

Tommy grabbed it. I wrote down the address in my notebook: Holland House, Wentworth Street, Whitechapel. East End, like Sir Norman had said. Frankie's old stamping ground.

'Bless you,' Tommy said, flipping the gold coin in the air. It spun, shining in the dim light. She caught it neatly and gave it a rub with her cloth.

Outside, Frankie was manoeuvring the car through the piles of rubbish and ankle-deep horse manure that was the aftermath of the market, a look of distaste on her face.

'I'll give it a good wash when we get back,' she said. 'Where are we off to now, Marge?' I passed her the address and she groaned. 'If you think this place is grubby, wait till you see Whitechapel. We'll be lucky if the Lagonda isn't nicked from under us.'

We set off, winding through the narrow streets to Aldwych,

and then east along Fleet Street where the great printing presses clanked and roared, past the looming dome of St Paul's cathedral, sitting like an enormous pudding basin above Cheapside. The traffic was increasing towards the evening rush, omnibuses and taxi-cabs fighting with horse-drawn carts, rattling across the junction by the Bank of England where dozens of bowler-hatted clerks armed with umbrellas streamed out into the street and down the steps to the underground electric railway. The clocks of the city churches struck five.

Frankie handled the car beautifully, nipping into gaps and darting across junctions.

'Who are we going to see?' she called.

'Dick Cooper.' I'd taken the seat next to her, despite Tommy's protests. He was sprawled in the back seat, gazing out of the window.

I filled Frankie in on the events of the day. 'So, it looks like Bert must have coshed Ernest Buckler and then fled. We're trying to find him. I thought Cooper might have some idea about where he'd go.'

She glanced sideways at me. 'You're sure about this, Marge?'

I shrugged. 'Mrs Jameson seems pretty sure, and she's usually right. You saw how Bert went for Peregrine on the morning his father died. He's been a soldier, hasn't he?' It was an uncomfortable fact that men who'd fought seemed quicker with their fists, more likely to resort to violence. The murder rate, Mrs Jameson had informed me, went up sharply after a war. Being taught to kill as soldiers changed something in men, removed a restraint that couldn't be put back, she said.

Frankie was silent for a moment. Then: 'Even if she's right, do you really want Bert to hang? Don't matter how much the bloke deserved it, does it? If a gardener bumps off a toff, he'll swing for it.'

'I suppose so,' I said, uncomfortably. 'But maybe the judge would be lenient, given the mitigating circumstances.'

'Not blooming likely. Especially with Bert's politics. They'll have a rope around his neck before they've found him guilty.'

We drove in silence while I contemplated her words. It was true, I supposed. But what else were we to do? People couldn't be allowed to get away with murder, just because one sympathised with their motivation. In the one case where Mrs Jameson and I had been unable to see the suspect put behind bars, the result had been another attempted killing.

We'd been driving along the wide expanse of Aldgate where it opened into Whitechapel High Street. Trams rattled alongside 'buses and delivery boys' bicycles. A high-sided wooden lorry had a close encounter with a tram as it crossed a busy junction, causing both drivers to turn white and shake their fists.

Frankie deftly swerved around them. 'Here we go. Hold on tight.'

I squealed as she swung the wheel left by a public house bearing the sign of the White Hart. At first it looked like she was about to drive straight into a wall, then I saw an arched passageway carved between a pawnbroker's shop and the pub, barely wide enough for the Lagonda to fit through.

We shot out the other side into a narrow alleyway, its cobbles hidden under layers of horse manure and other nameless filth. The air was thick with choking black smoke from rows of chimneys above a long brick workshop. I put my handkerchief over my nose to muffle the foul smell.

'Where are we?' I asked.

Frankie grinned. 'Gunthorpe Street. That's the furnace for the Board of Works' rubbish collection. Stinks, don't it?' She pointed to a doorway of a small shop on the opposite side of the alley. 'And that's where they found the first of the Ripper's victims, they reckon.'

I shivered. Forty years previously, the brutal Whitechapel murders of five unfortunate women by an unknown killer had entered London folklore. People seemed almost to revel in the stories, visiting the places where the bodies had been found and writing up theories about the killer. As if we had not experienced enough bloodshed. I hoped these old stories would soon be forgotten.

Frankie pulled up at the far end of the alley. 'Right. There you are: Wentworth Street, straight ahead. There's a boarding house three doors down. I reckon that'll be it. I'm staying with the motor. It won't be here when we get back, otherwise.'

I was glad of Tommy Eversholt by my side as I picked my way along the pavement. Men slouched against walls, appraising me frankly as I walked past, and hungry-looking children glanced up from their games. I kept my raincoat buttoned to the neck, thankful I was wearing my winter walking shoes, which had already been mired in mud.

Holland House was a six-storey building with a gabled roof and arched windows. A sign above the door indicated it had been erected 'as a residence for respectable working men' by a local philanthropist in 1884. A pitifully thin cat hissed as we approached, then arched its back and bared its teeth.

'Let's get inside, for heaven's sake.' For all his adventuring in foreign climes, Tommy seemed ill-at-ease in the slums of his own city.

We rang the bell. A greasy man with thinning hair and bad

teeth opened the door.

'I'm looking for Dick Cooper,' said Tommy firmly. 'Important message for him. Is he here?'

The man eyed us suspiciously. 'Who wants to know?'

However, Tommy's half-crown soon produced results. I wondered if Mrs Jameson or Inspector Chadwick would pay him back for all his carelessly dispensed coins.

'I'll see if he's in,' said the man. He beckoned us into the gloomy entrance lobby and began to lumber up the stairs, sighing.

We waited. I heard a heavy knock on a door. No reply. Bother. It had been quite a long shot, I supposed. Then the door from the street opened behind us.

'Dick! We were looking for you,' said Tommy. The man looked anxiously from him to me.

'What for?' he asked.

'Wanted a quick word about your chum Bert.'

Dick turned on his heel and flung himself out of the door. I flew after him and applied the toe of my shoe to the back of his knee. He stumbled down the steps and I grabbed his elbow, twisting it upwards. He let out a yell.

'No, you don't,' I gasped.

'Good Lord, Miss Swallow,' said Tommy. 'Hold on a beat, Dick.' He took hold of his other arm. 'It's important. Why don't you come and sit in our motor for a moment?'

Chapter 48

We walked Dick Cooper to the car. I got into the back seat, Tommy pushed Dick in beside me and sat on his other side. Frankie touched her cap.

'Where to, Miss Swallow?'

'What's all this about?' asked Dick. 'Let me go. You hurt my arm.'

'I'm sorry, Mr Cooper. But we need to find Bert. Did he come to you for help?' I asked.

'I'm saying nothing,' he growled.

'Have it your own way.' I leaned forward. 'Frankie, please take us to Pimlico police station. Inspector Chadwick can question him there under arrest. I expect Sergeant Williams would like to talk to him, too, about the lilies he's been selling at the Lord John Russell Tavern. And then Mrs Hall can tell us whether she wants to press charges over the sabotage of the lilies back in January.'

Frankie revved the engine. 'Right you are, Miss Swallow.'

'Wait!'

We waited.

'I dunno exactly where he is now. But I saw him this afternoon,' Dick admitted. 'He came to my lodgings and said he needed some money. He's an old pal. I couldn't turn him

239

away, could I?'

'How much?'

Dick hesitated. 'Quite a bit.'

'You had quite a bit to lend, then?' asked Tommy. 'Business must be good.'

'Ten pounds,' said Dick. 'He said he'd return it as soon as he could.'

My heart sank. With ten pounds in his pocket, Bert could get a third-class ticket to Dover and a ferry crossing to France, as Diana had suggested.

Frankie twisted around in her seat. 'Where've you come from, mister? Been seeing him off, have you?'

'None of your business,' he snapped.

Frankie swung the car around. 'He was walking down from the west,' she said. 'Liverpool Street Station, was it? Let's see if your pal's still there.'

We hurtled through the streets. Frankie dropped us at the entrance and Tommy and I ran inside. The railway station was full of men heading home into the suburbs, north to Tottenham and Wood Green or east towards Stratford and Barking.

'The boat train,' shouted Tommy, pointing. 'It goes from the far platform.'

We raced across the station and Tommy grabbed the arm of a passing porter. 'Boat train to Harwich?' he gasped. 'Are we too late?'

The man drew out his pocket watch, maddeningly slow. 'I'm afraid you are, Sir. The Harwich train was due to depart at five thirty-five sharp. It's a quarter to six.'

'And it left on time?' I asked.

'Oh, yes, Miss. It has to, see, to be there at half past seven.

Otherwise, they miss the ferry.'

'And where does the ferry from Harwich go?' I asked.

He looked at me curiously. 'Depends which ferry,' he said. 'There's a crossing to the Hook of Holland overnight, which goes at half past eight. Then there's the one north to Hull. That's a morning departure. Or do you mean the Rotterdam route?'

'I don't know,' I said, despairingly.

The man warmed to his theme. 'Then there's the Denmark ferry. Esbjerg. That only goes twice a week. Hold on a minute.' He pulled a small book with close-printed text from his jacket pocket. 'Tuesdays and Fridays, eight o'clock. It's an overnighter, too. But like I said, you've missed the train that would connect with that one. Where do you want to go, anyway?' An unpleasant smile crossed his face as he looked from me to Tommy. 'Running away, is it, Miss?'

I flushed. 'Never mind.' Tommy looked like he was about to punch the man, but I dragged him away. We scoured the station, but there was no sign of Bert Smith.

Eventually we returned to the station concourse, where Frankie was leaning against the Lagonda with a cigarette in her mouth.

'Where's Dick Cooper?' I asked.

She looked into the empty car, affecting surprise. 'Oh, isn't he there? Never mind, you'd finished quizzing him.'

I sighed. 'Frankie, we don't even know if this is where Bert was going.'

She finished her Woodbine and flicked away the butt. 'Ten quid in his pocket? He got the boat train, trust me. He'll be halfway to Harwich by now. If I was him, I'd go to Denmark. Very strong socialist movement over there. Or he could keep

241

going to Sweden or Finland. The Party would look after him.'

I looked at her curiously. She had more knowledge of the Communist Party than I expected. What did she do in her spare time, when she wasn't drinking at the Caravanserai club or practising jiu-jitsu?

She broke in on my musing. 'Where do you want to go now, Marge? Because I can tell you, this car won't get to the coast before the train.'

I felt deflated. We'd been so close – just ten minutes too late. 'I suppose we should go back to Chelsea. Tell Inspector Chadwick. He can get the police to meet the train at Harwich. They'll catch him there.'

We climbed back into the car and Frankie drove west.

'The trouble is,' said Tommy, 'Ernest did rather deserve it.'

I wasn't going to disagree with that.

'Bert's a decent bloke,' said Frankie.

That was probably true, too, if you ignored him having murdered Ernest Buckler.

'His poor mother,' I said. 'How will she manage? And how awful for her to see her husband murdered and her only son executed for murdering his killer.'

Tommy pulled out his pocket watch. 'Quarter past six. We've got loads of time to get back to Chelsea. The boat train won't arrive at Harwich until half past seven, the man said. It's been a hell of a day. Why don't we stop off for a quick brandy? I could certainly do with one.'

Frankie brightened up. 'The Pelham Arms is very cosy,' she said. 'Just a quick one. Marjorie, you won't tell on us, will you? They won't know how long it took us to find Dick Cooper, after all.'

I hesitated. It was very tempting. But I was on duty, and my first loyalty had to be to my employer.

'No. I mean, you do what you want. But drop me at Chelsea first. I need to tell Mrs Jameson what we've found out.'

Chapter 49

I did my duty. The Harwich police met the boat train and searched every compartment. Every ferry leaving Harwich that night was searched; every passenger checked carefully against their passport photograph. Not one of them was Bert Smith. It was rather awful, but I couldn't help feeling just a little bit relieved.

Four days later, Inspector Chadwick was slumped in an armchair drinking whisky. He had joined Mrs Jameson and me at home at Bedford Square for a late supper and was sunk in gloom.

'I'm in all sorts of trouble,' he grumbled. 'Not only did we let the suspect escape after having him under our noses, but I deployed the resources of two police forces, held up one train and two ferries and delayed the departures of all sorts of important businessmen. And we still don't know where Bert Smith is.'

I wondered if Bert had gone to Liverpool Street at all. We'd only had Frankie's word for it that Dick Cooper had been walking from that direction. Cooper had disappeared after Frankie let him out of the car and had yet to resurface, his room in Whitechapel remaining empty. Frankie was, of course, claiming complete innocence in the matter, but had been very cheerful for the past couple of days, whistling *The Red Flag* as she polished the Lagonda until it gleamed.

Diana and Tommy Eversholt had lunched with us earlier that day. They were still under police instructions to stay at their London address. So far, the Halls remained ignorant of Tommy's sabotage, but he was terrified of what would happen if they found out. Diana was furious at Tommy, both for the sabotage and for suspecting her of having murdered Ernest Buckler. However, her full insider account of the murder at the Chelsea Flower Show had been snapped up by the *Daily Post*, and she'd been invited to have dinner with the *Post*'s proprietor, Lord Bartleman, a keen amateur gardener. She had high hopes of persuading Lord Bartleman to fund a new expedition to Tibet.

The Halls had retreated to Kent in disgust, after Lord Lambourne announced that there would be no medals awarded to any gardens at Chelsea that year, as a mark of respect for Ernest Buckler's death. Peregrine had gone with them, hurt and upset that Lavinia was refusing to see him. She was putting on a great show as Buckler's grieving widow. A piece in the *Kensington and Chelsea Gazette* included a photograph of her looking beautiful and fragile in a most becoming black hat with a chic polka dot veil. She planned to stay with her parents, she told the *Gazette*, and expected to live very quietly.

Mrs Jameson sipped her whisky and soda. 'He'll turn up, Peter. You've done all you can,' she said.

'Four crimes,' I mused. 'And the problem at first was we thought that three of them must have been done by the same person.'

'Four?' asked the Inspector.

Mrs Jameson ticked them off on her fingers. 'The murder of

Tenzin, the Buddhist novice, in Tibet. Culprit: Ernest Buckler, to steal the lilies. The sabotage of the lilies. Culprit: Tommy Eversholt, in revenge for Tenzin's death. The murder of Harry Smith, intended to be the murder of Tommy Eversholt. Culprit: Ernest Buckler again, to stop Tommy from exposing the murder in Tibet. And the murder of Ernest Buckler. Culprit: Bert Smith, in revenge for his father's death. "And thus the whirligig of time brings in his revenges." If only people could leave their revenges to the law.'

Inspector Chadwick grunted. 'I thought you believed in natural justice, Iris.'

Graham, our butler, brought in my usual nightcap of warm milk.

'Miss O'Grady is in the kitchen, Miss Swallow. She asked if you could spare her a moment for a quick word?'

'Of course.' I excused myself and followed him down the back stairs.

Frankie was standing in front of the gas range with her cap in her hands, looking sheepish. Sooty, curled on top of the range, jumped down and pressed herself against my legs.

'What's the matter?' I asked, reaching down to scratch behind the cat's ears.

'Bert wants to go and see his mum, before he gives himself up. He's asked if I would take him,' said Frankie.

'Bert!' I exclaimed. She shushed me frantically. 'Where is he? Where has he been hiding?'

Frankie looked sheepish again. 'It might be best if I don't tell you that. But we can't let him be banged up before he has a chance to explain to Mrs Smith, can we, Marge?'

This was a dilemma. Harbouring a wanted man was a serious offence. And the policeman in charge of the murder investigation was sitting upstairs.

'Where is he, Frankie?'

She took a deep breath. 'In the car. I brought it round from the mews.'

I gave her what I hoped was a severe look. 'And he seriously wants to hand himself in to the police?'

She nodded. 'Honest. He knows he won't get away. And he can't stay hidden for ever, can he?'

Oh, goodness. I had every sympathy for Bert, not to mention his poor mother. But I couldn't risk his escaping again – aided and abetted by our chauffeur, with my full knowledge. What on earth was I to do?

Chapter 50

Graham intervened. 'Might I make a suggestion, Miss?'

'Please do.'

I listened to his proposal, a smile spreading across my face.

'All right. Perhaps Mrs Smithson could prepare a thermos flask of hot tea and cut a few pieces of cake for the journey.'

With these provisions and a rug for my knees, I slipped out of the basement door and up the steps into Bedford Square. The scent of wallflowers drifted in the night air.

'Hullo, Miss Swallow.' Bert looked at me apprehensively as Frankie put the car into gear and I took my seat next to him in the back.

'Hullo, Bert.'

He was clean-shaven and his working clothes were not muddy, as they had been last time I saw him. He hadn't been sleeping rough or hiding in alleyways for the past four days, that was for sure. My mind strayed to Frankie's spick and span rooms over the mews where we garaged the Lagonda.

I had no qualms for my safety. I suppose I should have worried about Bert murdering us both and fleeing with the car, but one look at his face told me he had no further thoughts of escape. He looked determined, but resigned. There seemed little point in quizzing the man about why he'd committed the crime. His motivation was clear enough. I certainly didn't want to have my suspicions about his recent whereabouts confirmed, so we drove off without further conversation through the restless London streets, crossing the Thames over Tower Bridge.

The journey to Hawkshill Manor would take us around an hour and a half. We stopped in the flat marshy land south of the Thames near Gravesend for Frankie to top up the petrol tank from the can strapped to the back of the car. I poured hot, sweet tea into enamel mugs and passed around wedges of Mrs Smithson's excellent fruitcake. Bert nodded his thanks.

'Good as my mum's, this.' He gave me a sad smile. I packed up our strange picnic and we resumed our journey down silent country roads.

Shortly before midnight, Frankie drove quietly into the entrance to the Hall Horticultural Supplies nursery, avoiding the grand drive to Hawkshill Manor. She pulled up beside the glasshouses.

'Here we are. All the best, Bert.' She reached round to shake his hand.

'You too, Frankie.' He ducked his head at me. 'And thank you, Miss. I won't forget this.'

He scrambled out of the car and walked quickly up the path to the gardener's cottage. The light was still on. I saw the door open, and a small figure give a cry. Bert stooped to embrace his mother and they went quickly inside.

About fifteen minutes later, we heard the crunch of tyres on gravel. A black car pulled up beside ours, Inspector Chadwick behind the wheel. He got out, then walked around to open the passenger door for Mrs Jameson.

'Mr Hargreaves gave me your note,' he said. 'You should

have waited, Miss Swallow, rather than setting off on your own. How did you get the tip-off?'

'Someone in a pub told me they'd heard Bert was back home,' said Frankie, lying with a facility that I still found difficult. 'So, we thought the best thing to do was drive straight down here and let you know to follow on after us. We didn't want to lose him again, did we?'

Mrs Jameson narrowed her eyes, but the corners of her mouth curled upwards. 'Very wise. Do you know if Bert is on the premises?'

'He is,' I said. 'We saw him go into the cottage, just after we arrived.'

'Right, then,' said Inspector Chadwick. 'I ought to wait for back-up, but I don't want to give him the chance to slip away again. Frankie, will you stand at the back door of the cottage in case he makes a run for it? I'm going in.'

Mrs Jameson and I watched as he strode to the front door and knocked loudly. A moment later Bert answered, and the inspector disappeared inside. We both sighed.

'How long did he have with his mother?' asked Mrs Jameson.

'About a quarter of an hour.' Not long, to say whatever he needed to say.

She nodded. 'Better than nothing,' she said, as if she was reading my mind.

Inspector Chadwick emerged with a handcuffed Bert and took him to the police car. Frankie rounded the cottage, the glowing tip of her cigarette like a firefly in the darkness.

'Do you want to go back to London tonight?' she asked Mrs Jameson.

'I daresay Constance and Walter would put us up. But I rather feel like I've had enough of Constance Hall for a while.

Are you too tired to drive back, dear?'

Frankie grinned. 'Not a bit of it.'

'Then let's go home.' She shivered. 'Blast this wretched British summer. I want to feel some heat in the sun. Let's go to the French Riviera, Marjorie. I think we've earned a vacation.'

A holiday! My heart leapt. I'd never had a proper holiday before. I imagined crossing the sea to relax in sunnier climes, sitting on the beach with a parasol. After all the sadness, how marvellous it would be to forget all about murder and murderers, just for a while.

* * *

Enjoyed Death At Chelsea? Read the prequel novella free.

So how did a nice girl like Marjorie Swallow end up working for a lady detective? And what happened during her interview for the job, in the Palm Court at the Ritz Hotel?

Subscribers to my Readers Club can download a free novella, *Murder At The Ritz*, which answers these questions and more! Readers Club members get a monthly newsletter with news about my books, events, exclusive short stories, recommendations and special offers. Sign up at my website, https://annasayburnlane.com/.

I loved writing *Death At Chelsea*. If you enjoyed reading it, I would be so grateful if you left a quick review to let me know. I read all my reviews, and they make a huge difference in helping other readers find new books to enjoy.

Historical Note

While the story of *Death At Chelsea* is pure fiction, it has historical roots. I try to keep as close to the historical world of 1920s London as possible.

The Chelsea Flower Show began as the Royal Horticultural Society's Great Spring Show in 1862, but the first event held at the Chelsea Royal Hospital was not until 1913. The show has always been seen as the start of the social season in London, and is usually attended by members of the British Royal Family. King George V and Queen Mary visited many times, including in 1923 when it did indeed pour with rain! The Chelsea Flower Show remains as popular and busy as ever, with elaborate show gardens by famous garden designers and wonderful displays in the floral pavilion. Lord Lambourne was president of the RHS from 1919 to 1928, and General Sir Neville Lyttleton was governor of the Chelsea Royal Hospital from 1912 to 1931.

Two real people inspired characters in *Death At Chelsea.* The writer and gardener Vita Sackville-West established a beautiful garden at Sissinghurst in Kent and wrote extensively about gardening. She was an inspiration for Constance Hall, and Sissinghurst for Hawkshill Manor. Frank Kingdon Ward was a botanist, explorer, plant collector and author. I pinched some of his adventures from *In The Land of the Blue Poppies* for my plant hunter, Ernest Buckler. Kingdon Ward sounds like a much more sympathetic character, however!

Sources for *Death At Chelsea* included the Royal Horticultural Society, the British Newspaper Archive, the writings of Kingdon Ward and Sackville-West, Charles Quest-Ritson's *The English Garden* and Michael Brown's *Death In The Garden*. I enjoyed inspirational visits to Walmer Castle Gardens, Sissinghurst Castle and Gardens, Chelsea Physic Garden and Chelsea Royal Hospital.

Acknowledgements

Thanks to my editor Alison Jack and my cover designer Donna Rogers. Thanks to Alison Savage for horticultural advice, book loans and a jolly visit to Sissinghurst. Thanks to Yang-May Ooi for pep-talks and enthusiasm. Thanks to my beta reader team: Radhika, Rosalie, Christina, Madeleine, Jean and Emma. Thanks to Phil for everything.

About the Author

Anna Sayburn Lane is a novelist and journalist. She writes historical cozy mysteries and contemporary thrillers.

Anna studied English and History at university, then began her career as a reporter on a London newspaper, later moving into medical journalism.

She published her first novel, *Unlawful Things*, in 2018, followed by *The Peacock Room*, *The Crimson Thread* and *Folly Ditch*. *Unlawful Things* was shortlisted for the Virago New Crime Writer award and picked as a Crime in the Spotlight choice by the Bloody Scotland crime writing festival.

In 2023 she began writing the 1920s murder mystery series of classic detective stories set in 1920s London. *Blackmail In Bloomsbury* is the first in the series, featuring apprentice detective Marjorie Swallow. *The Soho Jazz Murders* and *Death At Chelsea* continue the series. There will be more!

Anna lives between London and the Kent coast.

You can connect with me on:

 https://annasayburnlane.com
 https://www.facebook.com/annasayburnlane

Subscribe to my newsletter:

 https://wp.me/P9ZyRq-20X

Also by Anna Sayburn Lane

Step back into the roaring twenties with classic detective novels set in 1920s London. *Death At Chelsea* is the third in the series featuring plucky apprentice detective Marjorie Swallow.

Blackmail In Bloomsbury

Everyone at the party had a secret. Someone killed to keep theirs...

When a bohemian party ends in murder, there's no shortage of suspects. Half of Bloomsbury wanted Mrs Norris dead – but who wielded the knife?

Was it the handsome but troubled artist? The vivacious young actress? Or the aristocratic lady novelist? Marjorie and Mrs Jameson must find the true killer to save an innocent man from the noose. From the garden squares of Bloomsbury to the seedy backstreets of Soho, they navigate the glamour and peril of Jazz Age London in a thrilling story of secrets and lies. Marjorie needs all her wit, pluck and charm in this perilous hunt for the killer.

This classic murder mystery will keep you guessing to the very last page. The first in the 1920s Murder Mystery series, *Blackmail in Bloomsbury* will delight fans of Agatha Christie and classic crime.

The Soho Jazz Murders

It's January 1923 and London feels dreary after the festivities of Christmas. So Marjorie is excited about meeting the American Ambassador's niece, a genuine 1920s flapper with a love of jazz, dancing and fun.

But their night out at Soho's infamous Harlequin Club comes to a tragic end. Soon Marjorie is working undercover as a dance hostess in the club to unmask the drugs gangs that threaten the West End. It's a perilous occupation - and there are more deaths to come.

The Soho Jazz Murders is the second in the 1920s Murder Mystery series, featuring the irresistible apprentice detective Marjorie Swallow.

Printed in Great Britain
by Amazon

41554875R00148